Rogue the Durum

by

Steven J. Kolbe

Ezra James Mystery Series

Rogue the Durum

Cover Art by *The Wild Rose Press, Inc.*

The Wild Rose Press, Inc.
PO Box 708
Adams Basin, NY 14410-0708
Visit us at www.thewildrosepress.com

Publishing History
First Edition, 2022
Trade Paperback ISBN 978-1-5092-4557-4
Digital ISBN 978-1-5092-4558-1

Ezra James Mystery Series
Published in the United States of America

Lucia's partner joined her by the window and looked down at the snow. "No footprints," he said, echoing her thoughts.

She turned back to the wall thermostat. "If he wanted it to be cold, then why crank up the heat?"

Her partner cleared his throat. "The heater is on a digital thermostat. It was cranked to full blast at one a.m." He pointed to an expensive looking sound system. "The stereo, too."

"So what's significant about one a.m.?"

"These are great questions, Vargas, but you're missing the forest for the trees."

Only the open window and the locked door led to this room. Lucia knelt beside the office chair that held their victim. His head rested on the keyboard, but his open chest faced the floor. A generous pool of blood, too much to be absorbed, lay on top of the cream carpet. It was as if Torben Laakso had aimed his open heart directly at this spot on the floor. There were thick clumps in the blood as if someone had mixed it with flour.

Then she noticed something remarkable. She checked Torben's right hand. Empty. His left hand, too, held nothing.

"If he stabbed himself, then what did forensics do with the knife?" she finally asked.

A smile formed on Gorecki's lips. "Nothing."

She stood abruptly. "Then where is it?"

"Now you're asking the right question, kiddo."

No knife. Lucia was too perplexed to be offended that he'd called her "kiddo."

Praise for Steven J. Kolbe

ROGUE THE DURUM:

"…a twisty, contemporary thriller with a flawed but compelling protagonist…a plot whose roots sprawl from a Finnish tech company to a Southeast Asian island war… Fans of Bruce Coffin and Edwin Hill will find much to like here…"

~Karen Odden, USA Today
bestselling author

HOW EVERYTHING TURNS AWAY:

"…If you're looking for a good mystery to curl up with—whether it's hot and humid outside or freezing with inches of snow on the ground—you won't go wrong here…"

~Randy Overbeck,
Amazon Bestselling Author

"…Entertaining and well-paced, if this is the first book in The Ezra James Series, I hope Kolbe keeps his promise and quickly produces the second."

~Terry Korth Fischer, author
of the Rory Naysmith Mysteries

Acknowledgements

"It always seems impossible until it's done," Nelson Mandela once said about something much more important than writing a mystery novel. Still, it feels appropriate.

For many years, I had no idea how or when my words would find their way into an actual printed book. My life as a writer looked more like that famous Samuel Beckett quote: "Ever tried. Ever failed. No matter. Try Again. Fail again. Fail better." I failed a lot, but I failed a little better each time. For any aspiring reader glancing through the front this book, I can't think of better words of advice.

I want to thank everyone who helped me realize this novel: my wife, Susan, who sees everything I write before it reaches the light of day; fellow English teacher Steven Davis, who agreed to proofread the final galley; Mystery Writers of America mentor, USA Today bestseller Karen Odden, who looked at the early chapters; my beta-readers Fred Smith, Scott Duerksen, Katie Pearson, Mike Matson, and Charley Kempthorne; last but not least, my editor Kaycee John, who saw something in my first book and helped me revise it until it was publishable. Ezra would not be Ezra without Kaycee's guidance, and that goes double for Lucia and Remy.

A huge thank you also to everyone who embraced the first book, especially my family who accounted for 99% of those early sales. If people had not read and enjoyed book one, I never would have written a second one.

Prologue

Two Weeks Ago

Ezra missed his ex-wife so profoundly, in all the ways a man can miss his wife, that she regularly invaded his dreams, only to evaporate the moment the dream became interesting. He knew he must be dreaming now because there on his front porch stood Julia, sopping wet. Her chestnut hair curled riotously around her face and her cherry-colored blouse stuck to her skin in all the right places. Any moment his alarm would sound, tearing him from this brief moment of marital joy.

Only this time it didn't. Julia went on standing there, existing in the flesh before him as he slipped from semi-consciousness to groggy wakefulness. When she punched him in his good arm, he knew he was awake.

Instantly, she recoiled. "Oh God! I'm so sorry. I forgot about your arm!"

He raised the other arm, sling and all. His most recent surgery was a complete success, but it would still require another week of recuperation.

"Didn't you break both of them?" she asked.

"I only had a hairline fracture in the right forearm. Nothing too bad." He looked to the other. "The bullet hit my left, through and through, but it nicked the bone."

She crossed her arms, pulling her wet jacket around her body. "That's not what the articles said."

She had followed the story in the papers. So she did still care.

"Come in." He found a towel from the linen closet and wrapped it around her shoulders, closing the door behind her. "We struggled over the gun and then over a hunting knife. That's when the bone in my left arm shattered."

She turned skeptically toward the injured arm. "What do you mean?"

"It broke," he said lamely. He sometimes forgot Julia was a doctor.

"What kind of break? Compound? Comminuted? Greenstick? Is there nerve damage?" The questions came at him like friendly fire.

Her use of doctor-ese made him grin. "When I woke up yesterday, I knew it was going to rain. Does that count as nerve damage?"

"I can see the trauma hasn't made you any smarter."

He raised an eyebrow. "What trauma?"

She leaned down and kissed his better arm precisely where she'd punched it. "Are you healthy enough?"

"Healthy enough for what?"

She grabbed him by the waist of his pajama pants and led him back inside to their former bedroom.

****

In the early morning just before sunrise, he lay awake beside her, still unbelieving. He could rest his hand on her thigh; he could breathe in the lavender scent of her shampoo; he could lean over and place his lips on her bare white shoulder, which smelled faintly of vanilla. It wasn't a dream. She was here.

As the sunlight filled their room with an amber glow, Ezra crept from the bed and tiptoed out with his pants and shirt held in his hands. He would dress in the hall so as not to wake her.

Julia's favorite bagel shop was a five-minute drive away. He ordered them vanilla lattes, for her an asiago bagel, toasted with cream cheese, and for himself a bagel sandwich. Noticing a stack of *New York Times* beside the counter, he picked up a copy. Saturday. The crossword puzzle would be at its peak difficulty this morning. In Julia's absence, he hadn't done a single puzzle, let alone a Saturday, in nearly a year. Now that she'd returned, an entire avenue of his life had reopened. A life of leisurely weekend mornings had returned, and he intended to make the most of it.

****

Detective Lucia Vargas decided to visit Ezra at home that Saturday morning. She knew he'd be there. Aside from his outings with Father Remy Mbombo, a West African priest who currently served as head chaplain at a local catholic school, Ezra had spent most of the last three months at home recuperating from a GSW to the upper arm.

As she turned onto his street, she debated what they might talk about. Would he invite her inside for coffee? She had yet to eat breakfast, and she had the whole weekend off. Maybe they would make a whole day of it, catching up and… Her mind stalled before filling in the rest of the details. Instead, an image of Adrian, her boyfriend of three months, flashed in her mind. Loyal, successful, handsome Adrian.

She would just check in on Ezra, she told herself. She'd see how he felt about returning to work, and maybe she would have some coffee if he'd just made some. Maybe she'd have a pastry if one happened to be lying around. She clenched the steering wheel until her knuckles turned white.

The purple sedan that usually occupied Ezra's driveway was gone, and a yellow jeep occupied the curb. Had Ezra traded in his car? Also, why had he parked on the street? Her mind refused to contemplate the more obvious explanation. Ezra had an overnight guest.

She knocked twice at the front door. How awkward would it be for her to show up unannounced? Even if he did have some woman in the next room, she still had a valid reason to check in. After all, his injury was her fault. If she hadn't led him to St. Joseph and Mary School in hot pursuit of her sister's kidnapper, his left arm wouldn't look like a cyborg's—all metal bars and pins. Her finger, as though moving of its own accord, rose toward the doorbell. She stopped it in midair and turned to leave, but the sound of the door opening froze her in place.

"Can I help you?" a woman asked. Not Ezra, but a woman in blue plaid pajamas and a loose-fitting gray shirt, greeted her. The woman's hair, the color of roasted chestnuts, fell in ringlets to her shoulders.

Thinking fast, Lucia lied. "There've been some robberies in the area, and we were wondering if you heard anything late last night." She produced her badge, which the woman glanced at.

"Nothing last night," she said confidently. "My husband is a federal agent, so I'm sure he'll let someone know if he sees anything suspicious."

Lucia tried to sound surprised. "Oh! Your husband's an agent, well, that's a good thing to have around."

So this made the pajama-clad woman Julia, Ezra's ex. From his descriptions of her and the way he'd inconsolably clung to his wedding ring, Lucia expected nothing less than Helen of Troy. The real deal paled in comparison. Her beauty and physique were admirable but certainly not worth what Ezra had put himself through.

"So that's everything?" Julia asked.

Lucia nodded. "Yep."

Julia started to close the door but then looked back at Lucia with one eye closed as if taking aim. "You're a friend of Ezra's?"

"Yes," Lucia admitted, exhaling fully for the first time since she'd stepped onto the porch.

"You work together?"

"We have. Just one case."

"And you two…" Julia let the insinuation hang.

"No, never. He's very faithful," Lucia said. Was this the right word to use for an ex-husband? Maybe *hung up* would be a better, more accurate, description.

Julia's nod was curt. "Good." She began closing the door again.

"But aren't you and Ezra…" Lucia asked, hoping Julia would also fill in the blank.

"Yes?"

"Divorced?" She tried not to sound hopeful.

Julia looked back into the house, as if hearing someone in another room, and then shut the door. Lucia heard no voices, just the click of the deadbolt.

Since her early days as a patrol officer, Lucia had employed a simple trick that helped with everything from writing reports to keeping witnesses, victims, and perpetrators straight when it came time to give her own testimony at trial. For each person she met, she would boil down their essence into a single descriptive word.

The officer who taught her this strategy would always be "mama bear" in her mind. Her first chief had been "pugnacious," and not just because he looked vaguely like a pug. And her partner, Satchell Gorecki, was "Sac," his actual college nickname because, well, it just fit.

Lucia stared at the closed door and settled on a term for Julia, though it wouldn't be appropriate for a police report—especially not one Ezra could read.

****

Lattes and bagels in hand, the Saturday paper folded under his slinged arm, Ezra bounded up the steps to his front porch. Only after he reached the front door did he realize Julia's yellow jeep was missing from the curb. In his excitement, he hadn't noticed.

Had the city towed it? Had a vandal stolen it? His mind resisted the more logical explanation.

The house was perfectly quiet. He placed breakfast on the kitchen counter and investigated the bedroom. Julia had made the bed and left a single, pink sticky note on her pillow. "Had to run, J."

He texted her immediately. —*Had to run where?*—

—*Back to K.C. I have patients.*—

—*Today?*—

—*Every day.*— she replied.

—*When will I see you again?*—

No response came for a long time. He repeated the question.

—*I'm sorry*— It was all she said. All she needed to say.

He poured her coffee into the sink and tore her bagel into tiny pieces before throwing it in the trash. Then he wiped his dirty hands on a decorative hand towel and opened the newspaper to the crossword. His eyes fell on clue one across.   "French island making headlines, fifteen letters," he read aloud. Without Julia he'd be hopeless. "Nope!" he said to himself and clapped the paper shut as if the clue, and not his ex-wife, were the cause of his consternation.

Chapter One

Early Saturday morning

The room smelled like the kill floor of a slaughterhouse. Lucia had never personally been in one, but her *tia* worked at a beef packing plant in Missouri and had come home early every morning reeking of hot blood. Lucia, along with her mother and sister, had lived with her aunt and uncle for only two months. They slept on egg crate mattress pads in the basement while her mother looked for work. It had been a short chapter in her life, but Lucia remembered that time vividly, especially the smell.

Her *tia* would sit at the kitchen table while she ate her cereal and say sternly, "Go to college, *sobrina*. It does not matter what for. Just promise me you'll go."

Her partner, Detective Sac Gorecki, had woken her at two a.m. this morning with a phone call. "We got a fresh one."

"Where?" she'd grumbled, dragging herself from sleep.

He gave her an address on the west side of Evanston, a red-brick apartment building she could easily picture in her head. Then he added, "Fitzpatrick just left." Captain Fitzpatrick, a man in his mid-fifties, was fair but strict. That being said, she was glad it would just be her and Gorecki.

Lucia had left her apartment straight away. She didn't even stop for coffee.

Now that she stood in the too-hot, foul-smelling space, she was glad her stomach was entirely empty. Her smart watch read 2:26 a.m., a digital snowflake beside the number. Even though it was mid-March, snow still clung to the grass and ice still gathered on the banks of the river.

Gorecki pointed at the lilac colored watch. "Cute. Does that thing keep track of your steps?"

"And my punches." She gave him a warning look in jest.

He patted his paunch. "Ash got me one of those for Christmas. I should probably charge it." Ash was short for Ashley, his wife. Sac and Ash, the perfect combination.

They joined the first officer on scene, Giovanni Russo. "Someone turned the heat up full blast," Russo said as they moved farther into the apartment.

They followed the familiar click-click sounds of a forensic photographer until they came to a large study. Russo pointed out the cracked casing on the interior door jamb. "We had to break this one down."

"Locked from the inside?" Lucia asked, surprised.

He nodded. "Triple locked. I've never seen three locks on an interior door like this."

On the east wall stood a bookshelf with thick leather volumes; the language on the spines was unknown to Lucia. On the south wall, its sashes pulled clear and the glass pushed all the way to the left, a large double window let in freezing cold air and the light of a distant streetlamp. In the center of the room, facing the window, sat a wide wooden desk with a black leather writing mat.

A sleek white computer monitor sat atop it. At that crisp workspace sat their victim, slate haired, slack jawed, and hunched over the keyboard. His chest had been sliced open. His hands in black leather gloves hung limply by his knees.

Click-click, the photographer continued recording the scene.

"What did forensics say?" Lucia asked as they circled the body.

Gorecki consulted his notepad. "Vertical chest laceration, one-and-a-half inches wide, probably piercing the heart. No other obvious injuries. They'll know more after the autopsy." He pointed to the printer in the corner. "There's an apparent suicide note in the printer tray."

She donned a surgical glove and lifted the letter. The writing was gibberish to her.

"Guy's finished," she heard Gorecki say.

She nodded to the body. "A goner, clearly," she agreed.

"No, he's Finnish," he enunciated. "Torben Laakso. He's some sort of Finlox muckety-muck."

Finlox was the most recent in a long line of international social media companies to wash up on the shores of America and bogart the market.

Lucia sighed. "That's all my sister Areli does," she said. "We'll be having dinner, just her and I, and she'll be staring at her phone the whole time..." she searched for the right word, "...Finloxing."

"I don't think that's a verb," Gorecki said.

She placed the letter back on the printer tray. "I guess we'll have to find a translator. Why'd you call it a suicide note if you haven't read it?"

Gorecki shrugged. "Just a hunch. Hari-kari and all that."

"I think it's *hara-kiri*, and that's disembowelment." She snapped her fingers, thinking through the evidence in front of them. "Okay, we have a Finnish businessman, far from home, types out a note, prints it, then stabs himself." She walked over to the open window, examining a neighboring apartment building and then the street below. A thin layer of snow covered the ground. Lucia saw no sign of footprints on the grass or the sidewalk. Nor did she see any on the ledge outside the window. No one left by this route.

"So why open the window?" she asked out loud.

Gorecki answered, "Maybe he missed Finland? I've never been there, but it sounds like one of those cold, Vodka-drinking countries." Her partner joined her and looked down at the snow. "No footprints," he said, echoing her thoughts.

She turned back to the wall thermostat. "If he wanted it to be cold, then why crank up the heat?"

Her partner cleared his throat. "The heater is on a digital thermostat. It was cranked to full blast at one a.m." He pointed to an expensive looking sound system. "The stereo, too."

"So what's significant about one a.m.?"

"These are great questions, Vargas, but you're missing the forest for the trees."

Only the open window and the locked door led to this room. Lucia knelt beside the office chair that held their victim. His head rested on the keyboard, but his open chest faced the floor. A generous pool of blood, too much to be absorbed, lay on top of the cream carpet. It was as if Torben Laakso had aimed his open heart directly at this spot on the floor. There were thick clumps in the blood as if someone had mixed it with flour.

Then she noticed something remarkable. She checked Torben's right hand. Empty. His left hand, too, held nothing.

"If he stabbed himself, then what did forensics do with the knife?" she finally asked.

A smile formed on Gorecki's lips. "Nothing."

She stood abruptly. "Then where is it?"

"Now you're asking the right question, kiddo."

No knife. Lucia was too perplexed to be offended that he'd called her "kiddo."

****

The only witness to prove even remotely helpful was Torben Laakso's Jewish neighbor, Saul Posner. Wearing a gray cardigan, a black tie, and a bright blue kippah, Saul met them at his doorway and invited them inside for coffee. Through the window, Lucia could see the sky was still pitch black.

"Sorry to bother you so early," she said.

He waved off her apology and shuffled back into the apartment, his whole body moving in one slow mass like a miniature iceberg. Although, short and round, he resembled a beach ball more than an iceberg.

The small black coffee maker with its five-cup carafe suggested Saul didn't entertain often. Lucia began questioning him as he prepared the coffee. "Our colleague in dispatch said you made the initial call."

"That's right." He spooned sugar into the three cups and added a dash of cream to each. "I heard the music come on."

"It woke you?" she asked.

Saul shook his head. "I'm an insomniac."

"Is it because, how should I put this…" She paused.

"Because I'm old?" He smiled and swapped a coffee cup for the carafe just as the coffee began to drip. "No, it isn't age. Sleep has always eluded me. Age has just compounded the problem."

"Did Mr. Laakso know about your insomnia?"

Saul swapped coffee mugs out, handing the filled one to Lucia. "Yes, yes, Ben wasn't much of a sleeper either."

"I'm sorry, who?" Lucia asked.

"Ben. Tor*ben,*" he said, emphasizing the last syllable. "He went by Ben."

Lucia jotted down the nickname.

"We spent many an evening discussing books, playing chess, listening to records, and trying to while away the long nights," he continued.

Insomnia qualified as both a cause and a symptom of depression, and it could explain Laakso's suicide, if in fact this was a suicide.

Lucia recalled a Sylvia Plath poem about *the witching hour.* Plath, a depressive and insomniac, wrote a lot about that hour of night when all felt lost. "It is easy to blame the dark," one poem about a witch burning read. If ever there was a witching hour, this was it.

"Have you read any Plath?" she asked.

Saul Posner smirked. *A police detective who reads poetry?* his expression seemed to say. "I have."

"Do you remember how she died?"

"A head in the oven," Saul said.

She sipped her coffee. It was neither bad nor good. "Plath told her neighbor to set his alarm for early that morning. If the neighbor had awoken in time, he might've saved her life."

"Why didn't he?" Saul asked.

"The gas leaked into his apartment, knocking him out." She noted the look of concern on his face. "He survived, though; her children too."

"I'm sorry, but how does this all relate to Ben?"

"Could the music have been a cry for help?" she asked. "Could he have wanted you to intervene?"

"Ben was saying good-bye." Saul handed a coffee cup to Gorecki and turned to watch the third and final mug fill. "I went right away when I heard the music. I knocked, I hollered, then I called you guys." He glanced back at them. "Sorry, I suppose you're not all guys." There was no sarcasm in his voice.

The apartment was spare, no decorations on the walls, no children's artwork cluttering the fridge, only advertisement magnets and various coupons. Likely, Saul Posner had no spouse, no children, and no grandchildren. Perhaps, Torben Laakso was his only regular contact.

It pained Lucia to ask her next question. "You said Ben was saying goodbye. What song did he play?"

The older man's face crumpled and, like a dam bursting, his eyes filled with tears and his shoulders racked with sobs. She placed a hand on his shoulder and led him to a wooden chair. Gorecki retrieved a box of tissues and the last mug of coffee, and the three of them sat together at the kitchen table until the sobbing subsided.

"I know this is difficult," Lucia said, "but it may help us discover the truth."

Saul wiped his eyes and cleared his throat. "What happened is clear. The song was a recording of kaddish."

"What's kaddish?" Lucia asked.

Gorecki answered for him. "The Jewish prayer for the dead." Then he turned to Saul. "You knew what Ben had done the moment you heard the music."

He nodded. "But I didn't want to believe it."

Everything pointed in one direction, but if Torben Laakso killed himself, what happened to the knife? "Did he show any signs of depression?" Lucia asked.

"Doesn't everyone?"

They thanked Saul Posner and left. The uniformed officers would interview the rest of the residents while they paid a visit to the building's security company.

Secure Security occupied a nondescript concrete building in downtown Evanston. Lucia had worked with them on numerous B&E cases. They always had the CCTV footage she needed, and it nearly always led to a quick arrest and conviction. Between security companies, private doorbell cameras, and cell phone footage, almost every serious crime was caught on camera these days.

The tech, a middle-aged man with square glasses and thinning salt-and-pepper hair, met them in the parking lot and led them to the locked door. The sun had still not risen. Light from streetlamps reflected on the opaque glass doors so that Lucia could make out nothing inside.

"Thanks for meeting us so early," she said.

The man grunted in reply and unlocked the double doors.

The CCTV footage from the previous evening provided them with the following timeline for Torben Laakso's building:

Friday:

6 pm - Laakso left his apartment in a black peacoat,

took the elevator to the ground floor, exited the building, and traveled south on foot.

10 pm - He returned from the south carrying a shiny metal briefcase and wearing black gloves, which he wasn't wearing when he'd left. Laakso then took the elevator to the third floor and went directly to his apartment.

11 pm - Laakso took the elevator down again, exited the building, and stopped at the large blue USPS collection box in front of his building. He withdrew a standard size letter from his peacoat, placed the letter halfway in the box, but then thought better of it. Letter in hand, he walked north.

Saturday:

12:15 am - He returned home from the north and took the elevator up to his apartment. No one else entered the building after this point until after Laakso's death.

12:50 am - Laakso raced from his apartment, carrying the metal briefcase. He ran down the stairs at high speed, burst out of the building through the backdoor, and raced westward out of the camera's view.

12:55 am - He returned to the building, sans briefcase, and raced up the back stairwell to his apartment.

1:00 am - The kaddish began playing at high volume.

1:05 am - Saul Posner approached the door of Laakso's apartment and began knocking, then pounding, then shouting.

1:20 am - the first officers, Giovanni Russo and Tanya Lane, arrived on scene along with the building super. After a few knocks, the super let them into the apartment.

Lucia paused the recording and asked the clerk, "Do you have cameras that could follow him west?"

"Beyond this is just a park. The city might have cameras," he said.

"And beyond the park?" Lucia asked, just to clarify.

"The river."

She'd call Parks and Rec when they opened. If Laakso ran to the river with the briefcase and returned without it, there was a possibility they'd find it in the water.

Then Gorecki pointed at the screen. "Is that one of your cameras, too?"

Lucia could just make out a camera affixed to an adjacent building. The angle seemed to face the upper floors of Torben's building.

"It is."

"Can you show us the same time period?"

The tech located a new folder and ran through the footage with them. It showed the exterior of the window but not inside. He rewound to just before Laakso's death, then played it at triple-speed until the police car arrived in the background of the frame. No one had gone into or come out of the window. This seemed to knock the wind out of Gorecki's sails.

"Were you expecting some kind of ninja assassin?" Lucia asked.

"I was expecting some kind of something."

Then a face came to the window and looked out. It was Giovanni Russo.

They left the security office and stood by Gorecki's car. The first of the early morning joggers and dog walkers were beginning to appear, but the streetlights hadn't clicked off yet. In ten minutes it would be morning, but right now it was something else.

"A hundred bucks says we're dredging the river for Laakso's briefcase," Gorecki said. "I don't know what we'll find in it, but he died because of it."

"And we need to find that letter," she replied.

"What letter?" he asked.

"The one he almost mailed. If he didn't put it in the collection box, what did he do with it?" The question was posed to Gorecki, but she wanted to answer it herself.

Chapter Two

Fr. Remy Mbombo himself suggested the Saturday morning confession time, so it was Remy alone who took confessions then, sometimes before the sun had even risen. While there was rarely a crowd at 7 am, the penitents who did come usually had a good reason.

Confessions at St. Joseph and Mary, a parish and school situated at the heart of a wealthy Chicago suburb, took place not in a cramped wooden booth, but in a cozy room at the back of the church. Father Remy Mbombo, born Remy També, spent the first twenty years of his life not in Africa, as the members of the parish assumed, but in Paris. Twenty years in Paris, then thirty in Africa—Zaire and Senegal among his postings—and now this past year in Illinois.

Growing up in Paris, he had shown little interest in the religion of his middle-class parents. Nor had he set his sights on the priesthood. The business that initially brought him to Africa had nothing to do with religion, though he was happy to use the Church to his ends.

Despite his metropolitan upbringing, Remy allowed his parishioners to imagine him as a devout African boy for the simple reason that it allowed him certain freedoms at the pulpit. He could critique the ills of unchecked capitalism, for instance, and his flock would give him the benefit of the doubt. Had they suspected his Parisian childhood, they may have scoffed and labeled him a socialist.

Even though he didn't grow up dreaming of the priesthood, Remy enjoyed his work, especially the sacrament of reconciliation, or confession as it was more frequently called. As a young man, he'd taken a gossip's pleasure in hearing people's darkest secrets, though he never turned the information into actual gossip.

Now, his joy came not from this voyeurism but from the act of unburdening his flock. Parishioners arrived for confession heavy and sorrowful with the weight of their sins, then they left light and grateful. It truly was a gift he provided. If everyone had access to confession with a wise and understanding priest, there would be no need for prisons. Or so Remy often daydreamed. But then he would remember certain parishioners who confessed the same transgressions again and again, mechanically and without reflection or repentance, and he would amend the thought. Nevertheless, he hoped he'd kept some young people from the cold and heartless bars of the Illinois penal system.

As these thoughts came to a close, a man in a suit and tie entered the confessional. He stood at the door and closed it behind him slowly. Through the semi-obscure screen, Remy noted the man's short stylish hair, his dark oversized suit jacket, perfect for concealing a sidearm, and his white gold cufflinks.

Federal Agent, he thought. At first, he suspected the man was Ezra James, FBI agent and parishioner this past year. Except when Ezra confessed, he never stood hesitantly at the door. He instead came around the screen and sat face-to-face with Remy. The moment this man knelt behind the screen, Remy knew it couldn't be his agent-friend.

"Forgive me, Father, for I have sinned."

Remy cleared his throat. "How long has it been?"

"Twenty-six years?"

"Tell me."

The man turned his head from side to side, not sure where to begin. "I planted a bug."

"Yes?"

"A listening device," he clarified, "in the confessional booth used by a prominent general."

Without ever having met this stranger, Remy knew who it must be. "Assistant Special Agent in Charge, Jeremiah Cromley," he said.

Through the mesh of the screen, he saw Cromley smile. "Yes."

"To whom have you been speaking?" He felt ashamed over his next suspicion, but he had to ask. "To Ezra?"

"No, I have contacts in Washington."

Remy looked down at his scuffed dress shoes. "So, they are keeping tabs on me then?"

Saying nothing, Cromley fidgeted with his cufflinks.

"I am an ordinary priest," Remy said and paused. "What do you want?"

Cromley's sigh suggested coming here wasn't his idea. "The mayor of Chicago is diverting funds into a new community outreach program. We'd like you to be a part of one such program in north Chicago."

"You and the mayor, or you and the Bureau?"

Cromley answered with silence.

"What is it—this outreach effort?"

"A church program to keep kids off the street, specifically to help them exit gangs."

Remy shifted uncomfortably.

"We'd like you to be the Catholic component of the rehabilitation effort. You'd be working with a Baptist minister, Don Webber."

"I know Reverend Don," Remy said and then realized Cromley must've known this. "What would this program entail?"

"Counseling, leading the group in prayer, and teaching them chess. We all know your capacity in that arena."

Remy often engaged in games of *sans voir* chess with Ezra when they attended community events. At dull moments, they would exchange moves using standard chess notation until one of them achieved checkmate or they both lost track of the board and their position on it. The first week of Lent, Remy had received permission to enter a tournament in nearby Champaign, Illinois. He'd won second place and donated the proceeds to the maintenance of Catholic shrines in the Holy Land.

"So you want me for my chess skills?" he asked.

"You would also hear confessions," the federal agent admitted.

Remy nodded, certain Cromley would be able to see the motion through the screen. "I think I understand now. And if these confessions happen to tell me the name of their gang leader or their weapons supplier…"

Cromley scoffed. "You've broken the seal of confession before, Father Mbombo. Or should I call you També?

Remy didn't reply.

"As I understand it, if you're in for a dime, you're in for a dollar."

Instinctively, Remy's hand went to the scar running

down the left side of his face. "I was a young man then. I am not so young now, nor am I so naïve."

Now it was the ASAC's turn to shift uncomfortably. Perhaps he really was a lapsed Catholic. "Have you told Ezra about how you got that scar?"

"I suppose if I refuse, you will tell him about it?"

Cromley stood and came around the screen, abruptly taking a chair. "This isn't a shakedown, Father." Elbows on knees, he leaned forward and lowered his voice. "We are in a desperate situation. Maybe you can't tell us word for word, but you can still help."

The priest contemplated this offer. Best case scenario, he would be helping a troubled community make a fresh start. Worst case, he would let down the federal government by withholding information he simply couldn't share.

After another moment's thought, he said, "I'll do it. When do we start?"

"This afternoon."

"You realize this is the fourth Saturday of Lent. Next Sunday will be Palm Sunday."

Christmas and Easter were the two busiest seasons of the year for a priest—and now on top of all his preparations, he would have this.

Cromley smiled. "We'll be in touch." He returned to the other side of the screen and opened the door. "You really should tell Ezra."

"About the community outreach?"

He ran a thumb down the side of his face in the exact spot of Remy's scar. "About Rwanda."

"He would never understand."

"Maybe not." He grasped the edge of the door. "Then again, Special Agent James isn't so different from you or me." With that, he left.

While it was true Remy and Ezra had become close this past year, as close as he'd become with any parishioner, Ezra was still that: a member of the parish. He relied on Remy, not Remy the man but Remy the embodiment of Christian virtue. How could he possibly understand the decisions Remy had made under duress half a world away?

He closed the confessional room early that morning and went outside to sit on a bench beneath a blooming redbud tree and watch the sun complete its ascent into the sky. The sky had turned purple and orange, but below this the horizon glowed dark pink. Looking at it, he recalled, as he often did at sunrise, a morning thirty years before when he sat beside the banks of Lake Kivu. More exhausted than he'd ever been, he had watched the watery horizon, burning ever more brightly. He hadn't known that morning if the color came from the convergence of the rising sun and a massive flock of flamingos, or if the earth itself had just caught fire.

And he hadn't cared either way.

Chapter Three

For twenty minutes, he spoke without ceasing, almost without breathing, while dozens of expressionless eyes studied his every move. Then the strap of his sling caught the edge of the podium and it crashed to the ground.

Ezra James had always been such an expressive talker that he sometimes felt like a man doing charades. After toppling the podium, however, he made a concerted effort to keep his elbows pinned to his side. Either from this sudden lack of motion or from embarrassment, he found himself unable to remember what he was talking about. He couldn't even recall the topic.

The class instructor stepped forward. "This seems like a good time to ask Special Agent James some questions." Her blonde ponytail swished about as she made eye contact with each of her students in turn. "If no one asks anything, I *will* call on you," she threatened.

A young woman sitting in the front row shot up her hand. With her blonde hair and freckles, she could've been the instructor's little sister. "I read that you're bipolar."

This wasn't a question, but Ezra nodded.

"Is that how you identified the epsilons from the Coast-to-Coast Killer case? I heard the newspapers received letters that contained Greek epsilons."

CTC had chosen his victims from the coasts, flying, Ezra had speculated, from a location in the Midwest or Southwest in order to distance himself from his crimes. In all his correspondences with news outlets, the killer had written his e's in the Greek manner.

"A lot of people noticed the epsilons," Ezra said in a dismissive tone.

"But how did you notice?"

"My wife's family is from Greece. They came over during the junta years."

"Don't you mean your ex-wife?" the same student asked, a look of disgust on her face.

Another hand went up and a young man began speaking before Ezra even called on him. "But your disorder did give you irrational courage? Isn't that why you pursued your last perp into that school?"

Ezra sighed. "I almost couldn't open the door to the school, I was so terrified. If anything—"

"So your mental illness is a constant liability?" the front row blonde asked. Her tone became accusatory. "Is that why you wrongly accused George Lewis Straugh?"

Straugh, a director at a tech company in Chicago, spent two years wrongfully imprisoned thanks to Ezra's mishandling of the case.

"That's not what I said." He grasped for the podium but found it missing—because it still lay on the ground.

From the back of the class a voice rang out. "You sent him to prison!"

From the corner of his eye, Ezra watched the instructor approach, her arms crossed over her chest. "You're nothing special," she said. "Is that why you're here instead of in the field?" Her facial features shifted, her hair turned darker, and her freckles disappeared.

With each change she looked more and more like Julia. "Is that what you're saying? That you're a fraud?"

She let down the ponytail until it glimmered, curly and chestnut brown. He looked into her eyes. Only now they weren't Julia's eyes; they were the eyes of George Lewis Straugh.

Ezra awoke in a cold sweat. Bright light filled the living room where he'd been napping on the couch. Instinctively, he raised his left arm to see if, in fact, it had rebroken. The cast had been gone for nearly a week, but in dreams it still remained in its sling, still winced with pain, still impeded his movements. During his medical leave, his FBI supervisor, ASAC Jeremiah Cromley, sent him on nothing but educational assignments—giving police training sessions and presenting to criminal justice classes. While none of them went as poorly as his dream, a few had veered into uncomfortable territory.

Even after his recent success at crime solving, the details of the Coast-to-Coast Killer case from three years before still hung over his head. He'd falsely accused George Lewis Straugh, and the man served considerable time. Cromley had placed him on probation, which he technically was still on. While on probation, he had assisted Evanston PD to investigate a series of attacks at a local Catholic school, St. Joseph and Mary, and had put a killer in prison.

In the media coverage that followed that case, Ezra made the perhaps unwise decision to announce his bipolar diagnosis to the world. "I want to stop the stigma," he told a reporter from the *Tribune*. Most of the subsequent coverage painted him in a positive light, but the tabloids had a field day.

Luckily, the FBI didn't care about the tabloids.

Monday would be Ezra's first day back in the office and, he hoped, his first day back with real cases. Playing school resource officer may cut it for some agents, but Ezra needed to be in the trenches.

He would wear his emerald tie. It always brought out the green in his eyes.

His phone buzzed with a text from Lucia Vargas, the detective he'd worked the SJM case with.

—*Can you meet me somewhere?*—

He thought about the text for a long time. He also thought about Julia's face peacefully sleeping in the bed beside him two weeks earlier. Had her visit been closure or the promise of a return? Did that change anything?

—*Pretty please?*— Lucia texted next.

—*Of course. Where?*—

****

Ezra drove south to a mixed commercial-residential corner on the East Side of Chicago. Not knowing the building Lucia had described, he resorted to following the GPS system on his vehicle. He'd heard of Finlox, of course, but didn't realize they had a Chicago branch.

The first thing to strike him about the Finlox lobby was the overabundance of glass. Every wall was transparent, which made Ezra feel vaguely like a fish in an aquarium.

Lucia stood beside the front desk talking with a young man in his mid-twenties with a short-kept beard. The detective looked as sharp as ever in her two-piece black suit and emerald green blouse, but her eyes looked glassy and stray black hairs hung from her otherwise professional hair bun.

Ezra inserted himself into their bubble. "Am I in the right place?"

Introductions went all around. Dominic Torres was assistant to the late Torben Laakso, whoever that was. Ezra was "a colleague" of Lucia's.

"Are you ready to see the campus?" the young man asked.

With the exception of Dominic, the entire first floor was empty. No desks, no chairs, not even an occasional cubicle.

"This floor will be reserved for sales and customer service eventually," he said, gesturing around.

They took an open staircase to the second floor. Lucia stopped and peered down at the floor. It was transparent glass. She brought Dominic's attention to it and asked, "So here's my question, Dominic: how do you keep people from looking up your skirt?"

He smiled. "Simple: I don't wear a skirt." Then he gestured toward the ceiling, which appeared as opaque as white tile. "It's specially tinted glass. You can see down, but the lower level can't see up."

Ezra examined the ceiling, following it to the corner where it met the wall and dissolved into a transparent window like snow melting into water.

"Where is everyone's stuff?" she asked next.

"The executives have been working from home while the building passes inspection."

"When will that be?"

"Monday."

"Are these executives in Chicago?"

"Yes. They come and go, meeting with Mr. Laakso." He paused. "At least, they did."

Lucia continued. "Just to recap: the man in charge of this branch—the first of its kind in America—died the week before the site launched."

"I suppose that's correct," Dominic said.

Ezra wondered what this meant. Who was Mr. Laakso? How had he died? Also, what sort of name was Laakso?

Out the south window, he saw a neighborhood thriving with restaurants and shops, their signs written in various languages. Some he recognized—Spanish, Greek—but others remained a mystery to him. One he guessed was Arabic, but he didn't actually know. People had come from all over the world and settled into this one corner of Chicago. It was remarkable.

"What did this building replace?" Ezra asked.

"Just some ramshackle apartments," Dominic replied.

"Where did the people go?"

"What people?" Dominic asked innocently.

They continued their tour of the vast, clean office, though Ezra wasn't sure what he was looking for. Lucia had wanted him here for some reason; she just hadn't told him yet.

Lucia asked the next question. "Why did Benjamin Kirsi send Mr. Laakso to Chicago alone?"

Ezra mentally cataloged the new name, Benjamin Kirsi. Somewhere in the trivia portion of his mind dinged a tiny bell of recognition.

Dominic leaned up on the balls of his feet. "I'm sure he had his reasons. Mr. Laakso hired me over the phone in January and I met him here at the Finlox campus the day he arrived from Helsinki. The other executives arrived the following week. We're supposed to begin sales training on Monday, but…"

But what? Ezra wondered. He didn't enjoy being in the dark, but he also didn't want to interrupt the flow

Lucia had established.

"So plans for this campus, as you call it, began when?"

Dominic's head bobbed, noncommittal. Clearly, this question was above his pay grade, but he didn't want to admit it.

"How would you describe the late Mr. Laakso?" Lucia stopped walking and stared at the opaque ceiling.

"Outgoing, positive, almost bubbly even," Dominic said.

"How so?"

"If I can be honest," Dominic started, then stopped, as if waiting for her permission. When none came, he continued, "Mr. Laakso didn't seem like the type to do what they're saying."

Suicide then, Ezra thought.

"It's not always the type you'd expect," Lucia replied. "Is this the way to his office?" She headed toward the stairwell and Dominic and Ezra followed.

Thankfully, the stairs were concrete all the way up and down. Lucia took them quickly but carefully until she reached the top. There she paused and waited for the men to catch up. Dominic unlocked the door with a key fob. The third floor contained a single, vast, office space with a view of Chicago from every direction. It reminded Ezra of a vision of the future—all that glass and white, ergonomic furniture—but it also reminded him of moving. Other than the furniture, the wide office was bare.

"Did Laakso come into the office much?" Lucia asked.

"Every day."

"What did he do without files or a computer?"

Dominic didn't know.

****

Because their cars were parked in opposite directions, Ezra and Lucia lingered on the sidewalk outside the Finlox building for several minutes talking.

"So this Laakso fellow killed himself?" Ezra asked.

"It appears so."

"But you have your doubts?"

She chewed her lip in that absent-minded way she did when she was tired. "We've only just opened the investigation."

"You suspect his boss, this Benjamin Kirsi, was it?"

A broken bit of concrete lay beside her purple pump. "Of murder?" She rocked the concrete back and forth with the toe of her shoe, then kicked it into the street. "I don't know."

"Do you think this Kirsi guy cleared out Laakso's office before it could be searched?"

She glared at the building. "It crossed my mind. The problem is Kirsi's still in Finland."

"He could've contracted it. A murder, I mean."

She shrugged. "Laasko's emails are being translated. Gorecki and I will go through them."

"Where is *Sac?*" Ezra asked. Lucia's partner had never completely trusted Ezra and let him know it on a regular basis.

She yawned. "He's been working the case since we first got the call"—she checked her phone—"eleven hours ago." Then she smiled ironically at Ezra. "I bet you can't wait to be a full-time agent again."

Ezra rolled his eyes. He knew there would be long nights and early mornings, weekend assignments, and so many reports it would make grad school look like kindergarten, but he wanted to be of use again. He *needed* to be of use.

"I'm ready."

She smiled again, this time in earnest. "I believe it." She looked down the avenue in the direction of her car and asked, "Lunch?"

"I wish I could, but I have a doctor's appointment."

"Palacios?"

Dr. Palacios had been Ezra's psychiatrist ever since his cataclysmic manic episode and subsequent hospitalization nine months before.

"Last appointment before I start back next week." He didn't add that if Palacios didn't clear him, he wouldn't be starting back.

"It's a shame," Lucia said. "About lunch, I mean."

"I knew what you meant," Ezra replied, feeling a grin pull at the corners of his mouth. "How does breakfast tomorrow sound?" The moment he said it, he realized it sounded like a bad pick-up line.

She cleared her throat. "It sounds good. I picked the place last time."

"I'll text you," he said.

If they had been a high school couple, like the ones Ezra saw while running security at SJM, they would have hugged and intertwined their fingers, pulling away little by little until their last knuckles broke free with a burst of longing. But they were not a high school couple.

They weren't even a couple-couple. They were colleagues—and barely that. Lucia worked for Evanston PD and Ezra was still technically on probation from the FBI. Nevertheless, their bodies resisted separating until the last moment. Then they waved awkwardly and turned toward their separate cars.

****

The psych wing of Northwestern Memorial wasn't far from Finlox Chicago. Unlike the psychiatrist offices portrayed on television shows, the wing was busy, chaotic, and spare. Furthermore, Dr. Henry Palacios reminded Ezra of a pared down robot, one of those battle bots. His small but muscular physique intensified the comparison. His office contained a computer, a plastic office chair, and a ratty loveseat, all of it stuffed into a room roughly the size of a closet. And this was his *new* office.

In his usual manner, Palacios peppered Ezra with the standard clinical questions. Sessions with Palacios felt more like answering a survey than receiving therapy. As the questions went on longer than usual, Ezra realized Palacios was in fact filling out an electronic form, likely for the DOJ.

The doctor typed for several minutes, then gave Ezra a forced smile. "These formalities are unpleasant," he said. Although he'd lived in Chicago for decades, his voice still carried a hint of a Venezuelan accent. Not enough to cause misunderstandings but enough to add music to his speech. "But there, it is done."

"Did I pass?" Ezra asked.

"It is not for me to say." He looked at his computer. "But you have made as close to a complete recovery as I've seen." Then he added a caveat. "As long as you maintain this treatment program."

It seemed as good an opening as any to ask, "Have you been following this study on a bipolar allele?"

The doctor sighed. "I assume you have?"

Ezra launched right into it. "They've identified a polymorphism that could be the cause of my trouble."

The doctor raised a skeptical eyebrow. "And?"

"Could you imagine if they develop effective gene therapy?"

"What will happen then?"

"I'll be cured."

Palacios nodded somberly. "And how will that change your life?"

"I won't be crazy anymore."

"But you are sane right now. You are here talking to me just as normally and logically as anyone in the world—and about alleles no less. Is taking a few pills each morning such a hardship?"

Ezra let his gaze drop to the linoleum floor, feeling as morose as the linoleum looked.

"What you want, I think," the doctor continued, steepling his fingers, "is to be a new person—not the old Ezra who threatened his wife and his partner and made headlines for bungling one of the highest profile cases of the decade, but a fresh version who lacks the potential for such violence. I'm sorry to break it to you, but all people are capable of such things." Dr. Palacios had never spoken of Ezra's past so bluntly. It felt like a splash of ice water. "Everyone wishes to escape their past. Even children want their families to forget they once breastfed and ran around in the nude and shat themselves." He paused to let the words sink in. "Unfortunately, they cannot. And neither can we."

Now he swiveled his office chair back to his monitor and began reading through his notes. Ezra shifted uncomfortably on the loveseat.

"Last time we spoke, you mentioned an argument with your mother."

"It's fine."

"So you two have made up?"

They hadn't spoken of it. The day Ezra got out of the hospital after being shot, he and his mother had a knock down drag out argument. It began with a conversation about his divorce, which she vocally opposed to the point of tears—hers not his—then somehow it spiraled into every area of Ezra's life and all the ways he had failed to realize his potential. There was nothing overtly bad about the things his mother said, but the underlying current of manipulation, guilt, and desperation left Ezra feeling battered. He tried now to convey the conversation to Palacios—but failed.

"You don't have to explain yourself," the doctor said. "This isn't arbitration. What happened after the argument?"

"Nothing. I brought it up the next time I dropped off groceries, and she acted as though she had no memory of ever fighting. When I pressed her, she said, 'That's in the past.'"

"Do you think this is a healthy way to resolve conflict?"

"No, but..." Ezra wasn't sure what to say. He had an advanced degree in psychology, yet he didn't know what to do about his own personal relationships. It was embarrassing to say it out loud.

As if reading his mind, Dr. Palacios added, "It is one thing to solve someone else's problems. It's another to deal with our own. My own family relations aren't perfect. Nor can I force them to be." He frowned at the thought. "Has your mother considered counseling?"

Ezra laughed.

"Not even when your father died?"

He shook his head.

"Have you suggested therapy to her?"

"She's not exactly thrilled that I'm in therapy."

Now it was the doctor's turn to shake his head. "What would she have you do instead?"

During his initial hospitalization, his mother tried to have him released into her care. She told him during one of her visits that medication was not the answer. Only Jesus could save him from the devil, not some chemical, and if she could just get him to a Church-sanctioned exorcist… He didn't tell the doctor this detail. The embarrassment would have crushed him.

"She'd prefer I find a natural solution," is all he said.

"The Rosary perhaps?" He smiled knowingly. "Fear can drive all manner of behaviors."

"What does my mother have to fear?"

"Losing you, perhaps. You say she doesn't have many close acquaintances. Isolation breeds loneliness, loneliness breeds judgment, judgment breeds fear." He shrugged. "Anything else you'd like to discuss?"

"Julia visited me."

The doctor turned to face him. "Oh?"

"The divorce is finalized, but she paid me a visit…"

"What kind of—"

"…in the middle of the night."

The doctor grinned. "I see." Then he asked more seriously, "What does she want?"

"Who knows?"

"What do you want?"

Ezra considered the question. "Something stable."

"Something stable is always good." He shifted in his chair to look out his small window. On the other side of the glass, white and purple flowers were beginning to bloom. "Do you know anything about horticulture,

Special Agent James?"

Ezra shook his head.

"Lenten roses. That's what these are called. Yesterday, I asked the girl who sits at the front desk and that's what she told me. I moved into this office just last month," he said and paused. "Remarkable, isn't it?"

"What is?"

"That Lenten roses grow just outside my brand-new office."

Ezra failed to understand the significance. "Because it's Lent?" he asked.

"Do you know what I love about spring?" Palacios' face acquired an expression of warm remembrance. "Death and rebirth. It's a beautiful metaphor, spring."

"I suppose so."

Palacios typed something into his computer. "How does three months from now sound?"

"What do you mean?"

"For your next appointment. Unless something major crops up."

The longest Ezra had gone between appointments was one month. This felt like progress indeed. "Are you sure?"

"If you are."

He wasn't sure, but he wanted to be.

"Three months sounds good," he said and could not hide his smile.

Chapter Four

None of the local universities offered Finnish language courses, but a small community of Finnish expats did live in North Chicago. They even had their own school for children of Finnish immigrants. Classes met on Sunday mornings. One of the instructors, Enni Frost, happily translated Torben Laakso's typed note. Lucia found it on her desk late that morning, along with an explanatory note:

Dear Detective Lucia Vargas,

I'm not an expert in Finnish or in English, but I did spend most of my life in Helsinki before moving to Chicago. Teaching Finnish is not a vocation for me, but rather a passionate hobby. My career is firmly in the tech world, writing code and designing interfaces.

The letter you had me translate is less straightforward than it seems. Finnish is not a cryptic language but, like English, it's open to interpretation, especially when the author is as intentionally vague as this one seems to be. From my perspective, the enclosed letter could mean one of two things. It could be an admission of guilt—though the nature of the crime is obscure—or it could be an accusation. I'll let you read it and decide for yourself.

Sincerely,

Enni Frost

Lucia opened the manilla envelope and slid out two

pieces of copier paper. The first was a photocopy of Torben Laakso's original note, in Finnish. Behind that was Enni Frost's translation. She skipped the Finnish and went straight to the English version.

To Whom it May Concern,

For reasons various and obscure, I find myself at the end of my rope—literally. Whose fault is all this? Can it even be deciphered or is the blame like a tablespoon of arsenic disseminated among a thousand bags of flour? I will bear the brunt of the blame for this disaster, but history will be the true arbiter—history and fate, which have their own ways of assigning blame. My name might go down in infamy, but it won't be alone.

Once upon a time, I had a bright future here, but that is all over now. The promise of tomorrow is tainted, an illusion trapped in the past like a salmon in a frozen river. So clear, so promising, but lifeless. Only in death does the fish know it was in water. I have been in hot water, indeed, but I am done with that now.

Goodbye forever,

Torben Laakso, Director of Compliance

Blame for what? She'd read up on the Finnish social network but hadn't come across any sort of disaster. In her desk, she'd filed a number of things related to the case. She pulled them out now. The first was Laakso's C.V. A business card hung from the back, affixed with a paperclip. Written in English and in Finnish, it read not "Director of Compliance" but the far loftier title "Vice President of American Operations."

A thought pestered her. What if the note was dated? What if it wasn't a suicide note at all but an earlier letter of resignation? What if the promotion had been to shut him up? She flipped back and read Laakso's note a second time.

Because the task of translating Torben Laakso's company emails would have overwhelmed the local Finnish translator, not to mention taken several weeks, Evanston PD had the emails run through an online translation program while they waited for a Finnish company to produce a more accurate translation.

After finishing the letter, Lucia turned to the computer-translated emails, working backwards from the present. Nothing stood out from Laakso's time stateside. In fact, for a Vice President, he had shockingly few email exchanges. She wondered if Laakso had intentionally avoided email communications or if, as with his office, someone had gone in ahead of Evanston PD and removed evidence.

Then she discovered in his drafts folder a half-written email about a Swedish island. He discussed "the deteriorating situation" on the island and suggested "evacuating the durum." The email had never been sent.

Could this be what his note referenced? She ran a web search and immediately learned that Sweden contained some 10,000 islands. "Disaster on Swedish island" produced a list of various natural disasters, but nothing recent and nothing tied to Finlox.

"Durum" turned out to be a kind of grain used for making pasta. Though it was a warm-climate crop, one of the larger islands, Gotland, had successfully started growing durum. Lucia, however, could find nothing about a disaster on that island. Something was clearly lost in translation, but what?

On an impulse, she texted Ezra. Perhaps he would know more.

Or perhaps she just wanted to text him.

—Do you know anything about Sweden?—

He responded immediately. *—Meatball capital of the world? Have you tried the internet?—*

—What a novel idea! I'll get right on that.—

—Sarcasm?—

—Mmmhmm. Torben Laakso mentioned a disaster on a Swedish island.—

Just as she was about to send a follow-up text, her captain burst into the bullpen. Fitzpatrick only came in on Saturdays if he'd left his golf clubs at the precinct. "Vargas!"

She rose and met him. "Sir?"

"Have you been harassing Benjamin Kirsi?"

Lucia wrinkled her brow. "No, of course not."

He turned his tablet toward her. It showed a screenshot of her profile page. "Is this your Finlox profile?"

"Yes, but I never use it."

"You used it this morning."

He displayed another page, this time with messages sent from her to Kirsi. Some were so long they filled most of the screen. They called Kirsi an asshole and a coward and said she'd nail his ass to the wall. Kirsi himself hadn't responded to any of them.

"Sir, it's his company. He could easily make my profile say whatever he wants."

Captain Fitzpatrick looked unconvinced. "Why would he do that?"

Lucia considered her response. "Maybe he's trying to slow down the investigation."

Fitzpatrick gripped the tablet so hard Lucia worried it might snap in two. "To what end?" he asked through gritted teeth.

She didn't know, but that wasn't the point. "Maybe Laakso did something unsavory or he knew about something illegal and Kirsi's afraid it will come out. There are a million possibilities." She clapped her hands and turned back to her computer. "I just received a translation of Laakso's emails and immediately this happens. Doesn't that strike you as fishy?"

Fitzpatrick agreed but added, "The optics aren't great."

Her captain had attended a leadership-in-law-enforcement conference back in January and ever since then he'd talked about nothing but "optics," as if the appearance of rightness or wrongness should be the deciding factor of all future actions.

"We're under the microscope, Vargas," he added. "You say they fabricated these messages, but the president of the company says that isn't so. He says he learned only this morning of Torben Laakso's death."

She shifted to her back foot. "So how do I proceed?"

Her captain looked around the crowded bullpen and lowered his voice. "The Finnish authorities have requested that the case be bumped up."

"The FBI?"

He nodded.

"But don't you see how this sets us back?"

"We've already forwarded everything up the line. Plus the Finnish police are sending one of theirs to assist."

She looked instinctively to the elevator, deciding whether or not to storm out. "Fine," she said, "I guess I can go home then."

She half-expected him to tell her to stay, but he just stared. She tried to think of it as a kindness. She'd already worked an eight-hour shift, so going home and sleeping didn't sound half bad. Then again Kirsi was hiding something, a secret so damaging that he'd hacked her Finlox account to keep it safe.

"I'll see you Monday," Fitzpatrick said and proceeded to his office.

Lucia's hands automatically balled into fists. How could they do this? They'd successfully blackmailed a detective and her captain from across the Atlantic with nothing but a computer. "I'm deleting my Finlox profile today," she announced to Fitzpatrick's back.

He gave her a thumbs up.

When she tried to access her profile, it was locked. Then she tried opening the emails on her computer but found that her email too had been locked. What next? She tried her phone to see if it was somehow, miraculously still logged into either her Finlox or her email. No such luck. She did discover a text from Ezra, though, and two from her semi-serious boyfriend, Adrian. She marked Adrian's texts as "read" and continued to Ezra's.

—*Swedish island disaster doesn't ring a bell. What else did the emails say?*—

—*I don't know. But I'm going to find out.*—

****

Enni Frost was thirty with jet black hair cut in an asymmetrical bob. She had a small cubicle in the middle of an open-concept office. The white walls of her space were decorated with photographs of her family—a boy and a girl, both elementary aged, and a handsome blond man in spectacles. In each photo, the husband wore a different crew-neck sweater. Lucia sighed inwardly at the sight of the photos, but then she remembered that she was dating Adrian.

"Ms. Frost?" she asked.

The woman turned from her computer.

"I'm Detective Vargas."

"Of course." Enni stood and they shook hands.

"Do you have a minute?" Lucia asked.

She nodded.

"You mentioned the original Finnish letter contained some ambiguity."

"Sure."

"Could Torben Laakso have been writing a letter of resignation?"

"It's possible," she said. "There's certainly some overlap in the sentiments. 'I'm leaving this shithole for good!' That sort of thing."

"Would you be willing to look at one more email?" Lucia asked. "It's very short."

Enni checked the time on her phone. "Sure. Do you have it with you?"

Lucia looked around. "You see, I've sort of locked myself out of my email."

Enni looked puzzled. "Have you tried resetting the password?"

Lucia shrugged. "I can't get it to work."

"I'm sorry, but can I see your badge?"

She showed her. Enni examined it closely.

"Here's the deal," Lucia said in her most candid tone, "as far as I can tell, Mr. Laakso discovered something he wasn't supposed to."

"At Finlox?" she asked.

"They've been messing with me online all morning."

"I was in high school in Helsinki when they started."

She smiled nostalgically. "I was friends with everyone in my grade. We all were. It's a great service, but Benjamin Kirsi…"

"Yes?" Lucia asked.

"He's fiercely secretive."

"A recluse?"

"No, not like that. Trade secrets."

Enni motioned for Lucia to come into the cubicle and sit beside her desk. "He has a wife and a daughter. Nélya's the girl. She's a major celebrity in Finland. We've watched her grow up her whole life through Kirsi's posts and then her own. He let her traipse around Europe—going to music festivals and nightclubs. She even had her own reality show for a while. Their life is an open book, but what happens at Finlox HQ is another matter."

"Do you recall any specific controversies?" Lucia pressed.

"He put a few smaller companies out of business in the usual legal but immoral ways. A few others he bought out."

"What about a disaster on a Swedish island? Gotland maybe?"

Enni looked up. "No. I haven't heard of anything. This is recent?"

"Six months ago," Lucia said. "Again, if I could get into my email, I could say more."

A devilish expression on her face, Enni rose from her seat and brought her eyes level with the top of her cubicle wall so that she reminded Lucia of a prairie dog emerging from its hole.

"Let's see what we can do," she said.

When she'd first stepped into Enni's cubicle, Lucia

had struggled to form the perfect adjective for the translator. For several minutes, she'd hovered around the word *earnest* or perhaps *shrewd*, but neither quite distilled the woman's essence. The prior seemed too wholesome for the young, vibrant woman, and the latter conjured in Lucia's mind an image of a shrew, which Enni certainly wasn't. As the translator, in equal parts clandestine and nimble, hacked into Lucia's email, she knew the exact right word: *foxy*. The word conveyed all the deception with none of the ill-intent, all the brains with none of the subterranean squint.

Within minutes, Lucia was staring at her own inbox, but there was no file of Laakso's emails, neither in translation nor in the original language.

"There's usually a temporary file or a trashed version," Enni said and took hold of the mouse. She searched quickly and expertly through files that Lucia didn't even know she possessed.

"It's gone," Enni said, surprised. "Someone has cleaned all traces of it."

"Can someone do that remotely?"

"If they know what they're looking for," Enni said.

It seemed unlikely that the Evanston PD tech team, which once took three hours to switch her printer from Portuguese to English, had managed to deep clean her email over the course of the last twenty minutes. This had been done from outside her department if not outside her country.

She suddenly regretted not asking Dominic Torres, the young man who had guided her through the Chicago Finlox building, more about his own tech background.

Chapter Five

Shortly after returning home from his psychiatrist appointment, Ezra received a vaguely worded text from the Assistant Special Agent in Charge, Jeremiah Cromley. Cromley wanted him to come into the field office. Ezra pressed for specifics but got none. When he called, Cromley's cell went straight to voicemail.

As Ezra entered his office on the fourth floor of the Chicago field office, he nearly dropped his briefcase. A severe-looking woman sat behind the desk in his office, examining a case file. At least he thought it was still his office. Her light blonde hair was pulled back into a high ponytail that created a perfect line with her sharp cheekbones. Her charcoal, knee-length coat contrasted with her skin, giving it the color of a bleached eggshell. Had they reassigned his office without telling him? Were the training assignments Cromley sent him on a ruse to keep Ezra out of the office while they found his replacement?

"Can I help you?" he finally asked.

Without looking up from the case file, she replied, "I doubt it."

Behind him came the squeaking of leather shoes and then the boom of Cromley's distinctive voice. "Ah-ha!" He clapped Ezra on the shoulder. "I see you've met your replacement."

Ezra's jaw dropped. So it was true. All his worst

doubts about his worth came rushing in like an attack of vertigo. It felt as if the ground beneath him had vanished.

"I'm shitting you." Cromley laughed.

Ezra laughed too, through gritted teeth.

"She's your partner, for a week or so anyway. Director Åkerholm, this is Agent James," he said by way of introduction.

The woman nodded but did not extend her hand. "Leena Åkerholm, assistant director of the KRP."

"A pleasure to meet you." Ezra lowered his hand, unshaken. "KRP is the...overseas, you all do..." he stammered. "Where is it you're from exactly?"

Her disappointment filled the room. "*Keskusrikospoliisi.*" When it became clear that Ezra still had no idea, she added, "The National Bureau of Investigation for Finland."

Ezra felt as though a dumbbell had been lifted from his chest. "Of course, so you're Finnish then."

"Very astute," she said, then turned to Cromley. "Your American television exaggerates, I think. Maybe the FBI is not the agency we are looking for."

As if to demonstrate his sturdiness, Cromley gave Ezra's good arm a paternal pat. "Agent James is just returning from medical leave. He apprehended a murder suspect with nothing but a stun gun. He took a bullet in the process."

She didn't seem impressed. "I would have gone in with a shotgun."

Ezra shrugged. "There weren't any available."

"I suppose an American superhero like you doesn't need a gun, not when you can go in *with your jacket open,*" she said.

Ezra didn't know what this expression meant, but he

couldn't help feeling insulted. He felt compelled to share the whole story. "I had been drugged with a heavy hallucinogen."

"How did you allow that to happen?"

"I met the suspect at a restaurant and…" He immediately regretted bringing up the subject. He felt the ends of his ears turn red with embarrassment.

Cromley rapped on the wooden desk. "Had Agent James not interceded, the suspect would've skipped town, possibly the country."

As the heat subsided from his face, Ezra made a connection he should've made the moment Leena Åkerholm explained where she came from. "A man killed himself in Evanston last night," he said. "A Finnish national if I remember correctly." He looked from the Finn to Cromley and back, seeking confirmation.

His ASAC nodded. A glimmer of discomfort, uncharacteristic for the man passed over his face. "That was Leena's original purpose for coming."

"Do you know the name Nélya Kirsi?" the Finnish officer asked.

He'd just learned about a man named Benjamin Kirsi but decided to play dumb. "Should I?"

Again, Leena's disappointment was palpable. "Everyone in the world learns English." She looked him dead in the eyes for the first time. Her eyes weren't green or gray but yellow, a deep yellow, and it made him take a small step backward. She held his gaze. "We watch your television, read about your celebrities, study your literature in our schools, your Shakespeares and Twains, but what do you know about us? Nothing. Nothing at all about the rest of the world."

Ezra smiled, somewhat smugly. "I suppose that's the nature of infatuation. It's a one-way street."

During this exchange, Cromley had positioned himself more and more between the two adversaries until he finally stepped directly in the center, breaking their eye contact. He gave Ezra his best "step down" glare. "Nélya Kirsi," he said, "is the daughter of Finlox founder Benjamin Kirsi."

"I trust you're familiar with Finlox?" Leena asked sarcastically.

Cromley turned his glare on Leena this time. "Nélya is the *de facto* heiress of the Finlox fortune should anything happen to her father. And…"

"And," Leena continued reluctantly, "Nélya has gone missing. As of this morning, no one knows where she is."

"How do you know all this?" Ezra asked.

"Every morning at eight, she's supposed to call a phone number to confirm she's safe. This morning she didn't call."

Leena then explained more about the Finlox heiress, affectionately called "the last princess of Finland." She'd been living in Chicago for three months, posing as a college student to escape the spotlight back home. From a very young age, pictures and videos of every formative milestone, walking, talking, skiing, appeared on her father's social network. By the age of five, she'd become a household name in Helsinki. By ten, she was appearing on morning shows in Oslo and Stockholm. By her late teens, she frequently drew crowds at clubs and music festivals all across Europe, not because she was performing but merely because she was there. If Ezra had read any American entertainment magazines, he also would've known the name Nélya Kirsi, or at least he would've recognized her.

Once Leena Åkerholm showed him a photograph, he agreed it was a singular face—rounded and soft, a perfectly placed dimple in her cheek, and a frame of shoulder-length sunflower blonde hair. "She's been wearing it shorter since coming to America."

He returned the photograph reluctantly. "So what happened?"

"Ms. Kirsi attended a party last night at a lake house," she said. Now she produced a different photograph, this one of a young man in his twenties. He could've been in a magazine ad for tennis apparel. "This is Puck Hartford."

"Puck?" Immediately he disliked this kid.

Cromley sat on the corner of Ezra's desk. "Puck changed his name in college. His birth name is Clive Hartford the Third. He's a tech whiz. Puck dropped out of Stanford a few years ago to start a dating app, Roll the Dice."

"I've heard of it," Ezra said. Then quickly, he added, "But I haven't tried it." Technically, this was true. He'd set up a profile late one night but chickened out before "rolling" for matches.

Ezra scratched his beard stubble. It had just reached that length where he'd need to decide if he wanted to shave it or go for an actual beard. "So are the two of them an item?" he asked Cromley. "I assume you've been keeping tabs on her?"

Leena responded, "We in the KRP believe Puck is the reason Ms. Kirsi chose Chicago." Her Finnish accent thickened around the words "Kirsi" and "Chicago." She lifted the case file off the desk and handed it to Ezra.

It contained, among other things, surveillance photographs of both Hartford and Kirsi at different locales around Chicago. Here they entered The Art Institute; there they strolled along the cages of the Lincoln Park Zoo; a final shot showed them knee-to-knee in the upper deck of Wrigley Field. No club seating, no luxury box, just a couple twenty-somethings at a game. Behind the photos, Ezra found a typed timeline for both Kirsi and Hartford. Times that their locations overlapped were highlighted in green. Most of the page was green.

His gaze searched the room, then settled on a spot on the wallpaper. All agents were given a choice of wallpaper designs: variegated stripes, a floral pattern, or chevrons. Ezra had chosen the stripes immediately but then stalled at the color, unable to decide between Michigan maize, Air Force blue, and Harvard crimson. He stared now at one of the blue stripes. What mistakes had Cromley made in handling Nélya Kirsi and why had Ezra been chosen to clear things up?

Furthermore, was this truly a top priority or was it more busy work to keep Ezra occupied while they decided what to do with him? Cromley still hadn't made his return official. He was back, but he wasn't back. The wallpaper was still his, but for how long?

Leena pointed at the timeline, specifically where it stopped. "Puck Hartford is the last person to see Ms. Kirsi before she disappeared."

"Where?" Ezra asked.

"He has a sprawling mansion on Lake Michigan," Cromley said. "He calls it Château Bachique."

"Castle of Bacchus?" Ezra asked.

Cromley shrugged.

"Which side of the lake is it on?" Ezra asked.

"Wisconsin. The Door Peninsula."

Leena wrote down the name. "What is that?"

"It's a body of land that—" Ezra began.

She snorted. "I know what a *peninsula* is."

"Door County is straight north of here. Three or four hours," Cromley explained. "I've arranged for the two of you to fly into Green Bay on a Phenom 100. You will be the only passengers."

"When does it leave?" Ezra asked.

"I thought you two could visit the shop where Ms. Kirsi has been working. Then we need to interview the Hartford family over at Roll the Dice. They're back in Chicago or will be shortly."

Cromley wrote down two addresses, one for the shop, Nordique, and another for Roll the Dice. "You can leave as soon as we're done. As you know, the first forty-eight hours are crucial. After that, testimony of the night will become fuzzy. If it isn't already." He mimed the copious drinking that had likely occurred.

"So if we are handling the missing person, are we also assisting with the death of..." Ezra searched for the name.

"Torben Laakso," Leena said.

"We are," Cromley said, "but this takes priority."

"What if they're connected?" Ezra asked.

Cromley shook his head. "We have everything relevant. Let's find the girl first and hopefully that will clarify the Laakso case. After all, he's not going to get more dead."

The Finnish officer flinched.

"Detective Vargas was the lead on that case," Ezra said.

Cromley wrinkled his brow, surprised if not concerned that Ezra already knew so much. "We're handling it now."

Before the ASAC left them, Ezra asked, "What does Puck use the house for?"

"Entertaining," Cromley answered. "He's already acquired two smaller companies, start-ups in the dating app world. Both times he had raging parties at Château Bachique."

"I've seen the videos. *Raging* may be an understatement," Leena said. "The police have been called seven times in the last year for noise complaints. They drink, have firework displays, even bring in live music."

"What do the neighbors make of all this?"

"As I understand things, they're invited to these functions, which are beyond the scope of most of their social standings," Cromley said. "A few decline, and those are the ones who call the police. Last fall, he had a firework display put on by the same people that do the fireworks at Disney World."

"You sound as if you attended," Ezra said.

Cromley grinned but said nothing. He rose from the corner of Ezra's desk and patted him on the back for the third time, then retracted his hand as if he too realized the gesture was becoming worn. "We're expected at Roll the Dice at noon," he said and left it at that.

Just the two of them now, Ezra asked Leena, "Your car or mine?"

"I am driving a Volvo," she said as if this settled the matter.

The thought came to him again and he decided to ask the Finnish officer directly. "What does the missing woman have to do with the dead Finnish national?"

"We don't know, but we intend to find out."

****

When Ms. Kirsi wasn't galivanting around Chicago with Puck Hartford, she spent her afternoons working at a trendy apparel store in downtown Evanston. The front window of Nordique already featured outfits too scanty to wear in the chilly weather.

The groundhog had predicted an early spring, but as near as Ezra could tell, the oversized marmot must've been drunk when it made that prediction, because the FBI agent was still wearing his winter peacoat.

Two stylish young women with asymmetrical hairdos moved around, folding and straightening, or otherwise fussing with the merchandise.

As Ezra and Leena Åkerholm entered, an electronic bell dinged. At the sound, a middle-aged woman with a pixie cut emerged from the back. Ezra assessed her pale features and baby blue eyes and guessed that she owned the Nordic-themed store. Her name was probably something like Annika or Ingrid or Valda.

"Cathy McCormick," she said, extending a hand. She shook his hand with a grip that could rival a lumberjack's. "You two must be…"

Leena nodded. "That's correct."

Cathy McCormick led them to the windowless storeroom in the back. To Leena, she offered an office chair. For Ezra she found a metal folding chair and for herself she took up a stack of plastic crates.

"You are aware of Ms. Kirsi's true identity?" Leena asked.

"Of course. My mother still spends summers with family in Oslo. Not every summer." McCormick paused.

"I go with her when I can."

"So you recognized Nélya?" Ezra asked.

"Right off."

Leena spoke now. "Did you tell anyone?"

She shook her head.

"Not even your mother?"

"I understood the seriousness of the situation and respected Nélya's privacy." She checked her phone unconsciously, then continued. "The man who called this morning said she's missing."

Leena frowned. "Have any customers paid her special attention recently?"

Cathy smiled mischievously. "Everyone pays that girl attention. Men come in with their wives or girlfriends and suddenly they're helping Nélya replace lightbulbs and rehang shelves. Little boys wiggle away from their mothers and turn her into a living jungle gym. The girls ask her for every piece of advice. They want to know what makeup to buy, which boys to date, even what books to read."

"Is she well liked by her coworkers?" Ezra asked.

"Venus and Brandy are the worst of all. They positively fawn over her." Then she looked down at the bland carpet. "They'll be devastated about this."

Leena nodded. "We will need to speak with them."

"Of course. Let me just close up the shop."

She put their seats away and closed and locked her office door. Then she turned off the sign in the window. A few minutes later, they stood in a circle in the warm light that filtered in through the floor-to-ceiling storefront. The red-and-white transom window was painted to resemble the selburose pattern, symbolic of Scandinavian knitwear. Ezra owned a Christmas sweater with the same pattern, also in white and red.

"Your friend," Leena began, addressing the two young women.

"Nellie?" Venus asked.

"Yes, she's—"

"Missing?" Brandy asked. "We heard you talking in the back."

Ezra tried next. "Did Nellie mention any plans for this weekend?"

The young women looked at each other, brows knitted. "What was she trying to find?" Venus asked.

Brandy's face lit up. "A mask!"

"I know that, but what kind?" Venus asked.

They both looked up as if the answer hung just over their heads. Then they locked eyes and said simultaneously, "Penguins!"

Leena pinched the bridge of her nose. "Okay, explain."

Venus spoke rapidly, the words tripping over one another. "Nellie wanted penguin masks for her and her boyfriend—whom she's never even shown us a picture of!—because they were going to some sort of masked party, where you have to guess who everyone is like the Masked Musician—have you seen that show? I don't care for it, but I think that's the best way to describe it. Well, now that I think of it, there is a name for the type of party—oh, what is it?"

"A masquerade?" Ezra interjected.

"Yes!" She continued at the same breathless pace, "Nellie said her boyfriend was attending a masquerade out in the woods and they had to have the perfect costumes—penguins because they mate for life and even though she never said as much, and really never talks about her boyfriend even though Brandy and I talk about our boyfriends constantly, I got the impression this guy was the real deal, you know, one she wanted to keep."

"Did you know about Nellie?" Leena asked and let the question hang in the air.

Brandy let her gaze wander the walls of the store, settling on the colorful transom, which she pretended to find suddenly intriguing.

Venus met Leena's gaze. "We knew about Nélya," she said. "We knew who she was back in Finland."

"Did you tell anyone?"

"I didn't," Venus said.

Pretending to just realize she'd been asked a question, Brandy replied, "Oh, I didn't tell anyone either." Her words sounded sheepish; her eyes remained averted.

Ezra wasn't convinced.

Chapter Six

Fr. Remy Mbombo approached the abandoned theater. He knew the building's history well because he'd seen it happen elsewhere. Once a fashionable movie house in a decent neighborhood, it subsequently became a second-rate one in a declining neighborhood, then a venue for community events, until finally the only people interested in the building, or for that matter the neighborhood, were the churches.

He stepped through the side door and found himself blinded as his eyes adjusted to the dark. Soon he realized he was standing behind the movie screen, a thin white wall littered with holes from years of neglect. Beams of light streamed through, punctuated by motes of dust.

"Is that you, Remy?" a booming voice asked from the other side.

"It's me."

A door opened beside the screen, and Reverend Don Webber appeared, haloed by light. He reminded Remy of a photo negative. He was about Remy's age but with less white hair, and his skin was every bit as dark as Remy's. There the similarities in their appearance stopped. Don carried the same informality in dress and in demeanor that Remy saw in almost every American.

"Thanks for meeting me here," Don said. "I know it isn't the best neighborhood."

Remy smiled.

"Why are you smiling?"

"It's nothing." Concerns for his safety always amused Remy. The idea that he would survive not one but two civil wars just to die in front of a discount grocery or behind a vacant movie theater seemed absurd. "God has kept me safe through far worse situations."

They walked into the light, Don giving Remy the grand tour of the theater. The seats showed wear and tear, and the stage needed work, but the bones of the building were solid. Near the front entrance, a large office sat to the side of the lobby. Don unlocked the door. "We've had our ecumenical meetings here the last two months."

"Meetings I wasn't invited to?" Remy asked.

Don waved him off. "You're out in the suburbs."

"You say that as though it makes my job easier."

Don raised an eyebrow. "Tell me it doesn't."

Three months earlier, a young woman from Remy's parish nearly died after falling from the school's bell tower. Then her roommate was murdered. He considered sharing this story of parochial tragedy, but something told him not to compare notes with his protestant colleague. Certainly whatever happened in the suburbs also happened in the inner city.

Don pushed the door open into a sparse but clean room. "We had to run the previous tenants out first."

"Someone occupied the building?" Remy asked, incredulous. "For what purpose?"

Don sighed. "They were squatting." The pastor spread his arms out as if in resignation. "This space wasn't doing them any favors. Most of them spent their days on the needle or the pipe with no heat and no running water in the whole building."

Remy agreed this was no way to live.

Don opened the cabinets and began removing colorful books, pamphlets, Biblical maps, and board games. "A few are in the shelter downtown," Don continued. "Some found beds at a halfway house. One girl entered treatment."

"Really?" Remy knew the large price tag alcohol and drug treatment centers carried. "Who is she?"

"A young woman, sixteen or seventeen, who ran away from home. We found her after working with CPD and the family took her to treatment the same day." Don piled everything onto a counter and returned to the cabinets.

"So what's the plan then?" Remy asked.

"Do you have Finlox Plus?"

Remy was familiar with the streaming service for old movies and television shows. "I have just the standard twenty channels from the cable company. I don't even have the internet at home."

"Ah ha!" Don brought out four wooden chessboards and spread them out on the table. "I saw a program the other day about these teenagers in Glasgow. *The Scotch Game.* These kids are getting involved in drugs, crime, getting pregnant, but then this priest starts a competitive chess league."

Remy nodded. "I've seen it. Not that one specifically, but a similar plot line." The metal hinge creaked as he opened one of the chess boards. Inside, affixed to the board with small elastic straps, was most of a chess set. The white king was plastic, not wood, and there were four dark knights.

Don craned his head over Remy's shoulder. "Our youth group may have mixed up the pieces."

Beneath the four wooden boards were two plastic

ones. Six boards in total. Once opened and laid out on the long table, they made five full boards and one partial. They could use that one for extra pieces or to teach fundamentals.

Don began setting up one of the wooden boards. "A little birdie told me you were something of a chess savant."

Remy chuckled and helped him, placing the kings and queens while Don placed the pawns. "Your birdie exaggerates."

"Do you have time for a quick game?"

"Of course."

Eight moves later, Don sighed heavily. "No, I think *savant* is a fair assessment."

Remy smiled, twirling a knight in his fingers. "Or perhaps you are just very bad?"

"So you'll join us?"

"When do we start recruiting?"

They began boxing up the boards as they talked, putting away everything as they found it with the exception of the chessboards, which they placed toward the front of the cabinet.

"We have four young men coming in this afternoon. One is a volunteer from our youth group, a young man considering ministry as a career. As for the other three, well, attendance is mandatory as a condition of their diversion."

"What does this word *diversion* mean? Not a *distraction*, surely?"

The preacher made his hands into two sides of a scale, weighing them back and forth. "It's not jail and it's not probation."

"I think I understand. It's their last chance before

their last chance?"

Don laughed. "That's a good way to put it."

They left the conference room and Don locked up behind them. For a moment, Remy wondered if his friend knew about ASAC Cromley and the FBI's plan to collect intel on the local gangs. Was the good reverend collecting information as well? "Can I ask why you're doing all this?"

Don's usually warm smile became strained. "What do you mean?"

"It seems like a lot of work to help a few people."

The preacher broke eye contact and a concerned looked passed over his face. Clearly, others had asked this very question. "To leave the ninety-nine to save the one—that's the nature of the call. You, of all people, should understand that."

"I do," Remy assured his friend.

The two men served together on a state-wide pastoral council and even attended talks by visiting theologians, a noted bishop and a popular evangelical author among them. Nevertheless, Remy didn't know the man well enough to read his intentions.

"Do you have lunch plans? Our fellows aren't coming until this afternoon."

"I have a Saturday mass to offer," Remy said, "but I'll be back."

He walked out the same way he'd come. The weather had warmed considerably so that what little snow had covered the grass and sidewalk that morning had already dissipated to a barely visible dampness. The L was a five-minute walk from the theater. During that short walk, Remy gave no thought to the nascent chess club or Don or even Cromley's proposition.

What occupied his thoughts instead was a memory from thirty years ago. It occupied his attention so thoroughly that he nearly stepped into the street as a city bus pulled to the curb. Its doors opened, and a small crowd of hooded teens and grocery-toting grandmothers poured out.

"Well?" the blue-visored bus driver asked.

"Well what?" Remy asked in return.

"Are you getting on, Father?"

He touched his Roman collar, nodded brusquely, paid the fare, and found a seat. He didn't know where the bus was heading, but he could take a cab from wherever it stopped. For now, he needed to sit, to let his mind wander through the maze of his memory, and this city bus was as good a place as any to do that.

His gaze was fixed out the window at storefronts and apartments and a thousand forms of metal and concrete, but what he actually saw were bushy green acacia trees and beyond them a river, deep and wide, a river rolling slowly through the ancient countryside.

Chapter Seven

Before heading to Roll the Dice, Leena Åkerholm arranged a meeting with two Finlox executives. They decided on brunch at an Italian bistro on Michigan Avenue. Holly Ward and Larissa Peterson were the kind of women who advanced easily in life. Their exterior wealth and professionalism showed the world they could be trusted, while their lighthearted interiors told the world they were here to have a good time. Leena explained that they'd been handpicked from Finlox London for these very qualities as well as their Queen's English accents.

"Why brunch?" Ezra asked.

"If we bring them into your office for an interview, they're going to want a lawyer."

"And he's going to want them to say nothing?"

She nodded.

The other option was meeting at the Finlox building but, as Ezra already knew, it still needed to pass its inspections. "Brunch it is," he said.

Holly and Larissa knew Leena well. They spent the first twenty minutes discussing Leena's *pesäpollo* team. *Pesäpollo*, Ezra gathered, was a variation of baseball specific to Finland. Talking with these women, Leena smiled for the first time.

Their food arrived and Ezra took this as an opportunity to change subjects. "Did the two of you know Mr. Laakso well?"

"No," Holly answered for them. "We met him at the central office in Helsinki a few times, but this was our first time working with him."

"We have become colleagues, though," Larissa corrected her friend.

"How did he seem?" Ezra asked.

Larissa dabbed at her mouth with a napkin before answering. "He's all business, all the time. But positive, too." She frowned slightly. "I was shocked when I heard…" She trailed off and looked in Leena's direction.

"Is Mr. Kirsi in town?" Leena asked.

The two execs shook their heads.

"We haven't seen him since…" Larissa started.

"…the Christmas party," Holly finished.

On a hunch, Ezra asked, "How about Puck Hartford? His company Roll the Dice is an up-and-coming dating app."

All three women shared an expression of mutual distaste.

"Oh, we know Puck," Holly said.

"Smug little bastard," Larissa added.

"Then I suppose you didn't attend the masquerade at his lake house last night?"

Both women giggled.

"Did I miss something?" Ezra asked.

"His company," Holly quoted Ezra.

"His lake house," Larissa added, this time with air quotes.

"What?" Ezra asked.

Holly laughed. "Everyone knows Roll the Dice is a pet project."

"Who's pet?" Ezra asked.

"Puck's. He was supposed to take on a position in daddy's business."

"He was supposed to do a lot of things," Larissa added. "Go to University of Chicago, graduate."

"Instead he went to Stanford and dropped out," Holly explained. "Now Daddy has bought him an app."

"I'm guessing then that the lake house isn't his either?" Ezra asked.

"Daddy's lake house," Holly explained. "Daddy's masquerade. MTT has one every spring."

"MTT?"

This time Leena answered. "Midwest Telephone and Telegraph. That's Hartford's business. Just as the Kirsis are famous in Finland, the Hartfords are famous in the telecom world."

Ezra scraped a bit of breakfast casserole off his fork and speared a raspberry. "So then did you attend the masquerade or not?"

"Oh we went," Larissa said, picking up a thin breadstick and snapping it forcefully. He wondered whose neck she wished it was.

"Why?"

The women shared a look, then giggled again, more like schoolgirls than middle-aged women in thousand-dollar suits. Ezra wondered if they were still drunk from the night before. "What's funny this time?" he asked.

Holly answered, "We were just remembering Larissa's costume.

Larissa gave his forearm a playful pat. "My husband, Leo, went as a sperm whale, and I was an octopus."

"How'd you get back to the city?" he asked.

"The Hartfords have a fleet of jets," Holly

explained. "Ours left a little after two this morning. We were all home in bed by three."

"And just to clarify, Mr. Kirsi was *not* in attendance?" Leena asked.

"No, Leena. Like we said, he hasn't been around since Christmas."

Did you notice anyone unusual?"

Holly laughed. "With the Roll the Dice crowd around, everyone's unusual. Puck keeps strange bedfellows."

Something occurred to Ezra then. "Strange name, Puck."

"He was a theater major. This whole app business is just to appease the parents. I think that's why he's gone about it so backward. It's like he wants it to fail. He's hired the strangest people he can find, done the tackiest advertising, but somehow it's actually working."

Larissa's face lit up. "The Turk! I nearly forgot about him."

"This was another costume?" Ezra asked.

She tilted her head. "I don't think so."

"How did you know he was Turkish?"

"He had on these clothes. Long white robe, tall hat like an upturned flowerpot."

"A whirling dervish?" Leena asked.

Larissa nodded. "He even whirled for us."

"Did he know Puck?"

She shook her head. "I don't think so. He seemed to know the Kirsis, though. I heard them speaking in Finnish."

"The Kirsis? Do you mean Nélya?"

"And Marja."

This caused a reaction from Leena. She placed her

silverware down carefully as if with great effort not to shatter her plate. "Mrs. Kirsi is in Chicago?"

Ezra made a note of this: At the time of her disappearance, Nélya's mother was present, along with a mysterious Turkish man.

"You need to tell us why two Finlox executives like yourselves attended Hartford's masquerade," Ezra said, tiring of their tact.

The women went tight-lipped.

"If this is a business secret, I can assure you nothing will leave this table," he said. "I've given Leena here permission to dislocate both my shoulders." He gave her well-defined arms a comical glance.

This seemed to loosen their resolve, or perhaps they too had come to view the interview more seriously. Holly spoke first. "It's not public information, Mr. James. Not public," she repeated. "But this time next week, the Kirsis and the Hartfords will be substantially closer."

As it seemed fast for an engagement and marriage, Ezra assumed she meant something financial rather than personal. "It sounds like either Finlox is acquiring Roll the Dice or MTT is acquiring Finlox." As Holly didn't react, he added, "Or the whole lot of them are throwing into some kind of merger."

"We're not at liberty to say," she continued. "But there will be some form of acquisition, and if you do anything with this information, such as purchasing stocks, you'll find yourself before a federal judge on trial for insider trading."

Larissa nodded gravely. "Mr. Kirsi will make sure of that."

"Have either of you seen Nélya this morning?" Leena asked.

The execs seemed confused by the question.

"I believe she stayed with Puck," Larissa said. "You could check with him."

Leena finished her food and pushed the plate toward the middle of the table. "Nélya never checked in this morning. She's presumed missing until she does."

The response to this news was mixed, both women exhibited a mix of emotions. Holly scoffed at first, then laughed contemptuously, pointing at Larissa. Larissa in turn shook her head, then rolled her eyes.

"That girl disappears from her family quarterly," Holly explained.

"Wait!" Larissa exclaimed over her friend. "Have you heard of Evelyn Williams?" The question was directed to Ezra and Leena, but then she turned to Holly beside her. "Do you remember what people were talking about last night?"

Together they were able to relate the story from various fragments they'd heard during their inebriated evening.

At last spring's celebration, a woman had been shot. During a spur of the moment hunting expedition, Evelyn Williams caught a few shotgun pellets in the back of the head. It happened right at sunrise, and she was rushed to the ER. Luckily, she was admitted and discharged the same morning. No one took the blame, but someone— who was it?—said Evelyn had been wearing a deer mask, and Puck, drunk, high, and not a good hunter to begin with, had mistaken her for a real deer.

Ezra turned off his recorder. "You've been a great help. Thank you."

The four left brunch amicably. Outside the investigators watched traffic pass on Michigan Avenue, waiting to compare notes until the two execs disappeared around the corner. When they could talk freely again, they settled on versions of three distinct possibilities. Nélya could've vanished of her own volition; she could've been involved in some sort of drunken accident and the Hartfords were having her treated somewhere; or, more sinisterly, something had gone wrong with the merger negotiations and Nélya's disappearance was a threat.

Ezra found it hard to believe the Hartford family would kidnap her, but a third party could just as easily profit from her disappearance. Then again maybe it was a hoax perpetrated by the Kirsis themselves—a stalling tactic or a diversion.

"Would Mr. Kirsi sink that low?" Ezra asked.

"To gain an advantage? It seems extreme. Then again…"

Something about her tone as she had questioned the two execs suggested to Ezra that Leena didn't trust the Kirsi family. Now he felt certain that she trusted Benjamin Kirsi least of all.

Ezra's phone buzzed with a text from Lucia Vargas.

—*Have you learned anything about Laakso yet?*—

—*I just left MTT on a parallel case.*— he replied.

—*You'll have to tell me about it over breakfast.*—

He'd completely forgotten about their plans, and now he and Leena were supposed to fly to Door County.

—*I'm skipping town this afternoon and probably won't be back until tomorrow evening. Raincheck?*—

Nothing came for a minute. Then, she replied,

—*Sounds good*— No exclamation point. No punctuation at all.

"Do you mind, Agent James?" Leena asked and

waited for Ezra to look up from his phone. "I need to check into my hotel." She pointed down the road toward a red awning.

"Do you need help?" he asked.

"No," she said irritably. "Sorry, I need to sit on a bed, take off my shoes, and be alone for a minute."

He made a hands-off gesture. "I get it. Take your time." He found the address for Roll the Dice and texted it to her. "I'll meet you there at noon."

"I know the place."

Ezra wondered what else she knew that she hadn't felt the need to share with him.

****

If the tears in Dorris Hartford's eyes were fake, she must've majored in theater like her son. Puck and his father Clive were less demonstrative in their concern for the missing young woman. Mr. Hartford, understandably, was too preoccupied with tending to his blubbering wife to have emotions of his own, but Puck almost seemed unaffected, as though he were trying to remain perfectly neutral.

With his tailored suit, gold cufflinks, and brushed back mid-length hair going fashionably gray, Clive Hartford reminded Ezra of an aging actor. He had gravitas and charm but also a sense of decline. Dorris also looked Hollywood-fifty. She was trim and elegant, her face and neck wrinkle-free, but her hands were not. Whenever Ezra met wealthy people on an assignment, he examined their hands. Men dyed their hair, women had Botox—and vice-versa—but people rarely bothered rejuvenating their hands.

You could tell a lot from the state of a person's hands. Mr. and Mrs. Hartford's hands, with their red cuticles and slight tremors, told a story of anxious exhaustion. Their son's, however, told Ezra nothing as they'd remained hidden beneath the conference table since the three investigators—ASAC Jeremiah Cromley, Finnish officer Leena Åkerholm, and Ezra himself—had walked in.

Midwest Telephone and Telegraph occupied the two uppermost floors of a major high rise in the Loop. Roll the Dice occupied four offices of this space. From the high ceiling of the conference room hung a postmodern sculpture that made Ezra think of a black, barbed-wire chandelier.

"Mrs. Hartford, how long did your guests stay at Château Bachique?" Ezra asked.

Clive peered into his wife's downturned face, then must have decided to field this one. "Most stayed until morning," he said. "We don't like the idea of people drinking and then driving around the area. The roads are winding and difficult to navigate at night. Each guest had their own room."

"When did this tradition start?"

Mr. Hartford smiled. "The Ides of March Masquerade? My father started it during his tenure as President of MTT. The company was small then, but it soon became large and then massive. He liked the idea of bringing everyone together once a year as a kind of litmus test."

"To see if anyone wanted to stab him in the back?" Cromley asked.

Hartford chuckled politely.

Yes, yes, Ezra thought, *we all read* Julius Caesar *in high school.*

Around the field office, Cromley dressed well,

spoke well, but remained down to earth. When they had to interview these Fortune 500 types, though, Ezra couldn't help but feel Cromley distance himself from his organization. He never tried to impress anyone, but in these interviews he almost did.

An assistant wheeled in a tray of coffee, tea, and pastries. Hartford motioned for her to leave the way she'd come, but both FBI agents were already reaching for apricot danishes. The assistant offered to make them coffee as well, then showed them the assortment of milks and syrups they could choose from. Only after they were happily snacking and sipping did she disappear back through the glass doors.

Leena scoffed at this show of indulgence. "I guess American TV does get some aspects right."

"This latte is prodigious," Cromley told the Hartfords. "I can't believe she made it right there on that stand."

I can't believe you know the word "prodigious," Ezra thought. What he said was, "We understand the Kirsis attended your masquerade last night."

Dorris wiped her eyes with her husband's handkerchief. "I invited Nélya and her mother. I felt it was only fitting as they're practically part of the *family.*" The last word clearly came out with more emotion than she'd meant.

Ezra didn't know what to make of this.

"Puck proposed to Nélya on Valentine's Day," Clive explained.

Dorris sobbed audibly and Puck patted his mother on the back with a steady, immaculate hand, a frown frozen on his face as if by force.

"When did you last see Ms. Kirsi?" Cromley asked.

"One a.m.," Clive Hartford answered without thinking. "That's when Dorris and I turned in. Some guests were still awake, but most had retired, so we felt comfortable going to bed."

"Who was still awake?"

"Nélya and Puck," he said, nodding to his son across the table from him.

"What about Holly Ward and Larissa Peterson?" Ezra asked.

"Them, too. Holly and Larissa seem to go everywhere arm in arm." He thought for a moment. "Oh, and some of Puck's friends. Sorry, his *colleagues.*" He could not keep the sarcasm out of his voice.

So Clive dismissed his son's venture as well. Ezra jotted down the phrase "arm in arm" beside his notes from the interview with Holly and Larissa, not because it was new information, but because of what it said about Clive Hartford and his familiarity with the Finlox staff.

Clive Hartford called his assistant over the speakerphone and had her bring the guest list.

Ezra consulted his hunter green notebook where he had started a list of costumes for the evening. "When you last saw her, was Ms. Kirsi still wearing her deer mask?"

A strained look passed between the Kirsi family.

Dorris shook her head. "She wasn't a deer. Puck and Nélya were penguins."

"My mistake," Ezra said.

Puck added, "It's an inside joke. When we first met, I tried to impress her with all manner of penguin facts. You see, I thought Finland was overrun by penguins."

"She never complimented your intellect," Leena said. "And when did *you* last see her?" she asked, glaring at Puck.

Puck's smile looked forced. "Apparently, penguins are a South Pole animal," he told Ezra. "As for when we turned in, it wasn't much after my parents did. Maybe two or two-thirty."

"When did you realize your fiancée was missing?" Ezra asked.

"In the morning."

"You made the discovery yourself?"

"That's right," he said through a yawn.

"What did you do first? Panic?"

Puck shook his head. "I had breakfast. I didn't realize what had happened. I thought she was in the bathroom. Then I thought she was getting breakfast. Then I saw these chocolate croissants and I was starving. It took me a half hour to realize she was missing."

"When did you realize she was gone?" Ezra asked.

"I heard her phone ringing upstairs." He indicated Leena. "It was her calling."

Leena confirmed this fact. "Ms. Kirsi is supposed to send a ping through our secure system every morning at eight. If we don't receive it, we call at eight-fifteen, then every five minutes afterward. Puck answered on our third attempt."

"You called from the air?" Ezra asked her.

"The ground. I had just arrived in the states," she said.

The fact that Puck was casually eating chocolate croissants while his fiancée was missing was a point in his favor. At Quantico, Ezra learned about a kidnapping case where a mother went to the restroom, leaving her toddler unattended at a shopping mall for nearly an hour. When she emerged, the child was gone. She searched the area, then ran home and called the police. "My son has been kidnapped," she told them.

This was her first mistake. People never want to believe the worst, not in an actual emergency. They'll deny, evade, rationalize. *He must've gotten lost.* Or *A friend saw him and took him to their house.* Worst case scenario, *the police found him unaccompanied and took him to the station.*

The fact that she leapt to kidnapping suggested her guilt, and in fact the agents who worked the case did discover the full extent of her guilt. The fact that Puck hadn't leapt to something catastrophic suggested his innocence. Or it suggested he'd carefully rehearsed and thought through his story.

"Then you came home on the family jet?" Ezra asked.

Puck shook his head again. "I drove around. I thought she might've gone for a jog."

"Or a hunt?" Ezra asked.

A micro-expression of fear passed over Puck's face, then he regained his composure.

If Julia had gone missing, Ezra would've stopped at every convenience store and bar and hotel on the peninsula. "Did you talk to anyone?"

"I stopped everywhere. I phoned all the lodges and hotels. The sheriff told me they'd take over from there. I didn't want to…interfere and mess anything up…so I came home."

"Alone?"

"Alone," he confirmed.

Leena interjected with a question. "What about the days leading up to her disappearance?"

"What about them?"

"Did she seem on edge? Did she have any conflicts

78

with anyone? Did she learn anything new?"

"Such as?"

"Family secrets, perhaps, or information someone may have found compromising?"

Puck thought this over carefully, swishing his mouth back and forth like a man eating a fish with tiny bones. "I can't think of anything. Her work was going well. Her family is close."

"Not so close that she didn't run off every so often," Ezra said.

The family shared another look, this one of mild disappointment. Puck answered, "She's past all that. This is a different situation."

"Have you seen Nélya's father?" Leena asked Puck.

This seemed odd to Ezra. Clive Hartford seemed more likely to have seen Benjamin Kirsi, especially if the merger was between MTT and Finlox, as Ezra suspected. But the question unsettled the twenty-something. He almost looked to his father for the answer, but Leena's gaze held him in place.

"Not…for several months," Puck finally said.

"Not even after the proposal?" she asked.

"We held a big video conference with everyone on Valentine's Day."

Clive shrugged. "Mr. Kirsi doesn't come to the states often."

Cromley interjected now, "We'll need to speak with the Kirsis immediately."

Hartford reached into his suit pocket and pulled up Benjamin Kirsi's cell number.

"Call it," Cromley said.

Hartford complied. It rang and then played a generic answering message. "You'll have to leave a message and he'll call back. He never answers."

Cromley nudged Ezra, who began speaking hastily. "Mr. Kirsi, this is FBI Agent Ezra James. I am working on your daughter's disappearance and need to speak with you immediately." He gave his cell number twice.

Then Leena added, "This is Leena Åkerholm. We don't care if you're in the country or not, but we do need to speak." She paused before adding, "Benjamin, if you are trying to handle this on your own, don't."

There were times when Ezra felt all-powerful, like the end-all-be-all of the federal government, like law and justice and democracy itself. Then there were times when he felt like a man leaving a message on the voicemail of a far more powerful man and hoping desperately for a call back.

Hartford hung up, and Cromley made a similar call to the Kirsis' office back in Helsinki. An administrative assistant assured him the call would be returned. The FBI and the KRP had already left a dozen such messages with no such luck. No one seemed to know where Benjamin Kirsi was. Just like his daughter, he had vanished overnight.

As far as they knew, no demands had been made or messages sent, but the idea that the Kirsis were trying to handle this on their own hung in the air between the two FBI agents. They'd both seen hostage cases where the families were warned against involving police and these frequently ended in tragedy. The family could easily pay any ransom and would, but what if money wasn't what the kidnappers were after?

Through the glass walls, he watched employees file off the elevator and back to their offices. Apparently, the lunch hour was ending, and they would need to wrap up this interview or move it elsewhere.

"Has anyone expressed animosity about the merger?" Ezra asked.

"What's this about a merger?" Clive asked.

Ezra ignored the denial. "Would anyone benefit substantially if it fell through or had to be delayed?"

He sighed. "Competitors, I suppose. Many companies would like to acquire the Finlox platform, but I don't think this would make it happen."

Taking a final stab in the dark, Ezra asked, "What can you tell us about Evelyn Williams?"

An eerie silence fell over the room and this time no one looked at anyone. Then Dorris answered for the Hartford family collectively. "None of us have ever heard that name before." If the mother wasn't going to talk about it, none of them were.

They thanked the Hartfords for their cooperation and the three investigators gathered their things to leave. Ezra had already turned his back to the conference table, but he noticed something reflected in the glass wall. Something on Puck's face.

It was subtle, involuntary. The grin of a suspect who's thinking, *I can't believe I just got away with it.* In the academy, they called this "duping delight."

Ezra saw it all the time.

Chapter Eight

The review of Torben Laakso's CCTV footage revealed two things to Lucia. First, it showed Laakso leaving his apartment with a metal briefcase and returning without it. Second, it showed him almost deposit a letter into a USPS collection box but then change his mind. Lucia called Parks and Rec the minute they opened. While they didn't have any additional footage of the victim, they did arrange for a crew to dredge a portion of the Chicago River.

By the time Lucia arrived, the sun had reached its zenith, showering light on the whole of Chicago. If Torben Laakso threw his briefcase in the river, odds were it floated down river. All manner of man-made structures filled and redirected the river. With any luck, a pier or an abutment had snagged it along the way.

A flat barge with a yellow crane on top spanned the river nearly east to west. It always impressed Lucia to see the dredger. She knew that, like an iceberg, most of the mechanism extended below the surface and down into the riverbed. It reminded her too of this investigation. A few elements were visible, but what they meant was obscured by five, ten, or twenty feet of murky water. By the time they finished, who knew what they'd find?

After an hour, the boat master wandered over to Lucia and Gorecki. The gray-haired man looked from one to the other. "Which one of you's in charge?"

"What did you find?" Gorecki asked.

"No briefcase, sorry, but we found this." He held out a no-frills cell phone with a black body and a small screen. Buttons made up most of the phone's face.

"Burner phone?" Lucia asked Gorecki.

"That's what the kids call them. Or it's what they used to call them anyway."

The boat master sighed, perhaps from tiredness or perhaps as a way of asking if they could quit. It was Saturday after all. He nodded at the phone. "Do you think you can pull information off that?"

"Shouldn't be a problem," Lucia said. "These have model numbers, and the company has call logs."

The boat master laughed to himself. "Here I thought these drug dealer types were so smooth, but you've got their number. Literally."

"Everyone's smooth until they get caught," Gorecki replied.

"And do you catch them all?" he asked.

Now it was the detectives' turn to laugh.

They watched as he rejoined the other workers on the barge.

"Did they find the letter?" she asked.

"What letter?" Gorecki asked.

"The one Torben Laakso didn't mail. If he didn't put it in the collection box, then it's bound to be in his apartment somewhere."

"It isn't. I just received the forensics catalog. No ready-to-mail letter." He retrieved his notebook from a jacket pocket. "They found a receipt in his pocket for Blue Basil, though. Dinner and drinks for two, it looks like. Officer Russo and I spent some time over there this morning talking to the waitstaff."

"What did you find out?"

He snapped the notebook closed. "Diddly."

This didn't surprise Lucia one bit. The staff of the upscale restaurant was almost chosen for their inability to remember the names or faces of their patrons.

"So no letter?" she asked.

He shrugged. "It could still turn up."

Why the letter mattered, Lucia didn't know, but it did matter. The missing letter had to matter. You didn't write a letter hours before your mysterious death unless it explained something. She needed that letter.

"I'll run this cell phone by Judge Deering and get a warrant," Gorecki said.

She stretched her back. "Good. I'm going home for a bit," she said. "I'll stop by the office tonight. Hopefully, we'll have some names and numbers by then."

"What's your hurry?"

"Oh," she said breezily, "I'm comparing notes with Special Agent James tomorrow."

Her partner rolled his eyes at the mention of the FBI agent. True, she brought up Ezra from time to time, but that hardly warranted an eyeroll. "When?"

"Breakfast." She remembered then with a sinking in her stomach that Ezra had rescheduled. Probably it would be dinner.

He laughed and shook his head.

"What?"

"For an engaged woman, you sure do eat a lot of breakfasts at another man's house."

"Adrian and I aren't engaged." Lucia realized only too late that this wasn't the part she was supposed to dispute. "Also, I doubt it will be at his house."

Thankfully, they'd driven separately. Gorecki headed back to the station while Lucia drove home if only for a few hours.

She lived on the second floor of a third story on the east side of town. The apartment was small but close to both downtown Evanston and the precinct. From her two-foot by six-foot balcony, she had a view of Lake Michigan, albeit a distant one.

When she arrived home, it was broad daylight, but her body told her it was the middle of the night. She wanted nothing more than to flop onto her bed and let Gorecki's eventual phone call wake her up, but the second she opened the front door, an eerie sensation ran up her spine. She didn't know what had been altered in the living room, but something, possibly everything, had shifted ever so slightly. If it had been the middle of the night, she may have written off this feeling as late-night paranoia, but in the clear daylight, she knew something was amiss. But what?

Cautiously placing one hand on the butt of her sidearm, Lucia cleared the apartment one room at a time, until she made it to the bedroom and found what she was looking for. The blinking green light on her computer monitor told her the computer had been shut down but not the monitor.

Someone else had been using her computer.

Chapter Nine

The four-passenger jet felt somehow smaller than Leena Åkerholm's rental car. In the car, they'd faced in the same direction. In the jet, they sat across from each other, occasionally making eye contact and then looking away, either to the reports they'd brought to read or down at their phones.

Though that morning's snow had melted, the flight felt icily quiet. Ezra watched the scenery below change from commercial buildings to mostly residential, then back to commercial, and then eventually to stretches of nothing at all. Other than the occasional evergreens, the trees were bare, the grass straw-yellow and tawny-brown, and from their vantage point, thousands of feet up, the lake looked perfectly still.

After what felt much longer than thirty minutes, the jet touched down in Green Bay, Wisconsin. Ezra handled the renting of a truck. He chose an all-wheel drive model in case they needed to do some off-roading. Leena spoke very little, and Ezra didn't try to make her.

As they left Green Bay and drove farther north into the Door Peninsula, the beauty of the evergreens and the rolling lake in the distance softened Ezra's resolve to dislike his temporary partner. "So, what made you want to become a cop?" he asked.

She hummed a single solid note. For a moment, he thought she was ignoring the question, but then she replied, "The police are a well-paid, well-educated, and well-respected profession." She paused, furrowing her brow. "At least, they are in Finland."

"Forget that I asked."

"Here they are brutes who bully civilians, or they're cowboys who dash into gun fights like they are in some action movie."

"I said I got it." Longing for the comfort of the earlier icy silence, he fixed his gaze on the curvy road ahead.

"It has been a long day," she said, apologetic. "I left my house at four a.m. Helsinki time to catch the earliest flight direct to Chicago." She checked her watch. "Already it is ten p.m. at home. I have been on a plane; rented a car; taken another, smaller plane; rented this monstrosity; now I am driving out to God-only-knows-where—and still I have learned nothing new."

"We've learned not to trust Puck Hartford."

"As I said"—she sighed—"nothing new."

"This case seems personal to you," Ezra said.

"The Kirsi family," she started, but stopped to consider her words, "they are important to Finland."

He wondered if they were also important to her. Benjamin Kirsi, from the photos in the case file, struck Ezra as a charmer: salt-and-pepper hair, light blue eyes, a genuine smile, and the sort of designer suits that only a tech company president could afford.

"To answer your question," she continued, "I started in IT. I analyzed online profiles for KRP, that is, our national police."

"I remember," Ezra said. "*Keskusrikospoliisi.*" While in the air, Ezra had researched the KRP on his phone, saying the Finnish name of the agency again and again in his head until it sounded half-right. Even though he nailed the pronunciation, she didn't seem impressed.

"Cybercrime is how I found myself working with Finlox. Benjamin Kirsi has assisted a number of cases," she said, "in Finland and all over the world."

"He sounds swell," Ezra said.

She snorted. "Do not think my English is so poor that I do not catch your sarcasm. What do you have against Finlox?"

"My mother…" he started but trailed off.

"Yes?"

Ezra decided to drop it.

"Oh, let me guess. Some Russian swindler catfished her and she fell for it."

He didn't react.

"Or perhaps she is one of the poor rabbit-hole Americans who has had their minds taken over by social media. Did it take her all the way to Flat Earth?" There was playful mockery in her voice but also disdain.

"I'm pretty sure Flat Earth was her starting point."

He saw her smile briefly in his periphery. They could pretend it was only playfulness then. That was fine with him.

"This isn't exactly what I had in mind for today, either," he added. "On Monday I'm getting reinstated and assigned a new partner and a caseload. When Cromley called, I thought he was reinstating me today. Instead, I'm on a babysitting errand, tracking down a foreign celebrity who got lost in the woods."

"She is not lost." Leena spat the words. "This is more complicated than you know."

"Okay, so explain it to me."

She looked down at her short, clean nails, splayed

out for self-inspection. "I can't." Then she turned to gaze out the passenger window and said more somberly, "You wouldn't understand anyway."

He tried to sound more friendly. "Try me. I actually worked on a case that involved the tech industry."

"CTC. The Coast-to-Coast Killer," she said like a dramatic TV narrator. "Yes, I've heard all about it."

Ezra turned to look at her, to put an expression to her mocking tone, but as soon as he did, she gestured urgently toward the windshield. "Here it is!"

Nearly too late, he turned and they found themselves momentarily in the wrong lane. Thankfully, no cars were headed in the opposite direction.

According to the GPS, Château Bachique sat a quarter mile off the highway, down a lane lined with sugar maples, American beeches, quaking aspens, and red and white pines. The pine trees were the only ones to retain their foliage through the winter. Even with the sparse leafage, Ezra could barely see twenty yards ahead through the thick forest. A ten-foot-tall iron fence appeared as if from nowhere and Ezra slammed the brakes.

A lanky man with black oily hair and pale gaunt skin met them at the locked gate. He dismounted his four-wheeler like a gentleman alighting from a coach-and-six. Without addressing the two agents, he unlocked the gate, pulled it completely open, then reboarded his four-wheeler and drove back to the property. Ezra followed.

As the forest parted, one stark tree trunk at a time, a mansion, styled in the manner of a French chateau, slowly took shape. Ezra noticed the blue conical roofs of the two towers first, then the towers themselves. White brick, the towers rose three stories into the clear spring sky. Pairs of windows ran up the dual towers that framed the white limestone mansion, the oversized bricks darkened unevenly over time.

They pulled into a circular drive at the center of which stood a Greco-Roman fountain, Venus holding an urn over her head, the water pouring over her bare breasts and splashing onto the child Cupid at her feet. Behind the fountain, a square stone path led to the entryway, which is where the groundskeeper parked. Had he not been there to guide them, Ezra wouldn't have known which of the half-dozen Roman arches led to the front door. It was the sort of house Julia would've sold her own aunt to buy.

"I'm Special Agent Ezra James," he said once they reached the entryway. "And you are?"

The groundskeeper eyed Ezra suspiciously. "Simmons."

Ezra walked over to one of the French windows and peered in. He couldn't see much through the gauze curtains. "And you watch this property daily?"

"That's correct." Simmons unlocked the front door. "This and four others, all vacation homes."

Before they went inside, Leena nodded at the roof. "I have seen this design before."

"What?" Ezra asked. "The roof?"

As she ran a hand parallel with the edge of the roof, Simmons took a step back from the doorway and craned his neck to see. "Ah yes, the roof cresting. Cast iron. They based it on the design of the roof cresting on the Cathedral in Reims. Have you spent much time in the North of France?" Simmons asked.

Leena looked to Ezra as if the question had been directed at him.

Reluctantly, Ezra said, "Perhaps you could just show us around."

"Of course."

The grand foyer opened skyward all three stories. At the top hung a blown glass fixture, blood red and made iridescent by the light of two dozen windows that ran along the facade of the building. To the left and right of the entryway, spiral staircases with ebony banisters curved elegantly upward and then disappeared into the second floor. The space glistened with light, light passing through crystal panes and light passing through the ornate glass fixture, so that Ezra felt himself momentarily illuminated from within like the pious figure from some renaissance painting.

"How much did all this—" he started to ask, then rephrased his question mid-stream, "—how much do they use the property?"

Simmons, who was already walking toward the north staircase, his shoes tapping confidently on the hardwood floor, stopped abruptly. Without turning, as though he expected them to join him, the groundskeeper said over his shoulder, "Once a month. More during the summer months."

Ezra jotted this down in his hunter green notebook. The pages contained a grid of dots, thirty-seven across and fifty down, spaced roughly a quarter inch apart. Ezra knew this about his notebook because he frequently counted the dots during irrelevant or rambling interviews. Whenever he interviewed a witness or a suspect, he let his recorder do the transcribing and let his mind roam the dotted field, making chance connections, not through the logical narrative but through the tone of the interviewee's voice as it settled on or rushed past or repeated certain keywords—*faithful, negligent, never, always, alibi.*

"How often do the Hartfords use the property during the summer?" Ezra asked.

"The children stay for weeks at a time."

Leena piped in now. "Puck, twenty-four, and Ginnie, twenty-one? These are who you are referring to as the children?"

With a half-turn back to them, Simmons nodded, then returned his gaze to the staircase. "Shall we?"

The three continued onward, Simmons purposefully and the investigators ambling as they took in the massive home. Ezra saw no signs of a party, no champagne glasses or trash, no damage to the walls or floors, not even the scent of food that follows a feast.

"Did they entertain guests last night?" Ezra asked.

Simmons gripped the ebony banister of the staircase. "That's correct."

"Was Nélya Kirsi in attendance?"

"I couldn't tell you."

"You don't know or you're not allowed to share?" Ezra clarified.

Simmons averted his gaze. "I'd be happy to provide you with a complete guest list if—"

"Mr. Hartford already did," Ezra said.

Looking annoyed, he pinched his lips. "Then why are you asking me?"

"It never hurts to verify."

With a note of resignation, he confirmed that all invitees had been in attendance.

"And no one else?"

"No one else."

"Not even Benjamin Kirsi?" Leena asked.

"I did not see Mr. Kirsi. Only his wife and daughter."

"But you would recognize him?"

"From the papers." He flashed a smile of tiny teeth. They looked to Ezra like the teeth of a rodent, a mouse or a rat. "I've never met the man personally."

They continued through the property. Seven bedrooms, each larger than the last; six bathrooms, one with his-and-her sinks, floor-to-ceiling windows that overlooked Lake Michigan, and the largest tub Ezra had ever seen; two dining rooms, one cozy, one massive; a wine cellar; and a home theater—Simmons showed them each, giving careful explanation of their design and use. After explaining the different vintages in the wine cellar, he even allowed Ezra to choose one.

"Not a bribe, obviously," Simmons said.

Ezra didn't have the heart to explain that he didn't drink, so he chose a bottle at random.

"A fine choice. Mrs. Hartford picked that out herself on a trip to Portugal. She brought home a whole case, in fact. It would astound you to know the price."

"For a case?" Leena craned her neck to study the label. "$25,000?"

Simmons frowned. "That's surprisingly close."

"Perhaps I should give this bottle to you," Ezra told her.

"I don't accept gifts from suspects." Out a north-facing window, she noticed something. "What's that?"

Simmons jutted his chin toward a small shed just north of the mansion. "Those are my quarters."

"You stay there when the Hartfords are present?"

"I stay there always."

The building was small even for a shed. Ezra looked

back at Simmons' face and imagined there an expression like that of a priest gazing out the window of an ornate cathedral at his tiny hermitage that lay just outside its walls. What did Simmons worship?

The groundskeeper continued through a doorway and into the hall. "This is the rifle room." He unlocked a pair of carved ebony doors, which made a stark contrast with the smooth egg-shell walls.

"Why is it called the rifle room?" Ezra asked.

The moment the doors swung inward, it became apparent. Other than a few trophies, which included a snow-shoe hare, a full-size grizzly bear, and the heads of various deer, moose, and caribou, every wall of the great room was covered with display cases. Two hundred rifles, shotguns, old fashioned pistols, and recurve and compound bows stared at the detectives as if with four hundred hostile and haughty eyes.

"We'll also need a complete inventory of the firearms and other hunting supplies owned by the Hartford family," Ezra said then.

Simmons nodded, unsurprised by the request.

Before they left the rifle room, Leena leaned close to the wall of deer heads. "This wall isn't trophies," she whispered to Ezra. "They're masks." Then to Simmons, she said, halfway between a question and a statement, "There is a cemetery on the property."

"On a hill west of the main house."

"Can we have a look?" Ezra asked.

The groundskeeper shrugged a shoulder, resigned. He led them back to the foyer and then out to the circular drive, stopping at the fountain. Something in his patient silence made Ezra wonder if he had more to say.

"This is Venus?" Ezra asked.

"And Cupid," he confirmed. "The white marble is Italian, but the sculptor was American." He gave them the name with no hope that either detective would recognize it. They didn't. "When Clive, Sr. built this home originally, he spared no expense making it as true to the chateauesque style as possible."

"Hence the name," Ezra said.

"Bacchus," Leena said, "god of drunkenness."

"His followers," Simmons murmured, "would take to the forests to revel and indulge."

"And to tear people limb from limb," she added.

This recalled a certain image in Ezra's mind, a painting of a man being restrained by two women while a third held a small boulder aloft to club him with.

"I should mention that a speedboat went missing last night," Simmons said apropos of nothing.

"What?" Leena sounded genuinely angry. "You didn't feel you should tell us this when we called? Or the police when they came this morning?"

"What's the registration number?" Ezra asked. Before the last syllable left his mouth, he had his phone out and ASAC Cromley's number pulled up.

Simmons recited the number from memory and gave the make and model as well. "White with blue stripes," he added.

Cromley picked up on the second ring. "James?"

"I need every marine unit and coast guard unit we have in Lake Michigan to check the shoreline for an abandoned speedboat."

Cromley cleared his throat. "Are we talking Wisconsin, Michigan, Canada?"

"Everything, and if that doesn't turn up anything, we'll have to check each body of water that's attached. I think whoever took Nélya Kirsi transported her with a stolen speedboat."

They discussed the boat's specifications and what agencies would need to be coordinated. "Door County Sheriff's office canvassed the area first thing this morning, but they didn't know about the stolen boat," Ezra said, glaring at Simmons.

"Why are we just learning about this?" Cromley asked.

"That's a good question."

Simmons looked up sheepishly. "I'd only just made the discovery," he said, convincing no one.

They'd spent at least an hour touring the Château Bachique. Had Simmons been buying someone time? His boss maybe? Or the son Puck? Or a third person? Was he protecting Nélya Kirsi herself? As the investigators walked in the direction of the cemetery, Ezra called the Door County Sheriff's office to suggest they bring Simmons in for a nice long conversation.

****

It took Ezra and Leena two hours to survey the forested grounds of Château Bachique. By the time they reached the cemetery, a small disused family plot on a slight hill, the light was fading to soft pink and Ezra could barely make out the inscriptions on the gravestones.

Ezra read them over, one by one, searching for a Hartford ancestor. When it became clear that no Hartford's had actually been buried here, he concluded the family must have purchased the cemetery with the property and hadn't cared to remove the bodies. Ezra found no signs of a recent gravesite, a fresh body buried among those long laid to rest. Nor did he find a single remnant of last night's masquerade. Leena had mentioned previous parties involving fireworks, all-night drinking, and live performances, but these woods bore no indication of the aftermath of such an event. Perhaps, last night's celebration had been less of a spectacle. Or someone had already cleaned up the trash. What else had they cleaned up?

"Door County will need to comb this entire property," Leena said. Her head pivoted, looking from headstone to headstone, unsure where to settle her gaze. It was the first he'd seen her truly agitated. He remembered then how long her day had been.

"Do you need a breather?" he asked.

She shook her head. "We'll go to the sheriff's office now."

"There's a hunting lodge up the road. Cromley reserved us a room."

Her face turned red with either anger or embarrassment.

"Two rooms, I mean, of course," Ezra added quickly. "He reserved us each a room, you a room and me a separate room."

Her face still burned red and now he knew it was with anger. "We're not stopping. I have come too far."

"How well did you know Kirsi?" he asked. He waited a moment before adding, "Nélya, that is." He wanted to know about her relationship with Benjamin as well. Again he pictured the tech CEO, his charming smile and eyes the color of a Nordic river. Leena Åkerholm was equally elegant and other-worldly. While she wasn't Ezra's type, she was certainly someone's.

Leena answered neither the question he'd asked nor the one he'd implied. Instead, she marched toward the château and their rental car.

From the hill, he watched her recede into the woods, letting her get some distance ahead. He would've watched her all the way to the truck, but his phone rang: Cromley.

"What do you have for me?" Ezra asked.

"They found the boat on Rock Island."

"That's not far from here."

"Not far at all."

"And the Finnish *princess?*"

"No sign of her. There is one thing, though."

Ezra waited.

"A deer head."

"Okay."

"The sheriff's office is running it through forensics to see if there's any trace of Nélya's hair inside it."

"Why would her hair be inside a deer's head?"

"There's more, but you shouldn't tell the Finnish officer just yet."

"Get to the point," Ezra said, impatient.

"It's a deer mask—like the ones the Kirsi's wear at their masquerades—only it's made from real deer skin and antlers."

"We just saw a whole room of similar masks," Ezra said.

"This one appears to be the same mask Evelyn Williams was wearing when she was shot last year."

"How sure are they?"

"They pulled shotgun pellets from the back and blood inside."

"We'll head up to Rock Island tonight," Ezra said.

A gunshot rang out, pulling his attention from the phone call. Ezra looked up just in time to see Leena

Åkerholm's blonde hair splayed over her head as she hit the dirt.

"Shots fired!" he hollered into the phone before dropping it and drawing his firearm.

Chapter Ten

That Saturday's homily felt hollow. The mass was rarely well-attended, most parishioners sticking to Sunday. Fr. Remy hoped he hadn't said anything strange as his mind continually wandered from behind the altar. Then he saw the expressionless faces of the Saturday regulars and realized he had nothing to worry about.

Victoria Holcomb, the new school secretary stopped him in the narthex, a concerned expression on her face. "Are you feeling okay, Father?"

Of course Mrs. Holcomb would notice. She noticed everything. She knew when the HVAC filters needed to be changed by a faintly stale odor in the air. She knew when a romance between upper school students was about to end by the way they sat too close together or too far apart at lunch. And she knew when Remy's mind was drifting elsewhere. How she knew this last bit, he could only guess.

"I have a lot on my mind," he replied.

He wanted to tell her about the FBI agent pressuring him to break the seal of confession. Deeper down, he wanted to tell her about his time in Rwanda. Then again, he barely knew her and had no idea if she would understand.

She wrinkled her brow. "Is this about the city outreach program?"

He nodded tentatively.

"Not every neighborhood in Chicago is as nice as Evanston," she said.

"You misunderstand, Mrs. Holcomb."

She cocked her head. "What have I been telling you since January?"

He'd forgotten to call her "Vickie." The Americans weren't just informal—they demanded informality from everyone around them at all times. It both annoyed him and filled him with a strange admiration. Here in the land of the free, no one stood above anyone else. Even the bishop recommended, although he didn't require, that Remy have the parish call him "Fr. Remy" rather than "Fr. Mbombo."

He started again, "Vickie, you are familiar with my interest in chess."

She laughed. "That's all you and that cop buddy of yours talk about."

"Ezra is a formidable opponent," he admitted. "The outreach program involves chess. Not all my memories of the game are entirely positive."

Vickie smirked. "Do you have a lot of traumatic chess memories?" Then her gaze traveled to the long scar running down the left side of his face and she stopped smirking.

"Father Khonde, God rest his soul," Remy said, "was the pastor at *L'église Notre-Dame-de-Fatima*, my first post in Kinshasa."

The secretary raised her eyebrows. "Where is that?"

"The Congo. At that time it was known as Zaire, a most corrupt nation."

"You must've seen a lot."

The priest nodded.

"If you ever need to talk…"

Remy smiled. "Another time, perhaps."

Parishioners filtered out until only Remy and Vickie remained in the empty church. Then she too departed, leaving him alone with his thoughts.

He stared at the wooden statue of Mary beside the south doors. In his mind, however, he saw the all-white statue of Our Lady of Fatima as it resided on a side altar in the Kinshasa church. It was the statue he passed each time he mounted the stairs to Fr. Khonde's office. There one evening thirty years ago he found his superior, not kneeling for evening prayer, but standing over a chess board. Khonde looked back and forth between the board and a paperback book, which contained numerous chess problems—mate in two, mate in three, avoid mate, gain material. He studied his wooden pieces, then studied the book, switching several times. Then he spied Remy in the doorway.

Khonde cleared his throat and addressed his curate in Lingala, a local Congolese dialect. "Ah, Fr. Mbombo, I didn't see you there. Is compline already upon us?"

Remy smiled. "Upon us and passed. You will have to pray twice in the morning." Then he added more seriously, "I am being called away by Rome."

Khonde laughed somewhat spitefully. "Funny, because they have said nothing whatsoever to me, your superior."

Remy opened his mouth, then closed it. He wanted to point out that Rome was superior to all, but surely Khonde knew this better than Remy.

"Everything in Africa is political, Fr. Mbombo."

"Even the Church?"

A laugh from somewhere deep inside Fr. Khonde erupted as suddenly as a geyser. The pastor seemed to remember his position—that of a representative of the Church mentoring a new priest—and he regained his composure. He cleared the chess board and set it up for an actual game. Remy knew better than to wager anything of value on a game with his superior. His first month, he'd lost three games in a row with such quick succession that he realized only moments later that his chores had been doubled, then tripled, and then quadrupled. If Fr. Khonde meant to keep him in Kinshasa through a chess game, Remy would decline—he had to.

"Get that nervous look off your face," Khonde said in French. "If Rome has called you, you must go." He placed the last two pieces on the board. "I only wonder who has called Rome."

Remy said nothing.

"Where are they sending you?"

"Rwanda," he replied, looking his superior in the eye.

The suspicion fell from the elder priest's face, replaced with concern. He stepped toward the only window in his small room, and Remy joined him there. "What do you see?" he asked.

A few lights shown in the distance. "It is nighttime," Remy said.

He pointed now. "Where are those lights coming from?"

"Brazzaville."

"Exactly. And between our two cities?"

"The Congo River."

"One great river separating two very different nations—Zaire and the People's Republic of the Congo, one a democracy, the other a communist state. We were supposed to hate them and they us. Why? Because of economic policies we had no control over." Fr. Khonde paused, perhaps expecting a comment from the younger priest. When none came, he continued, "Now things are different. The Soviets are no more. It is the 90s, as they say in American television, yet this animosity between us persists."

When Remy first came to the parish in Kinshasa, the Marxists still controlled Brazzaville across the Congo River. In fact, Remy was sent here for that very reason. For months, Remy monitored his superior's every action, submitting reports at regular intervals. He watched as Khonde hung a rosary, sometimes white, sometimes black, from one of three nails beside this very window: two colors, three nails, representing six distinct messages meant for someone across the river. Remy suspected that either an agent of Zaire waited across the river and behind enemy lines or a Soviet station awaited a message from Fr. Khonde himself. Remy never did determine which. Then the Soviet Union collapsed and Remy remained at the parish for two years, awaiting new duties. The call about Rwanda was the first he'd received since the People's Republic of the Congo had officially ceased to exist.

Fr. Khonde touched the highest of the three nails absentmindedly and continued to study the lights across the river as if they were a constellation that held Remy's fate. "Rwanda is different," he said finally.

"How so?" Remy asked.

"Communists killing capitalists, Christians killing Muslims, and vice versa. This is the formula in Africa." He wrinkled his brow. "Rwandans are democratic—on both sides. They are Christian—on both sides. Still they murder one another in the street and wrestle for power."

Remy nodded. "The Hutu and the Tutsi. I know about them."

The wooden window creaked as Fr. Khonde opened it all the way to the top. River air, cooled by the late evening, filled the room. Winters were not cold in Zaire, but they were still cooler than the summer, especially at night.

"When do you leave?"

"Late February."

"Will you have a replacement?"

Remy shook his head and frowned. "I should return in a few months. June by the latest."

"*If* you return," Khonde replied, not looking at him.

"Yes." He thanked his superior for understanding and then turned to leave.

"Do you speak any Kinyarwanda?"

Remy knew this was a local language in Rwanda, but French and English were used more commonly for official matters. He rocked his head back and forth, equivocating.

"I thought not." His superior frowned. "Do not speak French there, Remy." It was the first time he'd addressed the curate by his first name. "Speak only in English."

"Why?"

Khonde regarded him with sad eyes. "They will peg you for a Parisian immediately."

For obvious reasons, Remy had never mentioned his country of origin. Remy believed that Khonde took him for a fellow African, but this illusion vanished like smoke. Remy wondered what else the pastor knew about him. He knew better than to ask. Here stood a man at the end of his career—full of wisdom and experience and, apparently, discretion. The young Remy, on the other hand, felt like a newborn deer stumbling and tripping through the forest.

He didn't deny his French citizenship, didn't insist he really was the Nigerian-born son of a Congolese expat, as was his cover story. Nor did he ask if anyone else in the parish knew. Instead, he thanked Fr. Khonde and shut the door behind him as he walked back into the dark hallway.

Now, his mind refocused as the daylight of Evanston and the image of the lifeless wooden statue of the Virgin Mary returned to him.

"How strange it is to be human," he said aloud to Mary, "to be able to occupy two places and times at once, simultaneously missing the past and longing for the future."

****

Joaquin Nuñez couldn't seem to decide if he was a rapper or the host of a late-night talk show or, as Remy had been led to believe, a future minister. That's how short guys were, especially when they were as intelligent as Joaquin. Their lack of height—and at fourteen-years-old Joaquin barely cleared five feet—made them too quick to seek the approval of the men around them, and their agile minds constantly sought out the answer. For Joaquin, this meant switching personas like a stage actor switches costumes.

As they awaited the other chess club prospects, Joaquin discussed the book of Ephesians with the holy men, but as soon as the first teenager arrived from the diversion program, he dropped the religious talk, his voice lowered affectedly a half octave and he slouched down into his chair, making himself appear even smaller.

"What's up, Davon?" Joaquin asked.

Davon, who already looked uncomfortable in a white shirt and tie that his grandmother no doubt picked out for him, glared at Joaquin.

"How do you know my name?"

Joaquin straightened in his chair. "English class." His voice raised to nearly a falsetto. "You're the only sophomore." The falsetto warbled now. "Not that it's bad. It's cool. You sit right in front of me?"

Davon scowled at him.

"We're in alphabetical order. Davon Miller, Joaquin Nuñez."

At the pronouncement of the full name, a light of recognition filled Davon's eyes. His scowl faded from specific to general and he turned from his small classmate to the far more imposing reverend. "So this is the place then?"

Don Webber smiled. "We're going to have a lot of fun." He grabbed Davon by the shoulders. They stood eye-to-eye. "You like games, son?"

The teenager raised an eyebrow. "Like basketball?"

Remy rocked back on his heels. "We were thinking something a little less physical."

"Where are you from?" he asked.

"Do you ask because of my accent?"

Davon nodded.

"Africa," the priest replied.

This seemed to impress Davon, but he didn't ask any follow up questions. "So this game is like cards or something?"

"Chess," Don said. "Father Remy here is a master and he's going to train you guys for a tournament."

Davon ran his tongue over his front teeth. "Is there any money in it? A man says, 'tournament,' I expect there's got to be a little money."

Remy had spent the morning researching chess tournaments in Chicago. Youth 847 was holding a round-robin tournament for thirteen to seventeen-year-olds at a nearby youth center.

"Güey, you know there's money," Joaquin said, rising from his chair.

Davon wheeled on Joaquin and puffed out his chest. "Fool! You know what that word even means?"

Joaquin dropped back into his chair. "What? No. What?" He looked from Davon to Remy.

The priest wondered momentarily if this might turn into the first fist fight of the chess club. If so, it would be a short one. "There is a cash prize," Remy said. "A hundred dollars for first place. Second place is a ten-dollar gift certificate to a game store."

Davon cooled. "What's it cost to enter?"

"Nothing," Remy lied. Technically, the entry fee was five dollars per player, but Don's church had already agreed to cover the cost.

Remy stared at Davon's face for a long moment. Something about his wide nose reminded Remy of a young officer, Hakizimana, he'd met decades ago in Rwanda. The name meant "God saves" in the original Bantu language. Or so Officer Hakizimana said when Remy asked about it.

Remy, a young man himself at the time, was crossing into Rwanda from Zaire. On his person he had nothing save a passport, a letter from a Rwandan archbishop, a prayer book in Lingala, a wooden rosary, and a single change of clothing. His mind, however, contained a code he'd committed to memory the day before.

Depending on what he learned in Rwanda, he would call his contact and insert one of three codes into an otherwise ordinary conversation. *"...le **R**ouen. Souvent, le bâillement"* translated as, *"Le **R**wanda semble bien"*—Rwanda seems fine—.

If animosity was rising between the Tutsis and Hutus, Remy would work into his message the phrase *"le saint sabbat,"* meaning, *"la situation s'aggrave"* – the situation is escalating—.

The final coded phrase was, *"...une grande ancre. Contre..."* for, *"un génocide a commencé."*

He hoped he would not have to use this last one. Hakizimana, an officer of border management for Rwanda, had rifled through Remy's bag, perhaps searching for weapons or loose money. Finding nothing of interest, he returned the sack to Remy and, unable to pierce the priest's mind, allowed him into the country.

"Welcome to Rwanda," the man said in English without looking at the priest and without sounding like he meant it.

Davon spoke again and Remy found himself staring at the teen's nose, measuring its width unconsciously. "What was that?" Remy asked.

"I said, what do I have to do?" Davon repeated.

Before Remy could answer, another young man pushed through the glass doors of the old theater.

Don beamed at him. "You must be Mateo."

He scratched his patchy beard. "Call me Matt." Then he thought better of it. "No, call me Money."

Don and Remy shared a look. "I think Matt will be fine," Don decided. "Matt, this is Joaquin and Davon.

I'm Reverend Don and this is Father Remy."

Matt looked from one face to another, taking them all in. "So what's the job? Moving cinder blocks?"

"No," Don said. "We're just going to play some games."

"For real?" He smiled, clearly relieved. "Because the last guy…" he trailed off, rubbing his head.

"Yeah?"

"He had me moving cinder blocks. Güey wouldn't even let me smoke."

Remy held up a finger. "You can't smoke here either. But if you all want, we can get some coffee or sodas."

"Pizza?" Matt asked.

"Sure," Remy replied.

The teenager brightened. "This beats the hell out of moving cinder blocks."

"Heck," Remy said.

Matt looked perplexed, then realized his mistake. "Shit, I probably shouldn't have said 'hell.' Shit, I shouldn't have said…" He blushed uncomfortably.

Don patted him on the back. "We'll work on that. Now we're just waiting on Jesus Suarez."

"It's Chuy," Davon said, barely audible.

"Chew-wee?" Remy asked, perplexed.

Don placed a hand on his shoulder. "It's a nickname for Jesús. You'll learn a lot around here."

The priest supposed his colleague was right. Perhaps, he'd even learn a thing or two from Chuy himself. But Chuy never came.

****

Twenty minutes later, they decided to start. Remy covered how the pieces moved, then their placement on the board; two openings at e4 and d4; two defenses against e4, the Sicilian and the French; and three defenses against d4, the Slav, the Dutch, and the Queen's gambit. As he repositioned the board yet again to demonstrate the four knights game, Reverend Don rapped the table with his knuckles.

"Perhaps we'd better let the young men play a game or two before we introduce any more theory." He gestured at their bewildered faces, which Remy had not even glanced at since beginning his demonstration. Even Joaquin, the future pastor, bore a confused expression, his eyebrows raised, his forehead crinkled.

"Ah, yes," Remy agreed.

Joaquin and Matt began right away on the board Remy had set up. As the fourth member of their "team" hadn't shown up yet, Remy set up a board for Davon.

The first game, Remy opened with e4 and Davon responded, surprisingly, with the Sicilian. Remy had planned to get him with the Scholar's mate, but Davon advanced his queen's pawn to block. Regardless, Davon lost ten moves later. The second game, Davon tried the French defense instead and extended the game to fifteen moves. After the third game, equally short, he threw his king at the board. It ricocheted and bounced across the floor.

"I don't get it!"

Remy gave him a questioning look.

"It's just moves," he complained. "Moves and moves. If I do this, you do that."

The priest steepled his fingers and exhaled into them. "Let's step back. You said you play basketball, yes?"

The teenager nodded.

"What is the first thing you want to do in any game?"

He thought it over. "That's easy: win the jump."

"Perfect. This square," he said and outlined the center four spaces with his index finger, "is the jump ball, right at the center. You want to control this area first and foremost."

With this piece of information explained, they began again, Davon extending the game little by little, until Remy switched from white to black and Davon had to begin building his progress all over again. They played into the evening, an hour past the allotted time, until everyone else had gone home and it was just them.

"My *tia* says you got to keep secrets," Davon said apropos of nothing, "otherwise you lose your job."

"That's true. If it's said under the seal of confession, that is. What is a *tia?* Some type of relation?"

"My aunt. She's from Puerto Rico. How come it's just in confession?"

"The Church believes the confessional is sacred."

"But, I mean, it's just talking."

"What is it you'd like to confess?" Remy asked.

"What? No, not me. I was just saying…"

"Clearly, your *tia* was giving you advice. Maybe she thought you needed to get something off your chest, so to speak."

"Look, I get that you're all, you know, godly, but me, I don't even know if I believe all that."

"Then you would have nothing to lose." Remy smiled. "As you said, I can't share anything or I will lose my job—and mine is not the type of job one can afford to lose."

Davon thought this over. "What do I have to do?"

"I'll walk you through it. First, you cross yourself like this and say, *In the name of the Father and of the Son and of the Holy Spirit.*"

****

Remy placed a hand on the teen's shoulder and felt the weight of Davon's sins slide away. The priest had not always agreed with the absolute inviolability of the seal of confession but in moments like this he did.

"So is that what happened to your palms?" Remy asked as they began packing up the board.

Davon regarded the straight burns on both hands. "Like I said, the brief cases were ice cold."

"Even the handles?"

"They were solid metal. I guess they're all connected."

"Perhaps so," Remy said, more to himself than Davon.

Chapter Eleven

After several hours of going through her computer and checking with the owner of her building, Lucia had found no trace of who broke into her apartment. She did find a suspiciously long delay in the CCTV footage and learned that around eleven a.m. the whole system in her building shut down. It took twenty minutes to reboot.

She now stood in Adrian's doorway awkwardly explaining the situation, her gaze traveling between him and his living room couch. They were originally going to hit the farmer's market that morning, but then the Laakso case came up. Something always seemed to come up when they had romantic plans for a Saturday morning. Adrian had claimed it didn't bother him, but his tone, his body language and, most important, his eyes said otherwise.

"Is it normal for your cameras to go out?" Adrian asked now.

"No. The owner of the building is checking with the internet provider."

"Maybe that's what turned your computer on."

"Maybe." Lucia didn't think so. Someone had been in her apartment and had accessed her computer. She was certain.

Adrian sighed and looked back into his pristine apartment. Everything had its place and Lucia couldn't help but feel there wasn't a place for her in it.

"Want to get dinner?" he asked.

Her gaze returned to his couch. "Or just crash," she said meekly. "Unless it's an inconvenience."

He approximated a smile. "Not at all."

They'd been dating less than three months, but already she'd learned that Adrian enjoyed his days most when they were planned out ahead meticulously, preferably on a color-coded spreadsheet. Lucia, on the other hand, loved surprises—the last-minute invitation, the chance meeting, the hole-in-the-wall restaurant discovered while wandering. If someone told her that in ten years she would be happy, healthy, and would have achieved all her career goals, a part of her would be sad, for then she would know everything that lay ahead.

"I'm sorry! Your place has been broken into!" Adrian added as if correcting his previous reaction. "Come in, come in."

"I'm sorry I'm such a mess," she said.

"Not at all," he said, half-convincingly. "I'll get you something to drink."

She brought her tired body over to the couch and sat. Even though she'd been here dozens of times, she couldn't help feeling like a burden.

As if to rescue her from these thoughts, her phone rang. It was Gorecki. "Did we get the warrant?" she asked. It seemed late in the day for that.

"Not that," Gorecki replied with a cryptic hesitancy. Was someone there with him?

"Then what?"

"You have a visitor."

"Okay. What kind of visitor?"

Maybe Captain Fitzpatrick was within earshot. Technically, the entire Laakso investigation had been handed over to the FBI.

"A certain gentleman has brought you a letter."

"A letter?" It took her several moments to register the new information. "Oh!"

"Yes, *a letter that was never sent,*" he said. "You know that evidence you've been begging me for?"

She'd hardly been begging Gorecki for anything. "I'll be right there." Lucia hung up and turned to Adrian, who was returning from the kitchen, a glass of water in each hand and a frown on his face. "Shit," she said. "I have to go back to the office."

"It's fine."

She rose to embrace him, hoping to close their emotional distance with physical contact, but he held the waters in front of him like two dumbbells. She touched his elbows lightly and pecked him on the cheek. "I'll call you tomorrow."

"Okay," he replied in a tone that could've meant "no" just as easily as "yes."

Adrian was damn near perfect in every way, she told herself. Like a beautiful smile with just the hint of a sneer.

****

The ground floor of Evanston PD was quiet, even for a Saturday. Lucia couldn't help comparing the external calm of the precinct with the agitation building inside her. Adrian agitated her as he ran hot then cold. Ezra too seemed to become available and then closed off—even if he was only a colleague. Then there were these Finns. Like the tide, the moment she drew closer to understanding the situation, a force mysterious and far more powerful than herself, pulled her away.

The elevator doors slid open and there at her desk

sat Saul Posner, Torben Laakso's elderly neighbor. Saul wore a white puffer jacket, which accentuated his beach ball shape. The halogen lights bounced with equal glare off the jacket and his pale papery skin. Enveloped in white, he resembled a cartoon ghost and his vacant expression only added to this impression.

"Mr. Posner?"

Lucia's words seemed to wake him.

"I found something." Saul sounded dazed. He reached into the pocket of his puffer jacket and removed a letter, folded in half, which was stamped and addressed to him. "I read it," he admitted, as if in apology.

"What does it say?" she asked.

Gorecki too had come over to hear. Saul unfolded the letter and laid it out on Lucia's desk, and the three of them looked down at it.

Saul,

If you are reading this, it can mean only one thing: I am dead. Otherwise, by the time this letter winds its way through the postal system, I will have warned you not to open it. I don't know who will pull the trigger, but I do know who is to blame: Benjamin Kirsi, founder and president of Finlox and hypocrite extraordinaire. Although, who am I to cast aspersions? We knew they were planning to rogue the durum. Miranda and I even visited the islands ourselves and witnessed the preparations—the sickles and the effigies. I should've left when I had the chance, when leaving would have mattered. By Monday morning it will all be too late. But what else could I do? My father was a company man and his father before him. I suppose it's genetic. I suppose I lack the lung strength to blow the whistle. Lacked.

Tonight Benjamin and I are having dinner at Blue

Basil. Tonight it will all come to a head. Or perhaps, as the poet said, it will end in a whimper. There's only one way to find out.

Adieu, mon ami,

Ben

The note made no sense. If he truly feared for his life, then why not go to the police? Why instead meet his would-be killer for a late dinner? Also why would Kirsi risk a public meeting right before killing Laasko?

"Are you sure no one saw Laakso or Kirsi at Blue Basil last night?" she asked Gorecki.

"We'll try the staff again, see if anyone recalls two gentlemen wrapped in Finnish flags or arriving by dog sled or…"

Her glare cut him off.

More seriously, he said, "Officer Russo and I interviewed every single employee. We showed them pictures, went over the reservation list and called the phone numbers. If Laakso made the reservation, someone erased it." Then he added, "We'll try them again."

Lucia needed to compare notes with Ezra and find out what he'd learned about the Kirsis, but she settled for Gorecki. "What's so special about durum?" she asked, pointing at the letter. "And why would roguing it be such a big deal?"

"Durum is a pasta wheat, and they can get pretty specialized. It can't mix with other wheats, so you have to go in and pull the non-durum before you harvest. It's a manual process. Time and labor intensive."

She nodded. "Laakso mentioned the islander's roguing the durum in one of his emails. It sounded negative."

"Huh."

"Laakso wanted to evacuate the durum from the island."

"Evacuate the durum? That doesn't make any sense. Are you sure the translation is accurate?"

"Nope."

Gorecki chuckled. "That about sums up this whole case."

"Unfortunately." She sighed. "What are these islands he mentions?"

"That I couldn't tell you."

"I spoke with the Finnish translator this morning, and she thought they might be Swedish islands."

Saul raised a hand. "I believe it's the Durum Islands," he said. "Ben spoke of them once."

Both detectives turned to him. They'd nearly forgotten he was still there.

"Just once. He didn't explain about all this roguing business, just about this woman, Miranda. It sounded like love."

"Was she a Swede?" Gorecki asked.

"I assumed she was Finnish like Ben, but I'm not sure."

Together, the detectives began researching the islands. Finally, they cobbled together a rough outline. The Durum Islands comprised five islands in the south Pacific. Over the decades, various empires had controlled them from afar, imposing different languages and religions, which changed with the tide. Like many post-colonial lands, the Durum Islands exhibited a cultural hodgepodge. The majority of the population spoke a French creole, with both Spanish and Malay influences, and they practiced a form of Theravada

Buddhism, though the adherents used Catholic rosaries and crucifixes in their prayer rituals.

The previous October, the main island, French Halmahera, had made headlines when a civil war broke out. Thousands of Islamic minority inhabitants were slaughtered at the hands of local authorities and a mob of their supporters.

Once they'd finished reading, Lucia concluded aloud, "It's more trouble than it's worth."

"What is?" Gorecki asked.

"Religion."

"Tell that to a Soviet-era farmer," he retorted.

"That's right," she said. "Your family is from one of those hard to spell countries."

He grinned. "Poland?"

"Oh."

"Some made it out in time, some didn't."

She turned back to her monitor. "This at least feels like religion gone bad."

"Or race or language or which alphabet they used. Who knows why those islanders chose sides?"

"So why these islands?"

Her partner then launched into a detailed explanation of crop fertilization, which essentially boiled down to the concept that premier crops had to be protected from lesser ones to prevent the overall quality of the crop from degrading through cross pollination. For this reason, the islands were ideal locales for the premier crop. The Pacific Ocean served as a wall against infiltration by competing crops that might contaminate the durum. Even with the precautions, the farmers had to rogue the crops, pulling undesirable plants by hand.

An idea struck Lucia then. "What if the farmers

weren't roguing *crops*? What if they planned to rogue the island of something else they found undesirable?"

"Like an Islamic minority?" Gorecki asked.

"And what if Torben Laakso knew about the plans ahead of time?"

"But how? And why did he visit the island?"

As if responding to a cue, Saul Posner cleared his throat. "I also found this in the envelope." He handed Lucia a small metal key on a keychain. Attached to the keychain was a plastic tag with the Greek letter omega on it. "The alpha and the omega," Saul intoned, "the beginning and the end."

She turned the key in her fingers. The beginning and the end of what?

She looked over at Gorecki just as his desk phone rang. He held it to his ear. "Uh huh...Yep, I'm the detective you...Do you need us to...Oh, you already have. How did you...Well, that's great! We'll send someone over there to pick it up." He hung up and beamed at Lucia. "Torben Laakso did have dinner with Benjamin Kirsi last night," he said.

"How do you know?"

"The hostess found a phone this afternoon. The phone company says it's registered to Benjamin Kirsi."

She considered this new information and then clutched the key chain in her palm. "Does the inventory of Laakso's apartment include a lock box?"

Gorecki shook his head.

"We need to see his office again."

"Evanston PD getting a federal search warrant on a Chicago property leased by an international company on a Saturday night: I don't think it gets any easier."

She disregarded his sarcasm, which she did without

thinking these days, and said more to herself than Gorecki, "Then we do it without getting a warrant."

"How?"

Again, she ignored him.

Tonight Lucia would sleep at her own place. If someone wanted to break in, so be it. Tomorrow she was paying Laakso's assistant, Dominic Torres, a house call.

Chapter Twelve

Fr. Remy Mbombo lived in a three-bedroom ranch style home in a quiet corner of Evanston. With its yellow brick and large windows, it looked like any of the family homes on that block. The only sign that suggested three priests, rather than a nuclear family, lived there was a medium-sized marble statue of Mary tucked into the purple hydrangea bushes, which Fr. Xavier, one of Remy's housemates, dutifully maintained.

As vespers approached, Remy grabbed his prayer book from the simple nightstand beside his twin bed and headed to the dining room. Every evening before dinner, he would pray with Fr. Xavier and Fr. Terry. Then the three of them would eat whatever delicious feast Xavier had concocted while they discussed their day. Tonight would be different.

Terry had laid out the liturgical accoutrement for vespers. A taper in a silver candle stand, an iron crucifix, and an oversized breviary made a semi-circle around him, and behind him Xavier was preparing dinner, also surrounded by the objects sacred to his duties: a wooden cutting board, an aluminum colander, and a chef's knife recently sharpened. The two men were so engrossed in their preparations that Remy felt rude joining them.

He placed his prayer book on the table. "Are we ready?"

"We're having wild caught salmon and Brussel

sprouts," Xavier said without turning. Xavier's sauteed Brussel sprouts with pecorino and pancetta were one of the greatest pleasures of Remy's life.

"I won't be able to join you tonight," he said.

Both priests stopped what they were doing to regard him.

"It's nothing," Remy lied. "I have an errand to run."

"Do you need the car?" Terry asked. He was already reaching into his pocket for the notebook he used to record car activity.

"Not today. The weather is just warm enough for a walk," Remy said.

"You'll pray with us, though?" Xavier asked.

"Of course."

After vespers, Remy put on a light gray jacket, removed a chocolate energy bar from the cupboard and headed outside. A mile from the house and certain he hadn't been followed, Remy hailed a cab. He felt a pang of guilt for deceiving his brother priests in this way, but he knew the lie came from necessity. If he had any hope of saving not only a life tonight but possibly a soul, this had to be the way—and it would only work if he came alone.

By the time Remy's cab pulled up to the north Chicago park, the sunlight had dipped behind the high rises to his west, suffusing the clouds with patches of deep purple and bright pink, the colors reflected and transformed in the rippling Chicago River. The washed-out reflection made a shade of red like water mixed with blood or wine.

At the edge of the park, partially obscured by a blue-green juniper, stood a young man. Wide in the waist, he reminded Remy of a gourd. A hoodie concealed the youth's face, but the red bull's head on his black leather jacket told Remy this was the man he was looking for.

In seminary, Remy learned that dreams, even the ones that seemed to last hours, were often the result of only a few minutes of REM. If he hadn't known better, he might have mistaken his wakefulness in that moment for dreaming, for even though his human eye beheld perfectly normal junipers and American elms just beginning to bud, his mind's eye beheld broad topped acacias and tall, skinny siala trees, and he smelled not the Chicago River, carefully directed and tamed, but the Nyabarongo, which snaked through the center of Rwanda, leading straight to Kigali, the heart of the country and—though he hadn't know it when he arrived to Rwanda—the heart of what was to come.

There along that ancient African river, he had first met Sister Therese, the most beautiful nun he would ever meet. She intercepted Remy at the city limits, her hair uncovered, her thin blue dress fluttering in the wind like an extension of the sky itself.

She led him up a long winding road to the top of a hill that overlooked all of Kigali. At the very top of the hill stood a red brick church, the *Kigali Eglise de la Sainte-Famille* Cathedral, its facade embellished with panels of an ivory color. It called to mind *Basilique du Sacré-Cœur,* the Sacred Heart Basilica, which crowned the highest point of elevation in Paris, his native city. While that white, ornamented basilica dwarfed this red brick cathedral, the idea was the same: a church on a hill.

Therese walked just ahead of the then-young priest as they approached the cathedral. Though he knew it was inappropriate, a French love song played in Remy's mind. He let the tune play on, *"Il y a longtemps que je t'aime, jamais je ne t'oublierai."* They mounted the last incline of the hill, and the great cathedral came fully into view for the first time.

The sight of all that red brick up close called forth the final verses of the love song tickling Remy's mind. *"Je voudrais que la rose fût encore au rosier, Et que mon doux ami fût encore à m'aimer." I wish the rose were still on the bush and my sweetheart loved me still.* As a teenager, Remy had wondered if that rose served a double meaning. Staring at the back of Therese's short sable hair now, the thought of *her* rose made him blush and avert his eyes the rest of the way to the cathedral doors.

The grounds of the cathedral included a clinic, a visitor's center, a school, a small house for the bishop in charge of the parish, and a larger quarters for the nuns who ministered the clinic and taught at the school. Unlike many of the schools in Rwanda, here both Hutu and Tutsi students were welcome.

"Some of the nuns who teach are also Tutsi," Therese explained in English for his benefit. "Just the upper grades. By then the students should have a strong enough foundation."

"Do you not believe a Tutsi is capable of teaching math as well as a Hutu?" Remy asked, attempting to keep any note of judgment out of his tone.

Sr. Therese smiled. "I take it you can't tell Tutsis from Hutus."

Only then did it dawn on Remy that Therese herself was a Tutsi.

"As Bishop Bahati will explain, we Tutsis lack the moral fortitude to be trusted with the younger grades. We are like *les animaux sauvages."*

"I think I understand," Remy said, careful not to slip into French himself. If Fr. Khonde was to be believed, Remy's French accent would out him as a non-African, and that could mean trouble. He stuck to English. "This is a lovely cathedral."

She ignored the compliment. "You are reporting back to Rome after this visit?"

"I'm not at liberty to say."

She smiled like a fellow conspirator. "Of course, of course."

From this vantage point, one could take in most of Kigali. The brick cathedral owed much of its majesty to its placement on the hill. Though spacious, with brown wooden rafters like the inside of an ark, the interior of the cathedral left Remy underwhelmed. The pews were little more than long wooden benches with no backs and the altar looked homemade.

The bishop approached them, smiling and holding out his hands. "Ah, my friend, welcome." He clasped Remy's right hand with both of his. "You must be our special guest."

Again the blood rushed to his face, this time with discomfort. "A normal guest," he said. "Ordinary even."

Two men carrying a wooden crate entered through the doors Remy and Therese had just used. They walked past the group toward the altar. Their box rattled and clanged all the way up the center aisle. Just before the altar, they turned and disappeared through a side passageway. Though he first imagined sacred vessels, chalices and patens, Remy knew this was wrong. Sacred vessels would've been packed away with more care.

"Who were those men?" Remy asked.

"No one," the bishop replied, his smile fixed on his

face. "I think you will be very pleased with what we are trying to accomplish here."

Remy stepped out of the taxi and Kigali and his memories of that place fell away, replaced entirely by Chicago and the present.

Yes, Remy thought as he approached the park, *that is why this meeting at dusk reminds me so much of Therese, and why all of this recalls Rwanda, thirty years buried and gone. The bishop with his instruments of chaos—this man, Chuy, carrying cargo just as deadly.*

The priest took a slow, deep breath, letting go of Kigali, the cathedral and, hardest of all, Sr. Therese. Then he stepped confidently toward his man in the black leather jacket.

"Chuy?" he asked.

The young man looked up and raised an eyebrow for effect. "A priest? Come on. A priest?" He sounded more amused than anything else. "Who sent you, my mom? This right here is a new low."

"God sent me."

He laughed. "Come. On."

Remy gazed at the river flowing near them. "Maybe I'm not here to convert you. Maybe I'm here to buy from you."

"Are you African or something?" Chuy asked.

"Something."

He laughed again, a deep, belly-shaking laugh that made the bull on his chest ripple like a flag in the wind.

"What's so funny?" Remy asked.

"I've just been hearing a lot of accents these days."

"What kind of accents?"

Chuy's lips went tight, the amusement draining from his face. "Look, I'm not selling pharmaceuticals, if that's what you're after." Under his breath, he added, "Even the priests now, man."

"I'm looking for something a little colder."

Chuy's gaze darted momentarily to a juniper tree on the edge of the park. Its long branches hung low to the ground. The green needles and many miniscule berries clearly concealed Chuy's stash. Remy noted the tree in his periphery.

Chuy's gaze returned to Remy. "Nah, I don't have anything like that. You're barking up the wrong tree."

"It's never too late," Remy said. "You're, what, sixteen?"

"Seventeen," he said as if this were significantly different.

"You're practically a man," Remy said. "Ignorance won't be an excuse much longer."

Chuy puffed out his chest. "I am a man, and I know full well what I'm doing." A curious expression transformed his face. Apparently, he had just put something together. "If it wasn't my mom, then who told you about me?"

"How do you know it wasn't your mom?"

Chuy checked the low juniper branches again for a split second, then came back to Remy's eyes. A white-throated sparrow alighted on a branch just above their heads. Remy turned from Chuy to the bird. "Perhaps it was a sparrow who told me, a travel-weary bird returning after a long winter."

"Come on," Chuy said one final time.

"Never too late," Remy replied, more to himself than Chuy and left the park the same way he came.

The priest traveled south a block, then east, then north, and then back west toward the park, approaching this time from Chuy's blindside. Locating the juniper tree was simple but climbing through its web of branches without alerting Chuy proved a challenge. As he pushed into the tree, his heart raced and his palms became slick with sweat. He peeled back the layers of branches in search of his target, and the branches, with their needlelike leaves, sticky with sap and ramified like many-tined forks, latched onto his palms. He stopped, put on a pair of black leather gloves, and looked around him. No one. Approaching from the east, he was concealed from view, but if Chuy came to check on his merchandise, Remy would not have time to disentangle himself and make his escape. Even if he could outrun the large young man, Chuy was certainly armed. Perhaps, he would not stoop so low as to shoot a priest, but lord knew Remy had seen it done. He'd seen much that he could not unsee.

A glint of metal, the corner of a briefcase, came into view. He could reach it if he just—

A long, dry twig snapped underfoot.

"Who's there?" Chuy asked, his voice low.

Remy froze. Immediately, his legs burned with the half-crouching position.

Chuy stepped closer to the juniper, his gaze going first to the briefcase and then to the branches above him. He made a visual sweep of the park, then seemed to relax. His attention returned to the juniper and for a long time he stared right at Remy; although, the young man clearly didn't see him. Remy needed to breathe, needed to move his neck and relax his legs, but he held perfectly still like a corpse.

"Hey Chuy!" another man's voice said, distracting him.

Remy couldn't see this man, but he sounded older. He spoke more clearly than Chuy. Through the branches, Remy saw snatches of an expensive suit, well-groomed hair, and shiny black shoes.

The two spoke in hushed tones for several minutes then turned their backs to Remy. He seized the opportunity to snap a picture of the briefcase with his phone before leaving it there. He stalked away on stiff legs at first, then he strode, and then finally he ran or moved as close to a run as a fifty-something in dress shoes could manage.

In the cab, enroute to Evanston PD, he stared at the photograph and tried to pierce the picture of the metal exterior with his eyes to see its contents. He knew from Davon's description what lay inside, but all he could see in his mind's eye was the contents of the wooden crates in that austere cathedral in Kigali, Rwanda, so many decades ago.

When he'd finally sneaked into the bishop's office and pried the wooden lid off one of the crates, he didn't find sacramental vessels or bribes in the form of jewelry or silverware as he'd expected. No, what Remy found all those years ago in East Africa would haunt him for the rest of his life. There in a tangle of metal and wood had lain hundreds of long, bright machetes.

Chapter Thirteen

Gun drawn, Ezra stalked in the direction of the fallen agent. He neither saw movement nor heard signs of life from the ground, but as he neared the crumpled form of Leena Åkerholm, she turned toward him, a questioning expression on her face. At least she was unharmed. He kept moving, scanning the area for the shooter.

Two men appeared from a copse of trees nearby. Both wore matching hunting apparel that looked new and expensive. They didn't resemble American hunters, but instead reminded Ezra of Englishmen in a 50s period piece, two noble lords stalking deer through some heathery moorland. These were not tourists who had wandered over from the hunting lodge. They were the Hartfords' kind of people.

"Hands up," Ezra said, pointing his 9 mm at them.

"Oh my," the shorter of the two replied. He took his rifle in both hands and lifted it above his head like a Viet Cong soldier fording a river. "Augustus Campbell," he said. "Pleasure to meet you. This is Duane." He nodded at his companion. "You can take our guns but leave us our field jackets!" he added with a smile. "We just had them pressed."

His hunter friend grimaced and also raised his rifle. "I thought we were the only two out here," he said, his tone more serious than that of Augustus.

During this exchange, Leena had picked herself off the ground. She studied the pair of hunters as they spoke. "That's the gun," she said in an accusing tone and grabbed the muzzle of Campbell's rifle. "See? It's still warm."

He gestured at the clear skies above. "It's the sun."

Both men were in their early twenties, but only Duane showed the anxious diffidence of youth. Something about their mannerisms or their physical proximity to each other suggested to Ezra that they were more than hunting companions. He looked from one to the other. "Who gave you permission to hunt on this land?"

"Puck," Augustus said. "Duane has always wanted to hunt out here, so I asked Puck last night."

"You were at the party?" Ezra asked.

"What party?" Augustus asked innocently, then changed the subject. "Duane's a country boy and always wanted that Door County experience. He's shown me everything I know about *hunting*." He said the last word with a sheen of innuendo.

Duane answered hesitantly, "Yes officer, we were in attendance." Neither his accent nor his diction sounded country to Ezra.

"As I've been telling you, dear Duane, you never answer a federal agent's question unless compelled to do so. If my father has taught me nothing else, it is the value of evasion."

So this Augustus character had made Ezra for a federal agent.

Leena fired the next question. "What sort of party was it exactly?"

"A foreign investigator," Augustus said to Duane

133

out of the side of his mouth like a stage-whisper. "The Hartfords must be in it deep. Might I ask from which Nordic ice floe you hail?"

She ignored him.

Ezra continued, "We know they host a secret masquerade out here every March."

Duane glanced from Augustus to Leena and back, forgetting to breathe in the process. His cheeks grew redder and redder and the rifle held above his head began to rattle. "I was a black bear."

"Duane, Duane, Duane," Augustus said in mock disappointment. "I guess now that the proverbial black bear is out of the bag, we might as well tell you all about it." He gestured southward with the butt of his rifle. "I own the property next door. It's not quite as regal, but I have a teapot and Duane here keeps it halfway presentable whenever we come. Why don't you join us?"

They still needed to interview the park ranger on Rock Island, but Ezra assumed they'd likely learn more from guests of the masquerade than from the woman who found Puck's boat. Also the ranger would still be there in the morning. Who knew when these two were planning to leave? Leena seemed to share Ezra's line of thinking, because she nodded at Augustus and began walking south before the men even lowered their weapons.

Over one shoulder, she asked the three of them, "Are you coming?" She proceeded toward the cabin without awaiting a reply.

Augustus Campbell's log cabin paled in comparison to the Hartfords' mansion. Whoever initially built this home wanted nothing more than a shelter and Augustus Campbell hadn't added much. The front door opened immediately to a one-wall kitchen and a living room. A small island separated the two. Beyond the living room were two doors which Ezra took for a bedroom and a bathroom. One bedroom, one bath.

On the refrigerator, Ezra noticed a save the date. On it appeared Augustus Campbell and Puck Hartford in a staged embrace, a lake in the background.

"The engagement photo was in jest," Augustus said.

"Seems like an expensive jest," Ezra replied.

Augustus laughed, not at the joke, Ezra thought, but at the FBI agent's concern over wasting a negligible amount of money.

"You can explain it to us, perhaps," Leena suggested.

He tapped his chin as though considering this gravely. "Fine, you've dragged it out of me. Puck's mummy and daddy are the withholding type, the type of parents who won't release your multi-million-dollar trust fund until you're happily married off and ready to propagate the family line."

Ezra produced a digital recorder. "Do you mind?" he asked. Augustus shook his head. "You were going to marry Clive Hartford the Third, aka Puck, so he could have his trust fund?"

"He promised to share."

"What a good friend," Ezra replied. "You must've trusted him implicitly."

Augustus laughed. "I trusted the prenup my family drafted."

"A very thorough jest," Leena said. "The date was last year. Why didn't you have the wedding?"

Duane answered, "They changed their son's trust fund." He scowled at Ezra, projecting his frustrations perhaps. "They added the word 'heterosexual,' a 'heterosexual wedding.' It's bullshit."

"Is Puck heterosexual?"

The young men didn't know how to answer, but Augustus tried, "He didn't love me, if that's what you mean. The engagement was a ruse, sure, but as far as his sexuality, who knows? Puck is his own person, and I doubt he'd relish the idea of two investigators classifying his entire identity into a black-and-white—"

"I get it," Ezra said.

"I don't think you do." All the playfulness had drained from Augustus' voice. But then he smiled and looked at Duane, and the moment of tension and perhaps authenticity passed.

"What can you tell us about Evelyn Williams?" Ezra asked.

Again Augustus pretended to think it over. "Do you mean that poor girl with the deer obsession?"

"Did the Hartfords put her in the deer mask, maybe as some type of game?"

"No, I believe that was her everyday wear."

Ezra produced his badge and placed it on the counter. "Have you ever heard of obstruction?"

Augustus smiled. "Is this a threat of imprisonment?"

Ezra returned the smile. "Federal obstruction generally concerns itself with property," he said, looking around the cabin, "and associated accounts. I assume this cabin is in your father's name?"

The young man's smile withered. Although the seizure of funds was not a likely outcome, Augustus didn't know this. Additionally, the threat gave the young man permission to do two things: drop the cavalier persona, which was wearing thin for everyone, and betray his longtime friend, Puck Hartford.

Augustus was silent for a long moment. Then abruptly, he went to the kitchen and busied himself with a tea kettle. As he filled it, Duane motioned for Ezra and Leena to sit in the living room.

"Nothing happened last night," Duane said, "at least not while we were there. I don't know why you're harassing Augustus when you should be speaking with the Hartfords."

Leena assessed her seating options while they spoke and finally chose the only wooden chair in the room. "Who says we haven't?"

Augustus joined them now, leaning over the back of the sofa.

"Did the Door County Sheriff speak with you two?" Ezra asked.

Augustus yawned as though bored. "We came home before all that."

"It seems strange you saw the police there this morning and didn't go over to give a statement," Ezra said.

"Strange that I didn't run toward the police?" he asked incredulously. "You and I may have different definitions of 'strange,' Special Agent."

"No one saw Nélya Kirsi leave," Ezra said to the room, offering them the chance to offer their own account. The two men remained silent.

"The water's almost ready," Augustus said. He returned to the kitchen and began rummaging through cabinets in search of tea and mugs.

They don't spend much time here, Ezra thought. Perhaps they hadn't seen anything last night, but if they attended the masquerade, they likely attended last year's as well. "Do you always attend the Hartfords' masquerade?" Ezra asked Duane.

Duane shook his head. His gaze traveled to the kitchen where Augustus leaned against the stove while the water gurgled in the kettle. "Just the last couple years."

"Last year?"

He nodded.

Given the level of cooperation from Duane, Ezra decided to pounce. "Did someone shoot Evelyn Williams intentionally?"

The tea kettle whistled, first low and then loud. Duane leapt up and ran to the kitchen. Ezra watched as the two young men prepared the tea in four mugs. A faint scent of peppermint soon pervaded the air.

"We all read 'The Most Dangerous Game' in high school," Ezra called to them. "Perhaps the Hartfords have a real-life version every year—or at least a mock one. Maybe with paintball guns? Maybe with real guns?" When neither responded, he continued, "Evelyn Williams didn't attend prep school or college with any of you. As far as we can tell, she was barely an acquaintance."

Augustus brought two mugs over, bags still steeping, and placed them on the coffee table. "Puck met that girl in town in one of those doleful 'sports' bars," he said with air quotes. "Don't misunderstand me, I enjoy slumming it as well as anyone, but then he brought her to the masquerade!"

Leena regarded her steaming mug suspiciously. "Who shot her?"

"Puck did, of course." He must've seen the alarm in their faces, because he added hastily, "No, you misunderstand. She wanted to be shot. Everyone was so unbelievably drunk…and high…and she stole this shotgun, a turn of the century double-barrel. Puck said it didn't work anymore, but she wanted to play William Tell; she wanted him to shoot the deer mask off the top of her head. She kept balancing it like an apple."

"And he did it?" she asked.

"She forced the gun into his hands and it went off."

Evelyn Williams, they knew, had been shot in the back of the head, so this account didn't add up. Augustus seemed genuine, however. If he was covering for Puck, he was doing a damn fine job. Either that or Puck had lied to him as well.

"Did you see it for yourself, Mr. Campbell?" Leena asked.

The last name sounded awkward in her accent, as if it contained too many syllables. Ezra wondered if she was exaggerating her accent to sound more foreign and therefore less threatening. Then he recalled how long she'd been awake. Outside, the Wisconsin sun nudged the sky from red and orange to purple and blue, but back in Finland, the night must've been on its way toward morning.

"Puck told me about it after the fact."

Evelyn Williams had probably signed a non-disclosure agreement, otherwise there would be more information readily available. Clearly, no one had meant serious harm to the woman, but that didn't mean a dangerous game hadn't been played, nor did it rule out Nélya's death—either intentionally or accidentally—due to a repeat performance.

Ezra leaned forward on the edge of the couch. "You do realize an NDA doesn't protect you from a federal investigation."

"There are enough lawyers in my family, thank you," he said somewhat evasively. "I have invited you here into my home, well, my cabin, of my own volition, and I have shared this information freely."

This still didn't address Ezra's question, so he persisted. "Have you signed one?"

"A non-disclosure agreement? No. Not for that incident nor any other incident involving the Hartford family."

"You say that as if Evelyn Williams wasn't the first or the last incident on the Hartfords' property."

Augustus Campbell answered with silence.

"So why did your friend choose the name Puck?" Leena asked.

The interjection annoyed Ezra, who felt the interview had been heading in a productive direction and that they already knew the answer to this particular question.

"You're familiar with *A Midsummer Night's Dream?*"

She nodded. "We have been known to read Shakespeare even in humble Finland."

"Puck's father hates it." Augustus paused. "Actually, what he hates is this eighties film about it. Preppie schoolboys and their overbearing parents."

"I've seen it," she said.

"The boy who plays Puck in the film commits suicide and blames his father. Puck, our Puck, thought it would be funny…" He started laughing. "You have to know Mr. Hartford. The man doesn't have an ironic bone in his body."

"Puck is a trickster," Ezra added. "In the play."

"That's our Puck, too. When you're raised around the solemnity of wealth, you tend to go the other way." He took a few long sips of his tea. "At least for a while."

"Do you believe Puck has become solemn?"

Augustus shrugged. "The last time we spoke, he mentioned going back to his birth name, *Clive the Third.*" He said the name as if he were stating the name of an English monarch or a Russian tsar.

"Will he change his name back before the wedding?" Ezra asked.

"Oh, he never changed it legally, just on his social media and with the press. They do lots of profiles on him—*Chicago, Chicago; Country Life Illinois, Windy Men.*

Leena wrinkled her brow as though straining to solve a riddle. "These are magazines?"

"Obviously."

Ezra gestured toward the Finnish officer. "My friend has had a long day and is working in a second language," he said in her defense. He would've continued defending her, but he noticed the waves of resentment pouring from her every feature. He shifted uncomfortably on the couch. "Who all attended last night's party?"

"Didn't they supply you with a guest list?"

"They did. I just wanted to know who stood out." Then he added, "To you."

"Or maybe you want to know if they left anyone off the list."

"The Hartfords have been nothing but forthcoming."

Augustus laughed mirthlessly. "Who was there? That's what you want to know? Let's see, a pair of giraffes, a pride of peafowls and cocks—there are some inveterate cocks in that group—forest and aquatic life, the whole menagerie really."

"Did any of these animals have names?"

"Oh there I couldn't help you. 'We shall everyone be mask'd' the invitations read, and I am so abominable at guessing."

Duane, tired either of the threat of prosecution or of his companion's endless posturing, finally broke. He explained that the party consisted of mainly upper-level employees of Midwest Telephone and Telegraph, the small staff of Puck's fledgling app, and several personal invitees.

"Who did you know personally?"

Augustus fielded the question this time. "Hmm, there was Puck's sister, Ginnie; the groundskeeper, Simmons; the chef, Stephanie something; Duane and myself; and the Kirsis, mother Marja, father Benjamin, and daughter Nélya."

"Wait, Benjamin Kirsi was there?" Ezra asked.

Augustus shrugged in the affirmative.

Leena seemed to wake up. "You saw Benjamin Kirsi?" she asked urgently.

"Briefly," Augustus replied. "He left before dinner."

"Where did he go?" she pressed.

"How should I know?"

Her fury was rising now. "You didn't ask anyone?"

"No, I didn't ask anyone where Nélya's *isä* went." He turned to Duane and asked theatrically, "Wait, where'd Mr. Kirsi go? How will we ever dine without the Finnish billionaire? My drink is empty, what will I do without Benjamin Kirsi to refill it?"

From the look on Leena's face, Ezra thought she might slap Augustus across the face.

Duane must have seen the look as well because he interjected, "I'm sure his wife mentioned something about Chicago. I think they were going to meet him there tomorrow—or today I guess."

"And where is Mrs. Kirsi now?" Leena asked.

"We saw her leaving this morning, the Hartfords and Marja all together," Duane replied. "I assumed they were headed to Chicago."

"Did you happen to see a Turk?" Ezra asked. "Someone dressed up as a Turkish man, I mean."

Duane shook his head, but his gaze never left Augustus. "We would've remembered someone like that," he said.

"So you didn't see a Turk?" Ezra clarified.

"No," Augustus said firmly.

Ezra turned off his recorder. If nothing else, he now had Augustus Campbell lying to a federal agent. Hopefully, he wouldn't have to use it.

"Do you not like your tea?" Duane asked them as they rose to leave.

"I should've told you," Ezra said, "I don't accept drinks from strangers."

Outside and out of range of the cabin, he called Cromley to tell him that Benjamin Kirsi was in the country. "How is it possible that he's here and no one knows it?" Ezra asked.

"Money," Cromley said flatly.

"Why keep it a secret?"

"Maybe he suspects a kidnapping situation and doesn't want to alert the perpetrator."

"We need to speak with the Hartfords again when I get back to Chicago—and the Kirsis."

"I'll set up a time for tomorrow afternoon."

Dorris Hartford had seemed sick at the thought of her son's fiancé going missing, but not sick enough to come forward about Benjamin Kirsi being in the country. He prayed they weren't trying to handle the situation on their own.

As they walked back to the rental truck, the sound of his chirping phone broke the silence.

The text from Lucia read —*Can you check the Finlox employee database for a Miranda?*—

—*Sure. Can I ask why?*— he replied.

—*The Torben Laakso case. Apparently, he was romantically involved. We think she worked with him.*—

—*I'll see what I can find out.*—

"Who was that?" Leena asked.

"The detective working on the Laakso investigation."

"Have they found out anything?" Her words sounded wooden.

"Do you know someone named Miranda?" he asked evasively. "A Finlox employee maybe?"

"Miranda? Maybe in the London office? It sounds British to me. I think there is a young woman there, but her role is…" She searched for the right word.

"Are you trying to find a nicer synonym for *unimportant?*"

She smiled. "I know how you American's hate being blunt."

Before they left the Hartford property, Ezra checked the small boathouse from which the motorboat had gone missing. By the faint light of a single bulb, he examined the tidy space. The locks on the doors showed no sign of tampering and the chain that had secured the boat was wrapped in a tight coil and placed on a hook on the wall.

Whoever took the boat knew the layout well and, most likely, had access to the necessary keys. No one had broken in here.

Then he saw it. "Leena!"

She turned the corner to join him.

"Do you see it?" He gestured to the wooden wall, which contained a circular pattern of splintering.

"Shotgun pellets," she said.

Ezra took a photograph of it and sent it to Cromley. "No blood," he remarked, looking around the immediate area.

She traced a finger around the pattern of bullet holes, careful not to touch the wood directly. "See how the circle is completely filled in? Whoever fired this gun, aimed directly at the wall."

"For this shot," Ezra replied.

They examined the other walls then the exterior but found no other bullet holes. Once they'd exhausted the extent of their investigative powers and the entirety of Ezra's patience, he asked, "Are you ready to call it a day yet?"

"Fine."

They drove to the hunting lodge in complete silence, the headlights of the truck their only light in the darkness. They could only see twenty yards ahead as the road wound left and right through the woods.

Ezra pulled up to the lodge and cut the engine. "Did you know Benjamin Kirsi was in the country?" he asked.

Leena gave him a blank look, like a woman asleep with her eyes open.

Then Ezra put something together. "I just realized something. You left your home at four a.m. today, but four in the morning in Helsinki is still eight the previous night in Chicago." He turned to look at her. "Torben Laakso died just after one a.m., which means you boarded a plane to investigate his death before he was even dead. Why did you really come to Chicago?"

When she spoke, her words came out measured and slightly slurred. "Ben has been dead a long time now."

"Ben Kirsi?"

"No," she said, her tone sharp and her face twisted either from frustration at still being awake or from disappointment that this American investigator could be so dense.

Chapter Fourteen

Sunday

In the quiet hours of the morning, Remy mentally replayed the previous night's dream, one so familiar to him that it had taken on the significance of a favorite novel, a classic film, a core memory. Perhaps its importance came from the fact that it was based on a real experience, the experience that most defined the trajectory of the rest of his life.

The dream always began with Sister Therese sitting in a simple rustic rocking chair and watching a gorgeous sunset in Kigali, Rwanda. A supernaturally large, yellow sun burrowed into the hills, turning the green grass gold and the evening sky a mixture of amber, rose, and baby blue. Remy saw her before she saw him.

"This reminds me," he said, coming up behind her. At the sound of his voice, she jumped. He laughed. "I didn't mean to frighten you."

She laughed too. "You walk so lightly," she said. "What were you saying?"

"This sunset, it reminds me of a poem by Baudelaire."

She raised her eyebrows in surprise. *"The* Baudelaire?"

"Yes. Why?"

"He is salacious, no? We do not even have his books

in our library."

Rather than answer to the poet's reputation, Remy recited a poem:

"The violin quivers like a heart afflicted
A tender heart, which hates the void, vast and black,
The sky is sad and beautiful like a great altar,
The sun has drowned in his own dried blood."

Therese closed her eyes during this recitation. Then she opened them again and looked up. "He sounds like St. Francis."

"How so?"

"Seeing the divine in the natural—in brother sun and sister water. You have read 'The Canticle of the Sun,' no?"

He nodded.

"If only you knew French," Therese continued, "then you could recite your poem in the original. I'm sure it is even more lovely *en français*." She shrugged. "Oh well."

After a moment's hesitation, Remy continued in French, reciting the rest of the poem until the final line— *"Ton souvenir en moi luit comme un ostensoir."* How could he know then how prophetic these words would be? The memory of Sr. Therese would indeed shine "like a monstrance" for longer than either of them could have imagined.

Therese smirked, a gesture that accentuated the fullness of her cheekbones.

"What?" he asked.

She shook her head playfully. "I knew you were *un parisien.*"

"Comment le saviez-vous?"

"I knew," she said and looked back toward the

Cathedral, "because you don't speak English like a Brit or an American."

"I attended seminary in Nigeria," he said weakly.

She shook her head, more serious now. "You speak English like our Belgians, only better. Why are you pretending to be African?"

"Can you keep a secret?" he asked.

She nodded.

Remy smiled. *"Je peux aussi."*

A dour nun, Sister Didi, appeared at the doorway of the parish hall and called to them, "Dinner!"

He nodded in the direction of the parish hall. "Do they suspect anything?"

Therese set him at ease with a look. "The bishop is oblivious," she said. "Sister Didi, on the other hand, has been suspicious of you since you arrived. She thinks you are a Vatican spy."

"And you? What do you think?"

She studied his face, narrowing her eyes. "I haven't decided yet."

"Sister Therese!" Didi called, louder this time.

"We had better go," she told Remy. "Coming!"

The dining room in the parish center was plain but large. The church staff sat at a long table composed of three rectangular tables placed end-to-end and covered with white tablecloths. The bishop sat at the seat farthest from the kitchen. Remy sat opposite him. The moment Remy sat, the doors swung open and closed behind him, and nuns appeared with full serving dishes. Fried plantains and boiled sweet potatoes appeared, then a pot redolent of cassava leaves and onions, and finally the *pièce de résistance*, a roasted chicken stuffed with onions, leeks, and peppers.

Another priest, Fr. Uwawe, sat down beside Remy and rubbed his hands together. "You are in for a treat, my friend! Sister Didi's roasted chicken is the talk of Kigali."

Bishop Bahati grinned. "Fr. Uwawe is still very much *un paysan*," he said by way of explanation.

Remy furrowed his brow as though he didn't understand the term.

"A peasant," Therese translated, another smirk transforming her face. "His Excellency means to say Fr. Uwawe is not yet accustomed to eating meat."

"Did you grow up in a village?" the bishop asked Remy.

He waffled his head, equivocating. "My village was just outside of Lagos. My father worked there, so I went back and forth a lot, helping him with his trading." The cover story rolled easily off his lips.

"You must've come across many languages," Didi said. "Not French?"

He shook his head and rested his palms on his knees. He could feel his legs beginning to vibrate but hoped no one else could. The sweat from his palms felt warm on the cotton trousers. A nun placed an amber beer beside his empty plate, and he clasped it carefully, sipping the cool liquid at a rate he hoped didn't give away his anxiety.

"Hausa, Yoruba, Igbo, and many dialects of English," Remy said more confidently. In seminary at Abeokuta, Nigeria, he'd studied the Bible, the catechism, and canon law, but he had also studied the local Nigerian languages and culture in hopes that he could pass as a local. He knew those tongues well enough now to pass at market but certainly not as a native. His greatest worry was that one of his two dozen dinner companions would test his knowledge.

"So what language did you speak at home?" Didi pressed.

"All of them."

Bahati smiled. "I attended a conference in Nigeria." He looked at Didi. "Last year, was it?"

Remy inhaled slowly and held it, counting in French, *un, deux, trois*, as he awaited the bishop's contribution.

"The proceedings were all in English, though."

Remy exhaled with relief.

"The choir sang the Gloria in Igbo, if I remember correctly." Then Bahati recited a line, poorly, in that language. "How is my pronunciation, Fr. Mbombo?"

Remy laughed and sipped his beer. Laughter moved freely about the table.

"Perhaps you can regale us with how it should sound?" Didi asked then, her face and voice a challenge.

Remy happily obliged, singing the prayer in his most elegant Igbo. So often had he practiced these standard ecclesiastical pieces that even a native would've found it hard to peg Remy as a foreigner. He thought then of how wise it had been to send him to a seminary in Nigeria rather than France or a French-speaking part of Africa. Now he could move anonymously, a man of no country and no agenda.

Everyone seemed pleased with the singing. Everyone, that is, except Didi. Once the merriment had died down again, she said, "Mbombo is a Congolese name."

Remy's heart sank momentarily. "My father's family immigrated to Nigeria years ago."

"Is that common?" Didi asked.

"It's not uncommon."

The bishop tapped his glass with his butter knife. "Before we pray, we would like everyone to turn in their identification cards, passports, whatever you have."

Didi rose from her chair, raised a wicker collection basket from a nearby cabinet, and moved from person to person. Each in turn rifled through their belongings before producing a plastic ID or a passport. When she reached Remy, he did not reach for anything.

"The situation is worsening here," the bishop said across the table. "These Tutsi rebels could seize our city any day, taking our IDs and destroying them or passing them off as their own." He nodded to the basket. "Please."

Remy laughed uncomfortably. "And how would that help them, pretending to be a Zairean priest?"

"Imagine," Bahati said and gestured around the room with open arms, "what authority they could claim for their cause."

"They could use God to justify their wrong-headed beliefs," Therese said then.

Remy wondered if Bahati caught her double meaning. Didi certainly seemed displeased by the comment. She tapped the table with her fingernails, making an unpleasant and unrhythmical sound.

"We were told you came here to help," Bahati continued.

Remy reached into his pocket and touched the corner of his passport, his only ticket out of here in case the situation in Rwanda became untenable. Then he removed it from his pocket and slowly placed it into Didi's collection basket.

Didi gave him a malicious smile and continued around the table. She took each ID and placed it in the basket, then she placed the basket in the cabinet and locked the small wooden door. Remy could easily break the door—as long as they didn't move the IDs later—as long as he still had the freedom to come here and break it—as long as…

Didi reclaimed her seat and the serving dishes of food began making their rounds. Everyone took a spoonful from each dish and passed it along. Not wanting to appear rude, Remy did likewise.

If someone wished to poison the bishop, he thought idly, they would have to poison everyone. Then he looked down at his beer. Only the men had beer—Fr. Uwawe, Bishop Bahati, and himself. With a dedicated practice like mithridatism, one could become immune to certain poisons by slowly imbibing more and more of the substance each day. Remy knew this could be done with certain snake venoms, for instance. To poison the bishop would require only the active cooperation of the other priest, Fr. Uwawe—and possibly the coroner.

The young priest didn't know why these thoughts ran through his mind. Bishop Bahati was to be monitored only. Something about his manner, however, disturbed Remy. He seemed like a man who was capable of anything. Then again wasn't Remy? Wasn't his willingness and capability exactly why he was sent to Rwanda in the first place?

"Does anyone have a topic for discussion?" the bishop asked.

Didi cleared her throat. "I do, your excellency."

He nodded.

She looked from Bahati to Therese. "Near occasions

of sin."

The bishop clapped his hands together with pleasure. "Yes! A wonderful topic for our day and age. Let us define our terms. What do we mean by *near* or *proximate?"*

It took Remy a beat to realize this question had been addressed to him.

"In this case," Remy started, quickly accessing the theological part of his brain, "*nearness* refers to the likelihood of sin. A temptation can be remote or it can be near."

The bishop clapped his hands eagerly. "This sounds like a game. Let us each present a scenario for Fr. Mbombo and he will decide if the likelihood of sin is near or remote."

Didi set her water glass on the table more loudly than necessary. No water spilled, but the force caused her silverware to rattle and all heads to turn toward her.

"Sister Didi?" Bahati asked.

"What makes Fr. Mbombo an expert on these matters? Perhaps one of the sisters could also play?"

Clearly, she had herself in mind.

He considered this a moment. "Fr. Mbombo has heard enough confessions, I'm sure, to understand how these *situations* can escalate." He indicated Didi with an upturned palm. "But perhaps you can present the first scenario."

She smiled inwardly. Remy wondered if this had been her true aim. Too, he wondered what sort of curve balls she had planned for him. Surely she didn't doubt he was a priest. She'd watched him offer masses, and she'd supervised his catechism classes with the children. He had debated the meaning of papal encyclicals with

154

Bahati in Didi's presence. And more than once she'd witnessed him taking confessions—the parishioners arriving anxious and burdened, then leaving solemn but contented. If anything, she meant to test not his authenticity but his intent.

"A young man and woman sitting unaccompanied," Didi said, "watching a sunset."

"Ah, but we do not know their relationship," Bahati interrupted.

"Both unrelated, both unmarried, both young." She raised an eyebrow contemptuously.

Remy considered this a moment and consciously looked at the ceiling to keep from looking at Therese. "While a chaperon would be preferable, they could be family friends. For all we know, their families have trusted them to be alone."

Didi shook her head. "There is romantic interest."

"Courtship then," Remy said, adjusting his approach. "They are outside, before the eyes of God and all the world. I will assume the good intentions of the girl at least," he said and nudged Fr. Uwawe with his elbow, "and I'll say the chance of sin is remote. Nevertheless, it should be monitored."

The bishop seemed pleased with this answer. "Evil is in the eye of him who sees it." He raised his glass to Remy. "This is the benefit of experience: to assume good intentions but to watch vigilantly nonetheless."

"And what if," Didi started, then paused to ensure she had everyone's full attention. "What if the girl in question is a Tutsi?"

This time, Remy couldn't restrain from turning to Therese. Instead of looking back at him, however, her face was downcast with shame.

Bahati's face turned serious. "That is a different matter. The Tutsis are different from any other race in Africa. Genetically and morally, they are like the animals of the field. A young man, properly educated in the faith, might be trusted. A young woman naturally carries the distrust of sin—'I will put enmity between you and the woman' as the scriptures say." He paused meaningfully. "But not so with a Tutsi woman. She is like neither of these. She is like a man who is uneducated in the faith. She is more beast than soul."

Throughout this diatribe, Therese neither stirred nor showed any sign of disagreement, so acclimated was she to such discourses.

They spent the rest of dinner presenting scenarios to Remy. These ranged from similar unsupervised encounters between young people to the discovery of lost billfolds and bicycles. Finally, it came to Remy himself. Rather than pass him over, the bishop asked Remy for a scenario of his own, saying, "I will be the judge this time."

Remy thought before answering, "One thing we haven't spoken of yet is violence." His heart raced as he uttered this final word.

"That is true."

"The Nazis, for example."

Bahati steepled his fingers and closed his eyes. "Go on."

"Supposing," Remy started, "a Nazi general came to his parish priest and confessed plans to commit genocide against the Jews."

"That is easy." The bishop opened his eyes. "The seal of confession protects the priest. There is no sin."

He moved on to Fr. Uwawe who had the next

scenario ready.

"But say the confessor then encourages the violence," Remy continued, causing the priest beside him a moment's confusion. "Suppose he leaves the confessional and makes public statements confirming German biases against the Jews."

The wiser nuns, sensing the rising tension between the two men, began to clear away the dishes. Therese joined them, but Didi stayed.

"That's beyond the scope of proximate sin, Fr. Mbombo. Now let's move on," Bahati said coldly.

"But is it a sin?" Remy asked more forcefully.

"You are out of line." The bishop wiped his face with his napkin and pushed his chair back. *Dinner,* the gesture seemed to say, *is over*.

In this manner evening prayer began.

Remy found his prayers more difficult than usual. As he stared down at his prayer book, the corner of his left eye drew stubbornly to his bookshelf and the spine of a brown and gold volume there.

He knew with a kind of predetermined certainty that if he pulled the book from the shelf, he would automatically flip to the cover page and read, *Les Fleurs du Mal*. Then he would page through it until he found the poem he had recited to Therese. Just as automatically, he would tuck the book under his arm and leave his room, walking quietly down the hall with all the casualness of a student leaving the library until he arrived at her bedroom door. He would knock and the door would inch slowly open. That was as far as he could see—or as far as he'd allow himself to see.

He debated what he should do for the entire length of compline until finally he pulled the book off the shelf impulsively and crept into the hallway. When he reached her door, however, he didn't knock. Instead, he leaned the volume of poetry against the doorjamb. Then he returned to his own room, hoping Didi wouldn't pass by before Therese found the Baudelaire, hoping Therese would actually read the poems therein and find the same things true and beautiful that Remy had found, hoping, hoping, hoping...

Every night the dream ended the same way, and then morning followed with its heart-heaviness and regret. Remy didn't regret much from his life, but every morning that followed this dream, he longed to return immediately to that moment and not only knock but whisper her name through the door, not only whisper her name but nudge the door open, not only nudge the door open but... Oh, how different his life might have been!

"Remy?"

The dark, Rwandan night dawned in an instant, giving way to the soft morning light of suburban Chicago. He turned to see Fr. Xavier standing in his doorway. "Yes?"

"You have a visitor."

Remy thanked his brother priest. Xavier pantomimed wiping away tears. The gesture both frustrated and embarrassed Remy.

"The dream again?" Xavier asked.

He nodded. "It is just a dream."

The house was small, so it surprised Remy that he hadn't heard a knock. The front door stood half ajar and through the opening Remy saw Detective Lucia Vargas.

"Good morning, Father." She handed him a print off of a cell phone photo. "Someone left this for me at the precinct."

He took the photo and pretended to study it.

"Chicago PD also received an anonymous tip," she added.

"Did they?" Remy asked.

The detective smiled. "The caller spoke with a distinctive accent that sounded, well, surprisingly like your own. Have you read about the suicide that happened late Friday, early Saturday morning?"

Remy ignored the question. "Did the tip prove fruitful?"

"They picked up Jesus Suarez last night. He had a gram of cocaine on him and a firearm nearby, which he denied knowing anything about. But there was no briefcase."

Remy handed back the print off. "That's a shame."

She held up the photo again. "Do you have any idea what this briefcase contained?"

He glanced at it. "Just from a photograph of the outside?"

"Something brought you there," she said.

"Whatever may have brought your informant there, he's probably not at liberty to share. Isn't that how anonymous tips work?"

"Fr. Remy, you've already come this far."

A car crept by the quiet street. Its windows were tinted and its paint job sleek and iridescent. They stopped speaking and watched it. Remy took a mental snapshot of the vehicle and its license plate. "Would you break the law, Detective Vargas?" he asked.

"What do you mean?"

"To catch a criminal."

"No." She didn't even need to think about it. "That would defeat the purpose."

"You have your laws, and I have mine."

Now she did consider his question. "But I would find a way."

"As would I, Detective, as would I."

Chapter Fifteen

In the morning, Leena Åkerholm was gone. Ezra knocked on her door, called the phone in her room, then tried her temporary cell number. Nothing.

He couldn't help recalling the last time he'd been abandoned at daybreak, that time by his ex-wife, Julia. She had come to him in the middle of the night only to vanish while he was out getting bagels the next morning. As he packed up his suitcase, Ezra recalled how Julia's chestnut curls had caught the early sunlight, how he looked back one last time from the bedroom doorway, and how, weeks later, he now wished with all his being that he had settled back into the bed and soaked up every last minute of their time together.

The guy behind the counter couldn't have been more than twenty-three, and he seemed to be lost in a reverie of his own. His nametag read, "Chaz, night manager." Ezra wondered if he had been staring vacantly at the wall all night. "Good morning, Chaz."

The night manager looked out the window at the pitch-black world outside. "If you say so."

Ezra ignored the sarcasm. "Do you know someone named Evelyn Williams?"

Chaz snickered. "Evie? Yeah, everybody knows her. She lives in a ramshackle mansion in town."

Ramshackle mansion? A contradiction in terms, like dark day or open secret. Nevertheless, he had a perfect idea of the place. "Where is it?" he asked.

Chaz gave a few directions, which mostly included landmarks.

"What's the street address?"

"Oh, you'll know it when you see it."

"Do you have a phone number for Ms. Williams?"

Chaz took out his phone and pulled up a screen. "Here's her Finlox ID."

Somewhat sheepishly, Ezra admitted, "I don't have Finlox."

Though the field office had an account and agents could access anyone's posts through warrants, agents themselves were discouraged from having accounts of their own.

While Chaz printed the receipt, Ezra set up an account. He then accessed Evelyn "Evie" Williams' profile and messaged her. Immediately, she replied, saying he could stop by anytime. He wondered if, at six-fifteen in the morning, she was just getting up for the day or if she hadn't gone to sleep yet.

Another screen popped up, not a message from "Evie" but a list of suggested friends. Julia's name topped the list although she was now going by her maiden name, Rollins. He clicked "add," half-expecting her to respond right away. Instead, the button remained yellow, the word "pending" in the center. He tried to access her profile but, unlike Evie's, it was set to private.

Chaz handed him the receipt. "Your other party checked out already."

"When?" he asked, then looked at the receipt. It said five a.m. He wondered idly what time that was in Finland. He would drop by Evie William's place and then take the ferry out to Rock Island. The first boat wouldn't leave until eight anyway and, who knew, maybe Leena would be on board.

****

All the lawns on Evie Williams' block were still a tawny brown, but hers looked somehow tawnier, more drained of life. With its patches of bare soil and tuffs of dead bushes, the lawn reminded Ezra of a sickly dog he'd taken from a trailer once. The house too showed signs of wear. Overflowing gutters threatened to buckle under the weight of fallen tree branches; an exterior glass door hung by one hinge; a shutter was broken, another was missing; and, most prominent of all, a sea of beer cans stretched from the concrete sidewalk to the front porch.

Despite its two-story columns, the house reminded Ezra of that same trailer where he'd found the mangy dog, so it didn't surprise Ezra when a half-naked twenty-something with tawny, frazzled hair answered the door. From her navel dangled an impressive chain of diamonds that disappeared into the dingy elastic band of her gym shorts. Ezra tried not to stare at it and not to speculate where the chain concluded.

"You the guy?" she asked

"The one and only," Ezra replied.

She extended a wad of bills that must've contained a few hundred dollars.

"The federal agent," he clarified. "I messaged you on Finlox."

"Shit." She stuffed the bills into her black sports bra, which she wore in lieu of a shirt, then motioned for him to follow her indoors.

The inside of the house smelled like a pizza joint—if said pizza joints catered exclusively to homeless people, most of whom had just come in from the rain.

The soles of Ezra's shoes stuck to the entryway tile as if it were the cheap linoleum floor of a seldom-cleaned movie theater. The beer cans of the front lawn paled in comparison to the cigarette butts and empty liquor bottles covering the floor and kitchen counters. On the coffee table sat a bong, two-feet tall and in the shape of an alpaca, its glass body purple and pink paisley. On the living room wall hung a tapestry of Nancy Reagan accepting a joint from Janis Joplin. Not a poster. Not a fabric print. Someone had actually hand-woven this scene.

"I'll clear this off so you can sit," the young woman said and began moving a blanket from the couch. A head emerged from beneath and a shirtless man sat up. Every inch of his torso was covered in colorful, swirling tattoos.

"I'll stand," Ezra said. "Or maybe we could just speak outside."

"Dealer's choice."

Evie picked up a pack of cigarettes from the coffee table and rooted around inside. She checked two other packages, then settled for a vape pen instead. Ezra must've given her a judgmental look, because she asked, "What? It's just nicotine." She inhaled from it as they walked through the house and out the backdoor. At the last step down from the back porch, she stumbled and looked long at the vape pen in her hand. "Nope," she said, "that's definitely not nicotine," and stuffed the pen into the band of her gym shorts.

The backyard contained even more proof of her rock-n-roll lifestyle. Behind three kegs, which stuck out of a sea of plastic cups like buoys, rested half a race car.

"Where's the other half?" Ezra asked.

164

"For cripes sake, Linda!" she said and looked around the lawn as if Linda were hiding behind a bush, waiting to jump out.

Ezra sighed and produced his recorder. "I have a few questions."

She looked at the recorder. "Thousand bucks."

"I don't have that kind of money on me."

"Too bad!"

Then he remembered the bottle of Portuguese wine in his truck. "I do have an expensive vintage of red wine, though."

"How expensive?"

"More than a thousand dollars. You could easily sell it to the right—"

"Is it alcoholic wine?"

Ezra nodded.

"All right, then."

He hit "record" and the official interview began.

According to Evie, she had, in fact, instigated the game of William Tell, but Puck hadn't objected. She'd chosen the deer mask herself from a wide assortment. Later, she took the antique firearm from the rifle room and together they crept outside with it. Just before dawn, she remembered standing with her back against an elm tree, drunk, high and pant-less, the deer mask balanced atop her head like an apple, taunting Puck to fire. At the last second, she realized the double barrel gun with its wide muzzles was likely a shotgun, not a rifle. She turned and dropped to the ground, catching a few stray pellets in the process.

"The deer mask caught the worst of it," she said.

"Did Puck know he was holding a shotgun?"

She shrugged and took another hit off the vape pen.

"Who knows? We'd been drinking vodka and snorting Molly all weekend. He basically ruined the drug for me." She looked accusingly at the vape pen again and threw it into the yard. "We did so much Molly, it basically stopped working. When I came down, I was depressed for like a week."

"Just to clarify, you mean MDMA? Ecstasy?"

She nodded.

"You probably ran out of serotonin," he explained.

She shook her head. "No. I was just sad that I couldn't do any more molly." She shrugged again. "Thankfully, that problem went away."

"You stopped doing ecstasy?" Ezra asked.

"No," she said and looked at him as if he were the dumbest person in the world.

Even if Puck didn't know the weapon was a shotgun, the story didn't paint him in a good light. Ezra could understand the family wanting to silence Evie Williams. If Puck had any ambitions for politics or business, a story like this could curtail them. Aiming a firearm at someone while intoxicated wouldn't sit well with voters or with shareholders.

"The wine?" she asked.

"Of course."

Ezra returned to his truck to find the bottle and brought it back to the house. After examining the label the way a squirrel might examine a socket wrench, Evie took it inside and placed it on top of her fridge.

"A fancy house like this and no wine cellar?" Ezra asked in an attempt at congeniality.

"I've got one, yeah, but there's so much broken glass in there, you wouldn't believe it."

****

When Ezra arrived at the dock, the first ferry had yet to leave for Rock Island, and the entire lake was still shrouded in a thick morning fog. Much to his relief, Leena Åkerholm sat on a two-person bench facing the bow. Ahead of her a family of four leaned against the railing and looked out into the lake. They looked like a family on a postcard. Leena looked more rested. Her blonde hair was down, suggesting a more relaxed attitude, but her face looked just as tense.

She raised a gas-station coffee as he joined her. "You found me."

Ezra unbuttoned his jacket, put his hands in his pockets, and tried to strike a nonchalant stance. "I was worried I wouldn't see you again. I checked your room and called your cell phone."

Leena removed her phone from her black jacket. The screen showed black. *"Huora,"* she said in a profane tone as she fiddled with it. The wind swept across the lake, throwing hair into her face. She brushed the hair away several times, becoming increasingly frustrated with the phone, until Ezra took it from her.

"Let me see." He located the power button and held it down.

"They gave this to me yesterday. Someone in your office. I don't know who."

The screen flashed on and Ezra handed it back. "I thought you were in tech."

She laughed. "Ten years ago. Everything is different now." She looked out at the water. She must've been twenty when she left the tech job, that or she was older than she looked. "And I did my work from a desktop computer, not a phone." She waggled the smartphone at him.

The ferry lurched to life. Ezra grabbed a handrail for balance, then sat down. "What do you do now?"

Leena smiled, flashing her ivory teeth and gold-flecked eyes. "Visit cold, foggy islands with strange men."

For the first time since meeting the Finnish investigator, he imagined how easily a man could fall in love with her. Even a powerful man like Benjamin Kirsi. "Exactly how close were you to the Kirsi family?" he asked.

All light and warmth vanished from her eyes as though someone had shuttered the blinds on a pair of windows. Mechanically, she answered, "I've worked with them since my tech days." But then she smiled again, the corners of her eyes turning up slightly. "I can still remember Nélya riding her tricycle around the original Finlox campus. CFOs and Vice Presidents blocking the stairwells lest she or Niko go…" Her lips closed tight.

"Who is Niko?"

She closed her eyes and sighed deeply. "Nélya's twin brother, Nikolas."

"Now she has a twin?" None of his research mentioned a second Kirsi child.

"The family has respected his wishes and kept him out of the spotlight."

Ezra shook his head in disbelief.

"You must understand, Mr. James, her father's success made Nélya a household name in Finland, but that wasn't the sort of life Niko wanted. He is shy. Even as a boy, he was scared of the lights and cameras and anonymous headset wearers that populated the marketing side of their business. The Kirsis decided to only post about Nélya, to put her front and center, and she loved the attention."

"Where is Niko now?" he asked firmly enough to get her attention, but not so commanding as to alarm the postcard family standing nearby.

"I don't know."

"Is he here in the States?"

Her tone turned from cold to angry. "I just told you that I don't know where he is."

"Did you know the Kirsis were in America?"

"How would I know that?" The postcard family looked around the deck, causing Leena to lower her voice but not drop her anger. "The American and Finnish governments were keeping tabs on Ms. Kirsi. If you're implying that I work for Finlox or am on their payroll or show them any sort of preference over any other Finnish company or citizen…"

Ezra hadn't been implying this explicitly, but it intrigued him that her mind went there.

"Then why did you board a plane hours before Torben Laakso died?"

"Benjamin Kirsi called me and asked me to evaluate the situation in Chicago, but he didn't say he was here."

"And your supervisor agreed to this, to a private business using you like an employee?"

"I am a director in the KRP. If I believe there is a pressing concern, I go."

He nodded. "And what was the pressing concern?"

"That is a matter of national security. I am not at liberty to share."

The questions came faster and faster to Ezra. "When did you receive the call?"

"Six p.m. your time."

Now what he'd wanted to ask since the moment he'd realized Leena was missing from her room that morning: "Did you have anything to do with Torben's death?"

"Damn you!" she said loud enough for the postcard family to turn and glare at them. The father kept an eye on them, first directly and then in his periphery. "I never—" she began, but the hard exterior that was Leena Åkerholm cracked, and tears filled her eyes. "I never would've laid a hand—"

Genuine anguish filled her face. It wrinkled like a punctured balloon. A minute of crying followed, no more than that, then she buried her emotions somewhere deep inside and wiped her eyes with her shirt sleeve. Her face resumed its statuesque rigidity.

They sat in silence for some minutes—her engulfed in what he recognized as grief, him disarmed by embarrassment—and watched the family talk and joke quietly. He should've seen the signs earlier, should've deduced the nature of Leena and Torben's relationship.

The family removed their phones and began aiming them toward the starboard side of the ferry. Through the fog, the island, with its rocky shore and wall of evergreens, loomed into view. Soon Ezra spied a stone structure with two archways that extended into the lake. Atop the stone edifice sat a red gabled roof. The ferry turned toward it. To the right of the dock, a park ranger stood looking purposefully at the deck of the ferry as though searching for them before they disembarked. The park ranger raised a small pair of binoculars, the style used by birdwatchers, and pointed them directly at Ezra, or so it seemed. A sensation of being caught ran down his spine.

They disembarked and walked toward the park

ranger. He'd called ahead, but still introduced himself and Leena, adding, "You must be Tana Vogel."

"You betcha."

The ranger's navy-blue tartan cap and brown scarf were obvious attempts to personalize her tan uniform and, unlike most of the fresh-out-of-college rangers he'd encountered, Tana Vogel was in the autumn if not winter of her life. The whole ensemble, not just the binoculars, screamed "bird watcher," and what better job for an amateur birder than being the park ranger on a low-key island in Lake Michigan? Short locks of white hair curled from beneath her tartan cap and, though she seemed happy to meet them, she frowned when she wasn't talking.

"Can you show us the boat?" he asked.

There wasn't much to show. The motorboat had docked on the east side of the island, suggesting Nélya or whoever took her, piloted the boat straight north from the Hartfords' estate, around the larger Washington island, and then stopped here.

"Any idea why this island or this spot?" he asked.

Tana reached in and turned the key in the ignition. It cranked but wouldn't turn over. No gas.

"Do the ferries document everyone who comes and leaves?" he asked.

"Yes," Tana said and gazed toward the dock. "Also, this morning is the first run since Friday morning. No civilians have come to this island except the people on your ferry and none have left." She corrected herself then, "By ferry, that is."

Leena asked, "Are there other ways on and off the island?"

The ranger waved a hand at the open lake. "Anyone

could've brung a boat by. Where are you from again?"

"Chicago," Ezra said, then looked at Leena. "Well, I am."

"Have you searched the island?" she asked the park ranger.

"Us and Door County Sheriff's office and the U.S. Coast Guard and—"

"And now us?" Ezra guessed.

She nodded. "No sign of the Finn. Just the boat, the deer mask, and this." She hiked a few dozen yards inland to the fresh remains of a campfire and a place where the leaves and twigs had been cleared from the ground and something rectangular had left an impression on the dirt. It could've been a sleeping bag.

A second boat may have been waiting for Nélya or her captor here on the island. They returned to the shoreline but could find no sign of another boat docking there.

"Could've dropped anchor offshore," Tana suggested.

That seemed needlessly complicated to Ezra. "If someone took her, I doubt they'd be worried about displacing some stones."

"I agree," said Leena. "It would be like scattering leaves in a driveway to hide the fact that you stole an SUV. Ms. Kirsi is gone. No one is trying to conceal that."

Ezra needed to think aloud. "Maybe she came here alone, camped, then hiked to a rendezvous point of some sort and left the island that way. It could've been another boat or a helicopter or"—he turned to Leena—"could Nélya swim?"

Her face distorted. A micro-expression you might call it. There and gone like a shadow or a race car. Was

172

it fear or surprise? It was too quick and too faint for Ezra to tell.

"She swam the open water 10k at HY."

"HY?"

"Sorry, University of Helsinki."

Tana chewed her thumbnail then gazed out at the water. "Ten kilometers would easily get her back to the peninsula. Then again, if she races the 10k, she could've swum much farther than that." She looked up, making a mental calculation or perhaps spotting a heron through the fog. "Could've swum up north. We're right on the line with Michigan after all. Next island's in Michigan waters, then there's the upper peninsula not far beyond that."

"Could she have made it to Canada?" he asked.

Tana thought it over a second, head tilting upward again as though a map of the Great Lakes and their many tributaries were there against the gray-white sky. "Not likely."

ASAC Cromley had already brought in every major resource in the area, but it wouldn't hurt to hit the upper peninsula of Michigan a second time. If she swam to the mainland, she would've found herself carless, phoneless, and soaking wet on a cold spring morning. She would've needed fresh clothes and hot food. Someone would've seen her.

Ezra called Cromley and gave him the update. He heard a pen scratching against paper in the background. "I want you back here immediately," the ASAC said. "We're hitting MTT again the second you get back to town."

"The ferry leaves in a half hour, then we can drive back to Green Bay."

"Come on, James, use your head," Cromley huffed then hung up.

Of course. Ezra turned to the park ranger. "Do you have a speed boat?"

"Yes, why?"

He'd call the rental car company later and tell them where to find the truck. Right now they needed to get to Green Bay and water was the fastest route.

Chapter Sixteen

Leena insisted on dropping Ezra off at the FBI field office and then running to her hotel.

"Time is of the essence here," he said.

"I will meet you there. I have to get something from my hotel room."

"What could be more pressing than this?"

She went red faced. "A feminine product."

"There's a machine in the lady's room," he said and pointed into the large federal building.

Her words came out measured and stern. "Respectfully, Agent James, do not tell me how or where to take care of my hygiene needs."

Reluctantly, Ezra went in alone and Leena drove off in the direction of her hotel. Before he made it inside, however, Cromley was already on the way out.

"Let's go!"

****

Their second interview with the Hartford family took place not at the MTT headquarters but at Clive Hartford's luxurious apartment. The courtyard patio of the apartment building featured a bronze sculpture by Chicago artist Neil Goodman, the lobby contained a series of Terry Evans photographs, and the moment Ezra stepped into the foyer of the Hartford's apartment, he found himself standing eye-to-pistil with a Georgia O'Keefe.

He pointed automatically at the painting. "Is that…?"

Dorris Hartford just smiled and nodded, then she led Ezra and Cromley to the dining room table. The table was impossibly large. It could've featured in a Victorian period piece. Each leg and edge contained flourishes of gold. It wouldn't surprise Ezra at all to learn they were real gold.

Clive Hartford sat at the table in a three-piece suit as if ready for a meeting rather than relaxing on a Sunday morning. Beside him, where Ezra expected to see Puck, sat a bald, mustachioed man Ezra pegged for legal counsel, which he in fact turned out to be.

"Where's your son?" Ezra asked.

"My client," the mustachioed man answered, "would prefer not to say."

"Do you or any of your family members know the whereabouts of Ms. Nélya Kirsi?" he asked.

The investigators stood across the table from Mr. Hartford, refusing to sit once they noted the presence of a lawyer. Whatever atmosphere of cooperation they had felt at the MTT office was officially gone.

"My client would prefer not to answer."

Ezra ground the knuckles of both fists into the table. "Where's Benjamin?"

"Again," the lawyer began.

Cromley cut him off. "If you are trying to handle this yourselves, I need to reiterate how reckless and ineffective that strategy is."

The lawyer opened his mouth, then closed it. He splayed his hands palm up as if to say they had nothing for the FBI, then he looked to his client.

Clive shook his head. "Whatever has happened…or

is happening…I haven't been told," he said with heavy pauses.

Ezra pulled a chair out and sat. He unbuttoned his suit jacket. "Not everything the FBI does is public information. If you're worried about this situation affecting your merger—"

Clive struck the table hard. "I'm not worried about the damn merger. What worries me are these techies, these drug-addled freaks my son has surrounded himself with."

His legal counsel made a tut-tutting sound.

"I don't care, Lewis!" he snapped. Then he turned to Cromley. "What's happening? Do you know? Your team is still following Puck, still monitoring his movements?"

Cromley confirmed that they were but refused to give details. Ezra knew they had a surveillance team keeping an eye on Puck physically and through his cell phone data they were tracking Puck's exact location when he was out of sight.

"He's moved around very little. Although, he did pay a visit to a private residence in Deerfield," Cromley said.

"That's his," Clive said. "He has a two-bedroom house, though he rarely uses it."

"We're going to need access to both properties," Cromley said.

Clive leaned over and conferred quietly with his lawyer, whose mustache twitched and bobbled as he whispered. While the lawyer listened, he shook his head, he nodded, he raised his eyebrows, he tugged on his ear. Finally, he spoke, "My client would prefer that you procure a search warrant first."

"If that's how you want to play it," Cromley said. Without another word, he turned and walked out.

It was such an uncharacteristic reaction that it took Ezra a moment to realize what had happened. He caught up with Cromley in the hallway beside the elevator just as Leena was stepping out of it.

"Are we ready?" she asked.

"It's all over," Ezra replied.

Cromley had his cell phone to his ear.

"Which property are we searching?" Ezra asked.

Cromley covered the receiver. "All of them. Every single property with the Hartford name on it—houses, apartments, offices." He spat the words. "I'm tired of these rich sons-of-bitches and their games."

It was such a transformation from their previous interview that Ezra almost wanted to congratulate his superior. Almost.

Cromley spent several minutes on the phone arranging the warrants and the raids.

As soon as he hung up, Leena asked, "Did your surveillance team see Benjamin Kirsi?"

"No," he said. "They've been on the lookout, but unfortunately no one has seen him."

The elusive Finlox CEO continued to move in the shadows, the unmoved mover, only his effects seen— never the man himself. What strings was he pulling? Was Puck his marionette or the puppet master?

****

SWAT executed the warrants on Puck Hartford's two properties; vested agents took care of the other Hartford properties within Chicago, plus the MTT office building. The Door County Sheriff executed the final warrant at the family's chateauesque lake house.

While they found neither Nélya Kirsi nor Puck Hartford during the course of these raids, they did find in the trunk of Puck's coupe the antique, double-barrel shotgun suspected of inflicting Evie Williams' head wound. Forensics determined that the weapon had been fired recently.

"Within the last year?" Ezra asked over the phone.

"Within the last week," the ballistics specialist answered. "Possibly over the weekend."

They'd found their smoking gun.

Chapter Seventeen

Lucia drove leisurely back to her precinct. She'd made no progress visiting with Fr. Remy Mbombo, whose prime concern seemed to be preparing for his Sunday morning sermon, not explaining the mysterious photograph he'd left for her the night before.

Her partner was already in the bullpen, leaning back in his swivel chair and talking on his office phone. At her arrival, he said something hastily into the receiver and hung up. "How was breakfast?"

"What?" she asked.

"Weren't you supposed to compare notes with your special agent?"

She pulled her hair back into a ponytail. "First off, he's not *my* special agent."

"Did you learn anything?"

"He rescheduled."

"Why? Did your not-fiancé rough him up?"

"He had to leave town."

"I'd leave town, too, if that muscular boyfriend of yours…"

Lucia glared at him.

"Anyway," he said and held up a copy of the briefcase photo Lucia had received the previous night. "Did you have any luck with your priest friend?"

The previous night, Remy had dropped off the photograph for Lucia, but when she went to confront him about it, he feigned ignorance. What did it contain? And how did it relate to Torben Laakso's death? The night he died, Laakso discarded a briefcase identical to the one Remy had photographed. Then again, weren't all briefcases identical?

She scanned the bullpen for any sign of their captain. The only person working was Kley, the new administrative assistant. "I spoke with Fr. Remy this morning, but he wouldn't say much."

Gorecki leaned toward her. Though they were the only detectives present, he still closed the distance between them and lowered his voice. "Did he at least tell you what the briefcase contained?"

She shook her head. "But if we can find the model, it may give us some ideas."

"Impossible," he said too loudly. Kley looked up from his desk; Gorecki gave him an apologetic wave, sending the admin back to his tasks. "That's impossible," he said at a normal volume. "All we have is the handle and the corner of a generic looking briefcase taken through juniper branches at night." He pointed at the fuzzy lines of the case. "Your priest couldn't use his flash, so the details are blurry."

"Maybe forensics can reverse engineer it."

"Or maybe Fr. Remy can just tell us what he knows."

Lucia felt her face warm uncomfortably as though she were covering for a criminal. "Someone told him something in confidence, and he obviously can't share what it was."

Gorecki scoffed. "And why is that again?" he asked, picking a pen off his desk and twirling it absentmindedly.

"He'd get excommunicated." Now she was the one

speaking too loudly.

They both looked across the bullpen at Kley, but he kept his head down and busied himself.

Gorecki continued in a steady tone, almost as a challenge. "I go to church. If my pastor learned that one of his flock wanted to blow up the Field Museum, I'd expect him to tell the police."

Lucia threw up her hands. "Look, I'm not defending the man."

He threw his pen down, so hard it bounced off the wooden desk and hit his computer screen. "But you are!"

Why did men feel the need to control situations with their emotions? How many of her boyfriends had slammed doors, punched steering wheels, or simply raised their voices to end an argument in their favor? Adrian didn't. He might not make her heart race with excitement, but at least he didn't make it race with terror either.

Lucia stood. "What if he had told us the contents of the briefcase?" She pushed her rolling chair into the desk and shut off the computer.

"Then we'd have—"

"We'd have nothing," she said, cutting him off. "Just some second-hand testimony and a blurry picture, and Chicago PD would have a completely silent Jesus Suarez in custody and no hard evidence. Just like they do now."

He shook his head and leaned an elbow on the edge of his desk. "Knowing the contents of the briefcase could help Chicago PD in their interrogations. When they picked Suarez up, the briefcase was gone, but knowing its content would give them leverage."

She took her jacket, a purple belted wrap, off the

back of her chair. "You and I both know Jesús Suárez wouldn't talk even if they found a dead body and a smoking gun in his hand."

"Where are you going?"

"I'm paying a visit to Dominic Torres. I need a closer look at Laakso's office."

Gorecki gave her a questioning look. "What makes you think he'll let you back into Finlox without a warrant?"

"Give me one good reason he shouldn't."

Gorecki began numbering points on his fingers. "One, this is officially a federal case now. Two, you aren't exactly on good terms with his boss. Three, it's Sunday morning."

"Four," she said, interrupting him, "I have this." She pulled the Omega keychain from her jacket pocket. "If Dominic knows what's good for him, he'll let me poke around Torben's office again."

"And if he calls the captain?"

"I'll have to make sure I have everything figured out before he does."

Gorecki made a show of rising out of his own chair.

"Are you going to stop me?" Lucia asked, unbelieving.

"I'm going to join you," he said, grabbing his own jacket, a simple brown journeyman.

"Why would you do that?"

He shrugged. "If this thing goes sideways, I'll be out a partner—and contrary to what you might think, Vargas, I kind of like working with you."

On the ground floor of the precinct, the medical examiner, Patty Ly, intercepted them. Patty handled autopsies for Evanston PD and frequently brought her findings directly to Lucia. The two women would talk at length about television shows, books, and the peculiar habits of their boyfriends, savoring the presence of another woman in their male-dominated environment, before getting down to the forensics.

Today, however, Patty got right to it. "The wound is consistent with self-harm," she said and handed the file to Lucia. Apparently, Patty didn't know Lucia had been taken off the Laakso case. "The angle is inward and upward, piercing the heart from below the sternum."

Lucia took the folder and fanned it open, examining the photographs and scanning the notes. She noticed the phrase *thoracic stab wound* several times. "Could someone have forced his hand?"

Patty frowned. "In that case we'd see some defensive wounds, no doubt."

Gorecki looked over Lucia's shoulder at the report. "What if they handed him the knife and held a gun to his head?"

"How would you rather die, getting shot in the head or stabbing yourself through the heart?" Patty asked, a hand on her hip.

While Gorecki had certainly grown on Lucia over the last four months, Patty had worked with the sometimes macho and racially tone-deaf detective for years and hadn't warmed up to him one iota.

"Good point," he replied. "Maybe they had something worse than death to threaten him with."

The notes on the knife wound mentioned frostbite. Lucia pointed at the word so Patty could see. "What's this?"

Patty squinted, then pulled out her glasses. They were black cat eyes with full rims. In them, she resembled a female NASA engineer from the 1960s. "We've been seeing this lately," she said. "Well, in Chicago anyway. They pulled a body out of the north branch of the river just last week. It was the second or third body with frostbitten stab wounds."

"Were the wounds all self-inflicted?" Gorecki asked.

She shook her head. "Chicago PD suspects gang violence. One kid got stabbed in the back, another had his throat slit." Her gaze fell to the autopsy notes. "In both instances, the wounds showed signs of frostbite."

Gorecki shrugged. "Maybe the water was cold."

"I don't think so. It only occurred around the entrance wounds."

"What does that have to do with our guy?" Lucia asked.

"I don't know," Patty replied, "but the wounds are the same." She crossed her hands over her abdomen to demonstrate. "Along both sides of the torso laceration there's frostbite. Also along the laceration to the heart."

This surprised Lucia. "The heart was pierced, you said?"

"An inferior puncture to the heart is what killed Torben Laakso. The thing is, there was frostbite even on that wound, on the inside of the heart."

"A frostbitten heart," Lucia said meaningfully.

"That's cold," Gorecki added. The two women glared at him. "Sorry." Then to Lucia, he added, "Do you want to bring that with us?"

She nodded. "You can read it to me in the car."

****

After a quick stop off at Dominic Torres' apartment and some metaphorical arm twisting, Torres agreed to meet them at the Finlox building.

Lucia knew the route, but her GPS kept redirecting her.

"It said left," Gorecki reiterated after she ignored three straight sets of directions.

Lucia turned her GPS off. "I just came here."

"Maybe they moved?"

"Ha."

A minute later, the GPS proved correct. An entire city block had been barricaded for a Burmese cultural celebration. The letters on the signs looked like scrawling, interconnected circles to Lucia. She tried sounding one of the banners out in her head but it came out, "Oooo-Ohhh-Oooo," which was definitely wrong.

She took a wide detour, stopping many times for pedestrians enroute to the festival. The men wore collarless shirts and billowing pants; the women wore long dresses in vibrant colors and sashes covered in the labyrinthine patterns that Lucia associated with Southeast Asia.

Dominic Torres met them out front. The building was completely empty this time.

He led them up the stairwell to Torben Laakso's floor, then to a supply closet, unlocking the door and pulling it open. The door led not to a closet filled with cleaning supplies but a floor-to-ceiling safe.

Lucia glared at Dominic. "You didn't feel I should know about this yesterday?"

"You didn't have a key yesterday," he said innocently and gestured for her to try the key.

To her dismay, the lock was a combination dial. The key in her hand likely belonged to a lockbox within the safe. "Okay, what's the combination?"

Dominic shook his head. "You think they tell me?"

Gorecki placed a hand on the young man's shoulder and gave it a firm squeeze. "If we find out you knew the combination, that's obstruction of justice. In a case like this"—he looked at Lucia, who nodded twice—"that could be up to two years in prison."

Dominic's previous indifference gave way to sheepish compliance. "I don't know the combination, per se, but Mr. Laakso did use one code for most things."

He wrote it down for them. Lucia thought it looked like a birthdate. She tried the code, and the safe clicked open.

While she searched for a smaller lockbox, Gorecki kept up a stream of chatter. "My money's on a mystery woman," he was saying. "I'm betting it's her birthday. It seems too long ago for an anniversary. We could run the islands for anyone with this birthday. Maybe we'll find her."

"I doubt she's an islander," Lucia said as if this were obvious. "I'll check the Finlox personnel files. If that fails, I'll run the date through MTT's employee database."

"The cable company?" he asked.

"They're involved with Finlox somehow. At least the FBI seems to think so."

"How do you plan on getting access to their system?"

Lucia almost didn't want to say it. "Ezra."

On the bottom shelf, she found it—one foot wide by two feet long, a metal lockbox covered with stickers from all over the world. She inserted the key and twisted it. The top popped open a half inch. When she pulled the lid the rest of the way, several newspaper clippings fell out and glided to the ground. News clippings filled the box to the brim, some in English, others in French and what looked like Finnish, and still others in languages Lucia could only guess at.

Beneath them, she found a leather journal tied with a thin leather strap. She opened it and tried to read the front page. It wasn't in English, but the handwriting matched the note Torben Laakso had left in Saul's mailbox.

"We're taking this," she told Dominic. "Keep this safe open. We'll send a team to go through the rest."

Lockbox in tow, Lucia Vargas exited the Finlox building with a renewed sense of purpose. Something in this box held the key to the company's involvement in the Durum Island civil war. Laakso's letter to his neighbor, Saul Posner, confessed that he knew the islanders were planning to "rogue the durum," but how much did he know? Did he know they meant to slaughter the undesirable inhabitants? If Laakso knew the plan was fatal, did he know the extent of their planning? And more importantly, could he have prevented it? Whatever Laakso knew, he'd taken to his grave, either willingly or by coercion. Hopefully, he wrote some of it down first.

The late morning sun turned the sky a burning amber and the clouds a sharp pink. Above a high rise to her right, the sun sliced through glass windows, rendering Lucia momentarily blind.

Which is why she didn't see the car shoot around a corner and plow into her.

She felt the impact on her hip first. It was like being smacked by a great wave. Then she was aloft, turning a crude sort of cartwheel in the air, the newspaper clippings from the lock box exploding and whirling around her like confetti, her dark hair turning majestically.

It all took both an instant and an eternity, challenging the nature of time or at least her perception of it. With a sudden jerk back into reality, she collided with the street. As she raised herself to see the retreating vehicle, her hands pressed against a half-dozen loose pebbles, her knees scraped the pavement through her thin slacks, and something warm and thick pooled around her.

She strained to make out the license plate, to call out, to get out of the street, but the world disappeared.

Chapter Eighteen

The pastry shop catered to all manner of tastes, from vegan and lactose-free to zero-sugar and fair-trade. They also handled custom cakes and assorted pastries. When his phone buzzed, Ezra was staring at one such assortment clearly meant for a bachelor party. It included artfully arranged donuts and maple eclairs, with a centerpiece of two oversized jelly-filled donuts frosted in white with two maraschino cherries meant to resemble bright red tassels.

Ezra took his eyes off the doubly alluring pastries to read Cromley's text.

—Benjamin Kirsi just received a ransom call. They're asking for $10 million.—

Ezra called immediately. "When?"

"I just got off the phone with Kirsi. He confirmed that his daughter has a history of disappearing. The family only became concerned after the ransom demand came in."

"Are they going to pay it?"

"I don't see why not. They're coming in shortly to discuss it."

Leena Åkerholm appeared outside the bakery, looking up and down the street. Ezra watched her through the window. Finally, he waved at her with his non-phone-hand until she spotted him.

"Hold on a second," he told Cromley. He waved

Leena into the bakery, mouthing "Come in." She looked around, then hopped up the steps.

"What did the kidnappers say?" he asked Cromley.

"They want to meet tomorrow night at five p.m. on a bridge over the Chicago River."

"What bridge?" Ezra asked, thinking DuSable or possibly St. Charles.

"West Argyle."

He had to picture the street in his head. Did it even cross the river? It must, but he couldn't remember a bridge being there. "That's hardly anything."

"They must want a quiet spot," Cromley said. "It might not even be the actual drop point."

"Do I keep watching the bakery?"

"Do."

Leena passed by Ezra's table and went to the counter.

"Any chance this ransom is a hoax?" he asked Cromley over the phone.

Cromley sighed. "Someone could've heard about Nélya's disappearance and is cashing in." Ezra could hear a shrug over the line. "We'll find out tomorrow."

After Ezra ended the call, he spied Leena, a cup of coffee in her hand and her gaze fixed on the covered entryway across the street. It was the main entrance to Puck Hartford's building.

"How much did you hear?" he asked.

"There's a ransom now?"

"Ten million." He sipped his coffee and studied her expression as it changed from neutral to mildly surprised. "Benjamin Kirsi is coming in to discuss the exchange."

Again, he watched her face. For a woman hell-bent

on tracking down Mr. Kirsi, she didn't seem terribly concerned by the news.

"What do you think?" she asked. "About the ransom."

"I'm still not ruling out a runaway situation," he said, "but I still don't know what it has to do with Torben Laakso. Then again, I trust the whole lot of them about as far as I can throw them."

"Do you distrust wealthy people?"

"Should I not?" he asked. "I suppose I distrust their means. If you're poor, when you break the law and get caught, you're caught. The wealthy have a way of wriggling out of it."

"You sound as though you speak from experience."

"None of my classmates paid for speeding tickets."

"Why not?" she asked, confused.

"Daddy's lawyer, or daddy's golfing buddy." He half expected a diatribe about American corruption.

Instead, Leena replied, "Ah, yes, this happens in Helsinki. Nowhere is perfect." It was a small kindness. "Perhaps the two of them are the kidnappers. Nélya and Puck."

"They could probably fleece both their families and walk away with enough money to never work again," Ezra added.

She followed Ezra's gaze past the pastry counter. "What are you looking at?"

He looked away quickly.

"Oh lord, the tassel cherries? You know that isn't a real woman. She is made of donuts."

He could feel his face flush with embarrassment. "It's been a while," he said weakly. Aside from Julia's recent visit, he hadn't been with a woman in nearly a year. He flexed his ring finger out to examine the tan line. In another few weeks, the spring sun would take it away entirely and no one would ever know he'd been married at all.

A young couple entered arm-in-arm, the woman leaning the bulk of her weight on the man's elbow as though he were a meat hook. She offered her weight and he bore it with ease, both of them perfectly content in this show of dependence.

"I was married until recently," he said. "That's misleading actually. She left a year ago."

"Why'd she leave?"

"Let's just say I was the guilty party."

"Infidelity?" she asked, her interest growing.

"I drew my service weapon on her in a crowded coffee shop."

"Paska! Really?"

"I drew it on my partner, if I want to be accurate. I thought, for a time, well…"

"So it was infidelity, just the other way around," she said.

His whole body dissented with this description. "No, no, I just lost my…perspective."

"Jealousy," Leena said with great weight. "She is a dangerous mistress." She studied his face. "I have a feeling there is more?"

"Julia was pregnant…for a time."

She covered her mouth. "You lost it?"

Ezra nodded.

"I didn't mean…" she started but trailed off.

"Have you been married?"

She laughed. "No."

He half-expected her to say marriage was beneath

her in some way.

Instead, she frowned. "The opportunity never presented itself."

He found this hard to believe. Though she was as cold as Finland in winter, she was also beautiful, even with her unsettling golden eyes. More likely, she'd found the wrong man to love and it ended poorly. "Have you ever been in love?" he asked.

She seemed to take offense at this question. "Yes, of course."

"What happened?" He didn't add the disingenuous, *if you don't mind me asking.*

She frowned. "If I'm going to talk about this, I will require a donut." She rose and reached into her purse.

Ezra perked up. "Can you get me one of the—"

"Yes, yes," she said, shaking her head. "You'll have your bosomy donut."

Moments later, she returned with two tasseled donuts, one for each of them, and told him about her former lover.

"So what went wrong?" he asked between bites.

She looked back outside. "It was doomed from the beginning."

"Why? Did you want different things?" he asked.

"No, quite the contrary. We were," she said, dreamy eyed, "like two berries."

"Excuse me? Two berries? What an odd expression."

She furrowed her brow, searching for the right English idiom. "Alike at heart. Compatible."

"Oh, like two peas in a pod."

She rolled her eyes. "Yes, that's so much less odd. Peas, berries, worlds of difference."

"So? Was he married or what?"

"Let's not get into the details."

"What was he like, this mystery man?" Ezra asked. "Is it a man? I don't mean to presume."

She nodded. "He was handsome, outgoing, and kind."

Ezra couldn't help noticing her use of the past tense. Had her mysterious lover stopped being handsome, outgoing, and kind? Or had he just stopped being these things to her?

"He had a way of connecting with people everywhere he went." She gestured around the bakery. "You and I have been here for thirty minutes, would you say? We've both noticed the flushed middle-aged woman who long ago finished her coffee yet remains here, checking the door, then checking her phone. We've observed the anxious teenager and his red and blue gym bag. And we've seen—" she nodded toward the back table.

"The homeless family, yes," Ezra said quietly. "What's your point?"

The bell on the door dinged and they both turned to watch a fifty-year-old man in a suit walk in. Was he the older woman's illicit lover? The teenage boy's father? A local pastor here to bail the homeless family out of a bad situation?

Leena sighed. "That's our training. Or it's the underlying personality that drew us to law enforcement. He—my 'friend'—was different. He would have already learned the woman's name and the teenager's favorite baseball player. The whole bakery would be showing him pictures of their kids, their dogs, and they'd be actively discussing what the woman should do about her situation—and he'd know what to do." She smiled a warm, unreserved smile. "He had a way of seeing the real you, because he genuinely cared. So few people do."

Ezra looked around the quiet bakery, everyone sitting at their separate tables like a chain of unconnected islands. The sight, so neutral when he'd arrived, made him inexplicably sad now. His companion also seemed sad. For a few minutes, they ate their donuts and drank their coffees and silently watched the street for any sign of Puck Hartford.

Eventually, Ezra did see someone on the street. He pointed. "There."

Together they watched a man in flamboyant Turkish garb pass the bakery. In a fez cap, baggy şalvar trousers, and a colorfully embroidered cepken jacket, he looked like a character right out of a children's book about the Ottoman Empire. Ezra half-expected to see a cartoon horse trotting along behind him.

"Let's go," Leena said.

They intercepted the Turk a block later.

"Leena?" he asked.

"Where is she, Niko?"

"Who?" he asked. The lie convinced no one.

"If you know where your sister is," Ezra tried, "you need to tell us."

"I'm sorry, but I can't help you," Niko Kirsi replied.

"A ransom has been made against her," Leena said urgently.

Niko looked down the street toward the upper floors of a distant building. "That's impossible."

Ezra produced his badge for Niko to inspect. "Your father just called our office. An exchange is being negotiated."

Uncertainty passed over his face for the first time. "But…" He scanned the pavement with his eyes, clearly trying to make sense of this information. "Nélya and Puck are at my place. I am headed there now."

Three blocks later, the three arrived at Niko's building. The elevator took them directly to the penthouse then stopped. Niko entered a four-digit code and the doors swung open.

"*Sisko!* Nel?" he shouted, moving through the spacious condo. A spiral staircase rose through the center of the first floor and into the second. Niko took the stairs two at a time, pulling himself up along the metal handrail. *"Sisko! Sisko!"*

Ezra heard his footfalls scouring the second floor. Then they stopped. Niko returned slowly, his fez cap knocked to one side, his baggy trousers swishing dejectedly as he came down the stairs.

There was urgency in her voice when Leena asked, "Where is she?"

"I don't know," he said. He turned his phone toward them. The screen read, "Sisko." He touched the speakerphone button. They listened to it ringing, then her answering machine picked up. Niko hung up and rang again. He rang a third time, then a fourth, and every time the call went to voicemail.

Leena grasped Niko's arm. He winced. "Listen, Niko," she said in a menacing whisper. "Did you actually see your sister here?"

He shook his head. "I've been with my mother since we came back to Chicago. She's pretty shaken up."

"When did you last see Nélya?"

He considered the question. "The lake house Friday night. Or I guess it was Saturday morning."

"So not since she left on the boat?"

"No."

"Did you see her leave on the boat?"

"Yes."

"Alone?"

"Of course."

Then Leena switched to rapid, angry Finnish. She seemed to be blaming Niko for something. The two of them argued. Ezra tried to pick up on cognates, words shared between English and Finnish, but nothing sounded familiar.

Finally, Niko shouted, "He didn't shoot her! Puck wouldn't do that."

"Then who fired the gun?"

"What gun?"

Ezra placed a hand on Leena's arm and shook his head. She'd already given away too much. Anymore and their later interrogation of Niko would be compromised. "Where is Puck Hartford?" he asked.

The young Finn leaned forward in his chair and covered his face with his hands. "This is all my fault."

"What do you mean?" Ezra asked. "How is this your fault?"

But he wasn't with them. Nélya's brother was far away.

Chapter Nineteen

Sunday afternoons always felt anticlimactic after the significance of morning mass. Lent was no different. Those solemn Sunday mornings emanated so much significance that the afternoon couldn't help but suffer. Remy laid out the homily he'd given and compared it with the Lectionary on his desk. Had his homily added anything to the readings—or had it simply explained what the scriptures already said? How had his parishioners reacted? Where had they smiled, nodded, looked up in surprise? Would he give this exact homily again or should he tweak it or even scrap it entirely? A knock at his door ended this contemplation.

Vickie Holcomb, the school secretary, smiled warmly, her black and gray hair curling around the pleasant features of her face. "You have a visitor."

"A parishioner?" he asked.

"No?" she answered in an uncertain tone.

"Davon," Remy said when the young man appeared in the doorway. "Come in." He closed his Lectionary and pulled out a chair.

"You said you wouldn't tell anyone."

Remy looked from Vickie to his door. She nodded and shut it behind her as she left. "I spoke with your friend, Chuy, and what he shared concerned me. That is all I told the police."

Davon frowned, more sullen than angry, his

shoulders sunken like a small child's as he awaits the principal. "Chuy's going to know I talked. He'll put it together."

"When you think of yourself, Davon," Remy said in a low, calming voice, "do you see a boy or a man?"

The teenager shifted from foot to foot uneasily, like a child seeing an adult's trap from miles away.

"Let me tell you what I see," Remy said and paused for a moment. "I see someone who wants to be a man but isn't sure he's ready for the responsibility."

Davon stopped fidgeting. "The cops have Chuy, but he's not the only one out there."

"He is in for questioning. That is all." Remy frowned. "I didn't tell them what you shared about the briefcase, and the authorities didn't find it."

"What if Chuy confronts you. Or…"

Remy pictured the well-dressed, faceless man from the park. "Simple. If confronted, I will lie. It won't be the first time I've lied to protect someone."

"I thought priests weren't allowed to lie."

Remy looked Davon straight in the eye. "I *will* protect you if I can."

He ran his hand over his short black hair. "What am I supposed to do in the meantime?"

"You chose this lifestyle and, as the teachers at our school are fond of saying, choices have consequences." This line didn't seem effective, so he asked, "Have you heard of the Trappist monks?"

Davon's expression told Remy that obviously he had not.

"I know some monks up in the Appalachian mountains. You could stay there until this dies down."

"I'm not Catholic."

He wrote down the phone number of the Abbey. "You don't have to be. Call this number and they'll arrange it."

Davon took the slip of paper and studied it. "I don't run."

He tried to hand it back, but Remy refused. "Having options and giving up aren't the same thing." He opened his Lectionary and nodded at the door.

"Is that everything then?" Davon asked.

"It appears so," Remy replied without looking up.

Davon snorted, crammed the paper into his pocket, and left.

****

That afternoon, Davon didn't come to chess practice. This didn't surprise Remy. After all, he'd taken something told to him in confidence and used it to have Davon's friend arrested. Chuy also didn't attend practice, though for the obvious reason that Chicago PD still had him in lock up. Therefore, they proceeded with a two-person team composed of loud-mouth Joaquin and oblivious Matt.

As they played, Reverend Don stood over their chessboard and made constant references to the parallel predicaments faced by Hebrew kings. "You're like Gideon, son, outnumbered by the Midianites, but not ready to give up!" Neither teenager paid him much mind and, when the outnumbered Matt lost miserably, even Don looked somewhat embarrassed about his running commentary.

After a few games, Remy ran them through pawn formation drills. These lost their allure quickly, so the priest relented and allowed them to just play more games.

"What if all the pieces were knights?" Joaquin wondered aloud.

"Then you couldn't checkmate," Remy pointed out.

"Okay, all the pieces *but* the king."

They mixed several sets together until they had a board of mostly knights, two kings, and a handful of pawns. Once that game concluded, Matt wondered, "What if all the pieces were bishops?"

In this manner, they whiled away the two-hour practice. Remy wasn't sure they learned much, but they enjoyed themselves and wasn't that the point of most activities?

Once practice concluded, Remy walked the mile and a half to the red brick apartment building where Davon lived with his mother, grandmother, and two younger siblings. Walking through the neighborhood in the fading light made him uneasy, but it was nothing compared to the war-torn neighborhoods and villages he'd passed through and survived.

A middle-aged black woman opened the door of the apartment but didn't unlock the chain. "What?" she asked, hostile until she noticed his Roman collar. "Sorry."

"Davon did not come to chess practice today."

She looked at him blankly. "Huh?"

"His community service."

"Oh," she said. "I didn't realize he was playing chess for the community."

"Didn't you ask him?" Immediately, he regretted his question and the implied judgment of her parenting.

The sound of two children arguing billowed into the hall like a thick cloud. From his vantage point, Remy could only see the off-white wall, but in his mind, he imagined elementary aged children bickering over a plastic toy. She disappeared back into the apartment and scolded them. "If the neighbors file a noise complaint again…" she said, then let them imagine their own punishment. Either she thought this would be more effective, or she didn't want to say it aloud in front of a priest.

"Davon's not here if that's what you're after."

"I didn't mean to imply…"

She snorted derisively. "Look, I've been lectured by teachers, preachers, principals, cops, lawyers, judges, and now a priest. When I met Davon's daddy, I never dreamed of him getting locked up for six years."

Remy nodded. "I apologize for bothering you."

She gave him a second glance, then shut the door with a soft click. He touched the wooden frame to bless it and a sliver of white paint peeled off and slid under his fingernail, cutting the sensitive skin underneath.

Making the sign of the cross, he prayed, *"In nomine Patris, et Filii, et Spiritus Sancti. Amen."* Then he offered a silent prayer for the safety of Davon, wherever he might be.

Had Remy not stayed those two minutes longer to pray, he likely would've missed Davon as he stepped back onto the street. This was precisely how prayer worked in Remy's mind, not by summoning people through spiritual magic but by slowing down the one praying. Sometimes the rosary was just twenty minutes of sitting silently in one place on the off chance someone might need you.

Davon nearly turned around when Remy spotted him. Then thinking better of it, he stood his ground and stuffed his hands into the pockets of his red bomber jacket. "What do you want now? You want my mother's social security number so you can go back to Nigeria and sell her identity?"

Remy smiled. At least Davon was joking. "I deserve that."

"So?"

"Let me buy you a soda pop."

He raised his eyebrows at the old-fashioned terminology. "A soda pop?"

"I can't very well buy you a beer."

Davon glanced back the way he'd come. "There's a Moo-Haha, but it's kind of a walk."

"I don't mind walking," Remy replied. "Moo-Haha is ice cream?"

"And shakes," he said, struggling not to smile like a kid.

****

"I am not from Nigeria," Remy said over their salted caramel milkshakes. He'd let Davon order for the both of them, and already he could feel his blood sugar taking off like one of those cartoon rockets that drags its unsuspecting passenger by a lasso all the way around the moon and back.

"I know," Davon replied. "It was just like, you know, those Nigerian prince scams. Do you have those in Africa?"

Remy grinned. "Yes, we get phishing emails as well. Although, in ours it's an American prince."

Davon laughed despite himself. "So where are you really from?"

"Have you heard of Rwanda?"

"Ms. B. told us about it in history class. They killed a bunch of people. Wait!" he exclaimed, nearly knocking over his milkshake. "Were you there when that happened?"

"I was. I wasn't much older than you are when I visited a parish in Rwanda."

"And you were there during the…" He stopped.

"During the genocide? Yes."

As they drank their milkshakes, Remy told him about his parish in Zaire and his call to Rwanda.

"When I arrived at the cathedral, the warning signs were already beginning. For one, the bishop received shipments weekly, large wooden boxes from all over. They contained weapons, machetes, machine guns, ammunition, and the crude ingredients for explosives.

"My second week, a terrible thing occurred. Then-president, Juvénal Habyarimana, was killed. Someone shot down his plane. The local media, especially the radio stations, blamed the Tutsi minority. Already, they blamed the Tutsis for so much in Rwanda. Radio personalities called them the *inyenzi*—cockroaches—and began the rally cry to exterminate their kind.

"In those days, there were still telephone booths on the street corners and outside certain shops. The morning the militia assassinated the president, I left the cathedral, jogged down to the nearest payphone, a small blue booth at the bottom of the hill, and called my contact across the border in Zaire with a coded message."

This caught Davon's attention. "Coded. What were you, some kind of spy?"

"I was a priest." This wasn't a lie. "I'd been sent to Kigali to assess the situation and was uneasy about what I'd seen. I sent the message, hung up, and waited. I waited a long time. Then a woman called me. She sounded French but wouldn't tell me her real name. She told me to stand by, continue assessing the situation, and call her again in a week. She left a new number for me to use.

"So I returned to the cathedral. I assisted the bishop in serving masses and taking confessions, many of which came from Hutus confessing the heinous acts of violence they were inflicting on their fellow Rwandans. I felt that these men and women were merely covering their bases—beating a Tutsi woman and her children to an inch of their lives on Monday, then finding absolution on Tuesday just so they could turn around and do it all over again.

"One morning, I awoke to the sound of machetes scraping along the pavement of the road outside my bedroom window. I raced to the telephone booth and called again. My contact asked simply, 'Is the anchor you're needing large or small?' You see, in French, the word for 'large' starts with a *G*, so that *une grande ancre* stood for *une génocide*. Already, key Tutsi leaders were disappearing as well as moderate Hutus, but I couldn't tell if this was a genocide or simply a grab for power, a *coup d'état*.

"On the radio, the calls-to-action were increasing. 'Clear the bush!' they cried. 'Cut the tall trees,' they urged more pointedly. The Tutsi were supposedly taller and more light-skinned, and the radio personalities had dubbed them 'tall trees' as well as 'cockroaches.' I told my contact that the anchor wasn't *grande*, not yet, but we were headed there. I asked for permission to take action. She denied it.

"The day after the assassination of Juvénal Habyarimana, the Hutu leaders began cleansing the government. By the weekend, the war had begun in earnest. I helped with the parish school. Sister Therese, oh she was most beautiful."

Davon grinned at this. Likely, he was picturing his own version of Sister Therese, not a nun, but a cheerleader or a basketball player from his school.

"Therese was wonderful, but the head teacher was a Hutu radical. Sister Didi hung an Interahamwe flag from the wall of her office. The Interahamwe were anti-Tutsi, anti-Twa, and even viewed with contempt Hutu moderates like President Habyarimana. When the killings began, the Interahamwe organized the efforts.

"Every day, fewer of our Tutsi students came to the school. The following Monday, I toured the classrooms and saw only Hutu faces. I only knew for sure they were Hutus because their educational files said so.

"I told Sister Didi this had gone far enough. I demanded she take down her flag. She refused. I told her we had to mobilize, to speak out against the racial violence. 'You think they treated us so well when they were in power?' she asked. We could at least help the Tutsis of our parish, I said, or just our Tutsi nuns. I was thinking of Sister Therese. I often thought of her. 'Bishop Bahati will not allow it,' Didi said. If Sister Didi was evil-hearted, the bishop was the devil himself. I suggested we set up a refuge within our church. We were located on the top of a hill that overlooked Kigali. We could protect those families. Also, we were a church. Even the Interahamwe, many of whom were catholic themselves, would have to respect that. Her lips curled into a strange smile. 'Yes,' she said then, 'we can do this thing. I will tell His Excellency.' Then she returned to her grading.

"I did not walk down the hill. I ran. I called every

contact I had and told them that the genocide had begun. I sent the information in coded messages. I told it straight out, not caring who knew. Each one of them told me the same thing. They told me to wait and see. And I am ashamed to say that is exactly what I did."

The story in full took them through their milkshakes, out of the ice cream shop, and all the way back to Davon's apartment building. From a dozen windows trickled the sounds of couples fighting, babies crying, and television sets cranked all the way up. These sounds collided with the whine of police sirens, which came from two separate directions.

"So." Davon gave the building a weary look. "If you could go back in time, what would you do differently?"

"That's the thing about life, Davon, you never know what you're going to do until you do it." The teen pouted, so Remy added, "But I know what I wish I'd done. I had regular access to the bishop's meals and access to strong poison used to kill rats and other pests. I would've taken care of that man myself before he could've led more people astray. Then I would've loaded up one of our buses and taken as many people as I could into Zaire. It wouldn't have changed history, but it could've saved some of them. Even if it could've saved just one of them…"

"And if your bus had been stopped?"

"They all would've died and possibly myself as well."

"What happened to them?"

Remy's nostrils stung, almost as if he were about to shed tears, almost as if he were smelling a horrific odor. "That is not a story for today."

Davon considered this a moment, then asked, "Why

did you tell me this story, Fr. Remy?"

"The opportunity to change the world for the better doesn't come every day. We must seize it when it does. We must do whatever little we can. By the time I decided to take action, the corpses of murdered men, women, and children already choked the Kagera River. And smoke blocked out the sky."

Davon shoved his hands into his puffer jacket. "So what do you want me to do? If I come forward about Chuy and…" he stopped before saying the name of their boss. "If I do that, I'm a dead man."

"There are many ways to die."

"You didn't do anything!" Davon was so angry now that Remy feared the young man might start crying.

Remy took him by the shoulders, but Davon broke free. "You're absolutely right, and there's nothing I can do about it now."

Davon dropped his head, his gaze finding the sidewalk that led to the front door of his building. "Whatever," he said and sulked homeward.

Was it impossible advice? After all, the teen had his mother and grandmother and siblings to consider. Who would help take care of them with their father in prison and their brother dead? In the end, hopefully, Davon would find the balance between the man he wanted to be and the one he was able to be—even if it took him the rest of his life.

****

Though a taxi or the L would've been faster, Remy elected to take a stroll through the darkened streets. It felt disingenuous to drop in and out of Davon's neighborhood like some religious airdrop, offering advice for surviving in a place he didn't even feel comfortable walking through, but also he had somewhere else he wanted to stop by on his way home.

Shortly after leaving Davon's neighborhood, he crossed the Chicago River. From there, he headed north on a road that followed the river. Soon, he came across Chuy's park. In Chuy's place stood a similarly dressed young man. He watched Remy approach, then looked away as the priest disappeared behind a wall of trees. Deep within the juniper tree lay a metallic briefcase. If he leaned in just right, he might be able to grab it without breaking stride.

Through the wall of trees, Remy could just see Chuy's replacement. Searching the ground, he located a pebble no larger around than his thumb. It might do. Closing his eyes and picturing the park in his mind, he cocked his arm back and hurled the pebble over the line of trees toward the river. It sailed through the air and struck a tree trunk. The sound was barely perceptible and didn't draw the young man's attention. He searched the ground again and came up with a stone the size of a golf ball. He closed his eyes, said a prayer, and launched it. Again the stone struck a branch or trunk, the noise subsumed by the sound of birds flying away. Chuy's replacement looked around, his sneakers rustling in the dry grass, but then he lost interest.

This time Remy grabbed a chunk of concrete that barely fit in his palm. Without thinking or even aiming, he chucked it as hard and as high as he could. Rather than strike the river, the concrete piece ricocheted between several high branches. Remy poked his head deep into the line of junipers and watched the gangster peer skyward at the noise. He searched for only a few seconds before seeing it, but not soon enough to avoid catching the falling meteor right between the eyes. He slumped over to one side and Remy slipped on a pair of leather gloves and grabbed the briefcase.

Not sure if he should thank God or ask forgiveness, Remy found himself humming, *"Acclamons le roi de gloire,"* acclaim the king of glory.

Perhaps the song came to him because Easter season was fast approaching or perhaps it was because, for the first time in several days, he had a victory to celebrate.

Chapter Twenty

Ezra and Leena sat talking with Nélya's brother Niko at an ornate marble table in his dining room. Niko's phone dinged and chirped and vibrated but never with a response from his *sisko*. It distracted him so much that they had to repeat their questions periodically.

"Sorry," Niko said for the umpteenth time, "what was that?"

"I asked if anything was missing," Ezra said.

They'd made a survey of the apartment, upstairs and down. They found no signs of a struggle—nothing broken, no blood or other bodily fluids, though they'd need forensics to be sure. Victims of sudden attacks often lost bladder or bowel control, leaving vital evidence behind.

Niko looked around the dining room. "I don't think anything's missing, but I don't know. She left all her stuff."

This wasn't a good sign. If she'd left of her own volition, she would've taken some clothes, toiletries, a purse, but all these items were strewn about Niko's spare bedroom and bathroom. The two agents who had camped out at Nélya's little-used apartment saw no sign of her. The only thing they couldn't locate was a phone.

"Did she have her phone?" Leena asked.

He gave them a sheepish look. "She has a second cell phone. An emergency one. Nobody knows about it except for us."

"You and her?" Ezra asked.

"The family."

The two investigators shared a look. So someone called her—they must've—and told her to leave her brother's apartment immediately, taking nothing. It had to have been someone she trusted implicitly. Or feared greatly.

"You said this was all your fault," Ezra said. "What did you mean?"

"We were at the Hartfords' party. I went as a whirling dervish; Puck and Nélya went as penguins." He paused for a moment, like he was trying to recall specific details. "It was just after two in the morning. We decided to take our little party outside."

"Who?" Ezra asked.

Leena left the table and searched the kitchen. She started at the sink, then moved over the fridge, studying the magnets and photographs. Apparently, nothing interested her, because she moved onto the trash can, then the gas stove, laying her hands on the cast iron grates one at a time.

Niko watched her, then checked his phone yet again.

"Who?" Ezra repeated.

"Sorry," Niko said. "It was Puck, Nélya, me, and two of Puck's friends—I can't remember their names."

"Was one of them a bear?"

"Yes! They were together—a couple, I mean."

"Then what happened?"

He squeezed his eyes closed. "Puck was pontificating. That's what he does. He gets just near the point of falling over drunk and then shifts into some kind of character from Shakespeare, delivering grand monologues on the nature of philosophy, love, existence. He was a theater major, you know. This tech thing, it's all for his father."

Leena moseyed back to the table and stood behind her chair.

"What did he say?" Ezra asked.

"I can't remember everything, but he kept coming back to this line. He said it was from *Macbeth.*" He nodded. " 'Realization is better than anticipation.' That was it, I think."

"That's backward," Leena said. "The quote is, 'Anticipation is greater than realization.' *That's Macbeth.*"

"Yes, *greater than*. That's what I meant."

Ezra, who was busy taking notes, stopped now. "Well, which was it?"

"Which?"

"Which did he say was greater, anticipation or realization?"

"Does it matter?" Niko asked.

It certainly could. Puck's speech revealed one of two sentiments. Either he was grateful over an engagement that exceeded his expectations, or he was dreading his impending nuptials to Nélya. Either he loved her beyond his wildest dreams, or he was wondering how to get out of the engagement.

Ezra decided not to tell Niko all this about his sister's fiancé. Instead he asked, "Then what happened?"

"Nélya got a call from Leena."

Leena shook her head. "*Not* from me."

"A call or a text?" Ezra asked.

"Our system sends out an encrypted text," Leena explained.

"I don't know," Niko said. "Her phone made its little alarm, and she went off toward the lake. I heard her talking with someone. We kept wandering the woods and then Puck joined her. He came back alone and told me to get a boat ready. He shoved these keys into my hands and pointed me toward the boathouse."

Leena's voice became suspicious. "He had the keys on him?"

"I guess so."

The investigators shared a look. Puck had the keys on him before the alarm reached Nélya's cell phone. It sounded orchestrated and, if Niko's memory was to be trusted, it sounded like Puck had been the one pulling the strings.

"I got the boat ready, and she drove it out into the lake alone."

"You spoke with the police?" Ezra asked. There'd been no mention of Niko on the sheriff's report.

"I hid out in the boathouse until the police cleared out. Then I came back to Chicago with my mother."

"Where was your father during all this?" Leena asked.

"He left early to take care of some business in Chicago."

Ezra recalled this from their interview with Augustus Campbell. "Do you know who your father was meeting?"

"No idea."

"You still haven't explained how this is your fault," Leena said then.

"I should never have let her get in that boat." He dropped his face into his hands.

Ezra realized something then. "What brought you to

Chicago?"

"I've been here since August."

This didn't seem like news to Leena. "Niko is studying linguistics," she said for Ezra's benefit.

"My work centers on the controversial Ural-Altaic language family proposal."

"Ah yes," Ezra said with mock understanding, "a tense issue around the holidays."

He ignored Ezra's sarcasm. "It would potentially give a proto-language to a whole host of languages from Finnish and Hungarian to Turkish and Mongolian."

"So is that why…" Ezra gestured to Niko's ostentatious outfit.

"I wear this when I'm working on my Turkish, yes." Ezra must've seemed unimpressed, because Niko continued. "Less than five million people in the world speak Finnish, most of them in Finland, and the population of my homeland decreases every year. By the time we have a solid understanding of the origins of our language, it might not matter anymore."

"And what will the history of your language add?" Ezra asked.

"You American's take everything for granted," he said sharply.

Someone entered Niko's penthouse and, in an American accent, called out, "*Pingviini!*"

"It's us!" Leena called back.

Puck Hartford came cautiously around the corner. "What's all this?"

Niko rose and met him in the hallway. "Nélya is missing."

"Yes, I know that," he said, giving the investigators the side eye.

"No, Puck, she's really gone."

"I know," he repeated even less convincingly this time.

"They know everything," he said through clenched teeth. He was no longer twisting and turning anxiously. His *sisko* was missing; saying this aloud seemed to make it feel real for the first time. Anger welled up in his eyes. "Where the hell is she, Puck?"

Then dropping all pretense, Hartford said, "She's here, Niko! She must be hiding."

Niko grabbed Puck by the collar. "If you did this…"

Puck broke eye contact and left the room. They heard him sprinting up and down the stairs twice. Finally, he returned, looking crestfallen. "This wasn't part of the plan."

"You'll need to come with us to give a statement," Ezra said.

"Who took her?" he asked. There was no mischievous grin now.

Leena rose from her chair. "The FBI is setting up an exchange for tomorrow night."

"What's going on?" he demanded.

"We don't know," Ezra said. "But we'll find out more tomorrow. Now, you need to come with us."

Puck agreed to go, but not before they answered another question. "Why? Why would someone take my fiancée?"

Ezra could think of ten million reasons, and despite this dramatic display of concern, Ezra still didn't rule Puck out as the culprit.

Chapter Twenty-One

Monday

As Lucia slowly regained consciousness, it was the sounds around her that returned first, one at a time. First, the rhythmic beep of a heart monitor—just like on the TV medical shows. Then came the endless messages from the overhead paging system. Somewhere a Code Blue needed the help of any available respiratory therapist. Last, she registered the annoying squeak of tennis shoes as they moved down the linoleum floors. As she processed all this, the noxious odor of cleaning fluids mixed with that of burnt coffee filled her nostrils in an unsettling, nauseating mix. Finally, her own body, as if stiff and unused, made itself known.

The sheets felt stiff and tight; the room lights were twenty watts too bright. Like the crow of a rooster, their brightness woke her the instant she realized they were there.

She opened her eyes then blinked rapidly, momentarily blinded. She felt someone sitting beside her narrow bed. She felt his warmth and smelled his cologne. "Ezra?"

"It's me." Adrian's face came slowly into focus. His eyes were downcast like the eyes of a boy whose mother had shown up drunk to the big game. *If you loved me, you'd be better,* those eyes seemed to say.

She opened her mouth to explain but couldn't find the words. "I'm sorry,"

"Am I defective in some way?"

"No!" she said, surprised.

"It was a rhetorical question," he said. "I have a good job, I come from a good family, and I'm not bad looking."

He certainly wasn't bad looking. If anyone was a poster child for the benefits of a gym membership, it was Adrian Silva. If he were a cartoon character, she could've played his abs like a marimba. More importantly, he was smart and kind. Looking at his heart-broken face, she knew the problem was her.

"I know this is a cliché, but it's not you, it's me."

His eyebrows wrinkled in a frown. "I don't know what your deal is, but if it's someone else," he said, leaving Ezra's name unsaid, "just pull the trigger and spare yourself the uncertainty."

He rose from the bed, grabbed his jacket, and left.

"That was awkward," Gorecki said.

Until he spoke, she hadn't noticed her partner sitting quietly in the corner. He grabbed a tissue box from beside him and brought it to her. With this subtle act of permission, the waterworks began.

"I must look like a fool," she said between crying jags.

He smiled. "There's nothing foolish about having emotions."

"I know, but…"

"Keep your 'but' to yourself," he said, smiling and sounding more rural-Illinois than ever. "There's nothing foolish about letting a good fish off the hook. No one likes being stringed along."

Lucia blew her nose. "Do you think I strung Adrian along?"

"You dated for two months. Let's not get carried away." He reached into his leather briefcase and removed an expandable organizer that bulged with color-coded folders. It looked surprisingly meticulous for one of Gorecki's casefiles.

"I know how you like everything in its place," he said and laid it on the bed.

"I know you're right," she said, "about Adrian, I mean. Still, why do I feel so terrible?"

"You didn't want to hurt him." He nodded at the tubes connected to her arm. "Also, they've been pumping you full of morphine all night. That alone is enough to make anyone's emotions run a little wild."

She looked out the window at a sky just fading from black to dark blue. "I've been here all night?" She sat up with a start and tugged at her sheets, but a pain shot through her right side as she moved.

"Whoa now."

"I'm not a horse, Sac," she said, using Gorecki's nickname derisively. More slowly this time, she pulled the sheets away. "I was supposed to meet Ezra."

The thought of their meeting filled her with a complex cocktail of excitement, anxiety, and sadness, which hit her with such blunt force that she found herself crying again. The idea that some people paid good money for drugs like these baffled her.

She wiped her nose with the sheet, then the hem of her gown on her eyes. "What did we find in the lockbox?"

Gorecki let the hanging folder flop open. Then he laid three files on the bed. "The news clippings fall into three categories: Torben Laakso's career." He pointed to the file labeled, *The Rise and Fall of TL*. "The rising racial tension and eventual violence in the Durum Islands." This file, the largest of the three, read simple, *Genocide*. "Finally, the media backlash and the response by Finlox." The thinnest file by far, it read, *Not with a Bang but a Whimper*.

"T.S. Eliot," she said, taking the thin file first. "Have you read 'The Hollow Men'?"

"I looked it up after we read that line in Laakso's letter. It's about the war, right?"

Lucia tilted her head, trying to recall the details of the poem. All that came to her were disparate lines. "We are the hollow men/ We are the stuffed men/ leaning together," she recited. That's all she could remember, a row of straw men with no will of their own. She remembered the ending, too of course, which her literature professor, a balding man with eyebrows that curled upward and around like the ornamental brows of a wise, old dragon in a fairy tale, had sung as though it were a children's rhyme. "This is the way the world ends/ This is the way the world ends/ This is the way the world ends/ Not with a bang but a whimper."

"I didn't realize you were a singer, Vargas."

Had she been singing aloud?

"Very much so," he replied.

Somewhat dreamily, she flipped open the file and perused the articles within. The first headline asked, "Is Finlox to Blame for Civil War?" The article recounted the events but failed to make a clear judgment. A handful of other articles, each more lackluster than the last, were also included.

"What do you think?" he asked.

"A whimper indeed," she said. She looked up too fast and made herself dizzy and slightly nauseated. "Whoa. The room just moved."

"Nope."

She settled herself. "It sounds like Finlox was the only form of internet these islanders had. If they were planning a genocide ahead of time, they could've been using the platform to organize it."

"The internal investigation found no evidence," he said, quoting one of the articles she'd just read.

"Or maybe it did. Maybe Torben Laakso knew, but his boss made him bury it."

"Rogue the durum," Gorecki said.

"Exactly." Then abruptly, she asked, "Who ran me over?"

Her partner frowned. "We don't know yet. The car took alleyways to and from the Finlox building and managed to avoid cameras. It was as if they had access to every surveillance device in the area."

"Dammit!" As her fist came down on the bed, pain shot through her pelvis.

"You're lucky they had to take alleyways," he said, "otherwise that car might've hit you going sixty instead of twenty."

He looked out the open doorway. "The translation of Torben's journal should be ready first thing tomorrow morning. Your translator, this Enni Frost person, has a full-time job, but she agreed to fit it in after work."

Taking up the file labeled *Genocide*, Lucia perused the contents. The articles were written in a variety of languages, and she had to continually use a translation app on her phone to read even the headlines. From what she gathered, the violence began slowly in a trickle of isolated hate crimes. These culminated in the burning of a young Muslim family in their straw home. The husband, wife, and two small children were unable to escape in time.

Months of apparent outrage and repentance followed the tragedy. It looked like the violence might stop. Then tensions rose again. Every Muslim family from throughout the island chain was relocated to a special housing development on French Halmahera. The local officials called it a housing development, but the pictures showed a ghetto. Once they were concentrated there, a fence was erected and, late one night, a fire was set. Those who escaped the conflagration were picked off by farmers, their sickles and plowshares transformed into weapons in some sick inversion of Isaiah.

In the aftermath, the island officials characterized the night of bloodshed as the start of a civil war incited by the Muslim minority. What would incite a small, powerless group to wage a civil war? This question was never addressed.

"Last but not least," she said aloud and took up the file on Torben Laakso's professional life.

After earning a business degree from the University of Helsinki, Torben joined a start-up social network his college roommate had started in their dorm room. Finlox went public, grew exponentially, and to everyone's surprise Benjamin Kirsi never jettisoned his college buddy.

"Tech IPO gives Finnish investors the Bens," one article joked then went on to claim Benjamin and Torben were a force to be reckoned with. Over time, however, Kirsi relegated Torben to smaller and smaller roles within the company. Eventually, Torben found himself in charge of legal compliance, working in tandem with Finnish national police.

Here the articles about Laakso stopped, and stories about an up-and-coming KRP investigator began. Time and again, this superhuman investigator cut through the bullshit and international obfuscation to deliver both justice and honor to her homeland.

"Who's Leena Åkerholm?" she asked her partner.

To her surprise, Gorecki was gone. The room too had changed. It shone with full morning light. She grasped the morphine drip in her hand. "I am asking for less of this," she declared to no one.

****

"Knock, knock," a cheery faced woman dressed in scrubs and a sparkling white lab coat said from the doorway. Her blonde ponytail swished back and forth. Her ID badge said Henrietta Lange, MD.

"Come in," Lucia replied.

Lange lifted a clipboard hanging from the end of the bed and scanned several pages. "How are we feeling?"

She held up her morphine button. "I don't love this."

The doctor tilted her head to the side like a perplexed dog.

"I don't like feeling out of control."

"How's your pain?"

"Fine," Lucia lied.

"You will tell us if that changes." She turned back several pages on the clipboard. "You suffered a number of injuries, but nothing life threatening. Your MRI showed bruising on your right leg, a cracked rib, and a hairline fracture to the pelvis." She looked up and said with the direction of a TV doctor, "It's not a big break, but you'll need to be on crutches for a few weeks."

None of this felt real to Lucia. She wondered if she was dreaming or still lying unconscious in the street or…

As if by magic, a person bearing the ID badge of a physical therapist came in, carrying a set of crutches.

"No, no." As Lucia sat up, excruciating pain shot down both legs. "I'm feeling much better, really. I can walk."

The medical professionals frowned in unison. "You're sitting now," Dr. Lange said. "Imagine how much more pain you'll be in when you stand, let alone try to walk."

"It'll be fine, really." *Please, God. Let me be fine.*

The doctor came to stand directly in front of Lucia to keep her in bed. Lucia pushed her aside and swung both legs over the side of the bed. She stood, on one foot, then both. The pain, indescribable for intensity and duration, took her breath for one second. Then the floor seemed to wobble, but she used everything she'd learned since childhood to help her maintain, to take that first cautious step.

And the room went dark.

****

When she opened her eyes, the physical therapist, Dr. Lange, and two nurses in green scrubs looked down at her. Each wore looks of pity on their faces.

"Okay, Amazon woman," Lange said. "You just passed out on us. We're going to restart the morphine drip and when you're ready to try again, we'll bring the crutches."

As soon as Lange adjusted the IV drip, a warm fuzziness crept up Lucia's arm. Her breathing eased; her legs relaxed. Maybe… "Wait," she said. "I remember being covered in blood."

She stopped in the doorway and looked up, as if she was trying to remember something.

"I felt the blood," Lucia clarified.

"Oh!" She smiled. "You had motor oil all over you. It's warm and viscous, and you were concussed so I can understand your confusion."

Lucia asked, "Did the motor oil leave a trail?"

The doctor nodded. "Your partner waited with you for the ambulance to arrive. He followed the car, but never found it."

Somehow, Gorecki had failed to mention this.

"I'm sure that's why he left here once you woke up," she continued.

"Why?" Lucia asked.

"To figure out who did this to you."

Lucia laughed.

"What?" the doctor asked.

"It's just…he's not bad. He's an asshole when he's talking, but what he actually does…"

The doctor smirked. "With a job like yours, you need someone you can trust."

It had taken a while but, miracle of miracles, Lucia did trust him.

Chapter Twenty-Two

They let Puck Hartford spend the night in federal custody—a small but comfortable room inside the Chicago Field Office. In the morning, they led him to a larger room for questioning.

The interrogation room in the basement didn't look like the typical interrogation room. In fact, it looked like nothing. That was the whole point. However, the nondescript room didn't fool Puck, especially when Ezra brought out his recorder.

The young man crossed his arms and refused to sit. "I don't mean any offense, but I'm not doing this without a lawyer."

In fact, the Hartfords' lawyers—now a whole team of them—were already in the building. Upstairs, ASAC Jeremiah Cromley and his boss, Special Agent in Charge Eileen Banth, met with the Hartfords, the Kirsis, and their gaggle of lawyers to plan for the following day's exchange of ten million dollars for one Nélya Kirsi.

Leena checked her watch. "Look, we're running out of time. You need to tell us what you know."

"You said there's a ransom," Puck said. "That means you know who took her."

She shook her head. "The message was left anonymously with a computer recording."

"We haven't been able to trace the call," Ezra added.

"They know what they're doing," Puck replied.

Ezra sat down in a small leather chair. "You said this wasn't the plan. What was the plan?"

He shook his head. "My father would kill me if I spoke without our lawyers here." He looked down. "He's already going to kill me."

"Tell him," Leena said to Ezra.

Puck looked back and forth between them.

Ezra sighed. "Your father's strategizing upstairs."

"Take me there. I'll tell you whatever you need to know."

Ezra looked to Leena for an answer.

"Don't look at me. It's your call."

"Fine."

Cromley wouldn't like having his party crashed, but Ezra couldn't see any other way.

****

The conference room bustled with activity. Cromley stood in front of an oversized map of the north Chicago bridge. Yellow post-it notes and bright green arrows highlighted various features. Across the room, Eileen Banth explained an illustration of a duffle bag. Several squares showed enlargements that detailed the bag's features, which included trackers, listening devices, and an exploding cap to mark the bills.

"What if they anticipate all this?" an elegant Finnish woman asked SAC Banth. Ezra had only seen a few pictures of Nélya's mother, Marja Kirsi, but he was sure this was her.

Banth pulled up an image of a second bag. "They will. You'll also have a second bag, an oversized purse. The ransomer might tell you to lose the duffle bag. If so, you can empty the contents of the purse and load as much of the money as will fit. The purse will be fitted with the same features as the duffle."

While Puck joined his family by the map of the bridge, Leena scanned the room. "Where's Benjamin Kirsi?" she asked loudly. All heads turned toward her.

Cromley answered. "He's with tech going over his part of the deal."

"What floor is that on?" she asked.

"Not here. They are setting up at the drop site." He checked his watch. "At least, they were. It's daylight now, so they've likely moved on."

"To where?" Leena asked.

No one answered. It was only then that Ezra realized his bosses either weren't allowed to share everything with the Finnish investigator or that they didn't fully trust her.

She gestured to the diagram of the duffle bag. "Why does he not need to see this?"

Banth stepped away from Marja Kirsi and lowered her voice to a whisper as she addressed Leena. "Mrs. Kirsi will be making the exchange. Her husband will accompany her."

"Out of the question." Leena shook her head adamantly. "This is too dangerous for Marja."

"They're expecting both of us, Benjamin and me," Marja said.

"Then I will be you."

"But Leena, you're blonde," she said as if this were their only difference.

Not to mention twenty years younger, Ezra thought. Although, their silhouettes were about the same. He wondered momentarily if Leena's eagerness was driven by heroism or if guilt played a role—guilt over losing Marja's daughter, failing to locate her. Or perhaps it was something else entirely…a subconscious desire to take Marja's place. Ezra still suspected an affair.

"I'll wear a scarf and sunglasses," Leena said. "They'll never know the difference."

As they continued negotiating, Puck rejoined Ezra. His father and their mustachioed lawyer flanked him. "Nélya's security team notified her of a threat, so I helped her get away for a while."

"Leena Åkerholm says she never contacted Ms. Kirsi," Ezra replied.

Puck clenched his fists. "Someone did. Otherwise, she wouldn't have gone into hiding. Niko put her on a motorboat headed for the islands. From there, she was supposed to wait for sunrise and then swim back to the peninsula and wait for me in the boathouse."

"Did she?" Ezra asked.

"I already said she did," he answered.

The other agents and family members stopped what they were doing to eavesdrop. Ezra still wasn't sure it was worth listening to.

"I had to answer the sheriff's questions and make the rounds as if she were missing. Then I had to return with my family to Chicago and meet with you people. Only then did I return to Nélya. She was hiding in the corner of the boathouse, wrapped in blankets and looking more scared than I've ever seen her. I put her in my car, and we drove back to the city. I have a little place in Deerfield. That's where we went first. Then I asked Niko for the code to his place; we hid out there."

"What about the security cameras?"

"We hacked them," he said.

"We?"

"Nélya and I both know our way around a simple

network. I set up a loop in the feed and distracted the doorman. It was easy. Then, all we had to do was wait."

"For what?" Ezra asked.

"Word." He nodded at Leena. "From her."

The accusation hung in the air. It sickened Ezra. Here Puck's fiancée was missing, possibly dead, and his biggest concern was not getting blamed.

Leena scowled. "It wasn't me."

The emotional tenor of the room had shifted so fast, Ezra thought for a moment it might come to blows. Either Leena herself would throw the first punch or one of the Kirsis would.

"If it wasn't you," Puck snarled, "then why haven't you reached out to her?"

Now Leena did act, grabbing him by the collar so hard it became a noose around his neck. Nobody stopped her. "Don't you think I tried? Whoever contacted her also must've told her to disable her phone. Has she used it since she's been on the run?" Leena relaxed her grip just enough to let him answer.

"Well, no," Puck admitted sheepishly.

She turned on Marja Kirsi now. "Have you been in contact with her this whole time?"

"No."

"Not even through her emergency phone?"

"Don't you think we've tried? I didn't know anything about this insane plan!" She regarded her son, Niko, as he sat forlornly in an armchair. Ezra saw equal parts anger and terror in her face. Anger that her children had left her out of the situation; terror that now she and Niko were on the outside looking in.

Leena scanned the room like a she-wolf in search of prey. Finding none, she whipped around, her blonde ponytail slapping the side of her head like a flail. Whatever gentleness Ezra had glimpsed in her the day before was long gone. Had she been holding a firearm, he would've coaxed it calmly from her hand and placed it on the ground. Instead, he watched her anger build like the steam in a volcano until she dismissed the whole room with one final glowering look.

"Tonight," she said and stormed out.

Marja Kirsi must've noticed the shocked expression on Ezra's face because she said, "Leena can be like that."

He scoffed. "Do you trust her to make the exchange in that state-of-mind?"

"There's no one I'd trust more."

Cromley clapped his hands twice. "You heard the woman. Director Åkerholm is our new Mrs. Kirsi." He stopped to make sure he had everyone's attention. "We have less than twelve hours, folks. We need to be ready for anything."

His gaze shifted straight to Ezra.

****

As soon as they dispersed, it dawned on Ezra that he'd never connected with Lucia. He set up the coffee maker in the breakroom and, as it brewed, he called her. She picked up on the second ring.

"There she is!" he said. "I never heard from you yesterday. What happened?"

"Someone ran me over with their car," she said flatly.

"Funny."

"I'm not joking, actually."

Ezra's heart skipped a beat and his breath caught. "What? Who was it?"

"I don't know. Gorecki's looking into it."

"Where are you?"

"Mercy Hospital."

"I'll bring you some coffee."

"I'll be out today or tomorrow. It's not worth it."

"That's ridiculous. I've already left."

****

Ezra had no trouble finding Lucia's room, but she made him wait outside, holding a hot latte in each hand for five minutes, while she straightened up. He realized as he waited that this was the closest he'd ever come to entering her bedroom.

"You aren't meeting with the queen!" he hollered while at the same moment that she said, "Come in."

The sight of her, connected to an array of machines by wires and tubes like a reclining marionette, upset him. He'd never seen her so vulnerable. Betraying his own unease, he forced a smile. "Nice gown. Is that one of those that doesn't close in the back?"

"Hence my remaining in bed." Her words came out slow but clear.

"Is this related to the Laakso case?"

"I was leaving his office with a lockbox of his things when it happened."

"What sort of things?"

"Newspaper clippings, his private journal."

He pointed at a stack of case files lying on her bed. "Can I see?"

With a slow nod, as if it hurt to move her head, she pulled out a user's manual and turned to a diagram of a metal briefcase. "You should start with this first."

"What am I looking at?"

"A supercooled briefcase. Fr. Remy brought a photograph of it by Saturday night. Then he left the real

233

thing at our precinct yesterday."

"What's it used for?"

Lucia regarded the photograph for a long moment. "We believe this one stored knives."

"I don't understand," he said. "I thought he died from a GSW."

"Stab wound. They found loose clumps of polyester mixed with Laakso's blood at the crime scene. Initially, they thought it came from the carpet, like maybe Laakso kicked it loose with his shoes or the leg of his chair. When it didn't match the carpet, they thought maybe the polyester fibers came from his clothes."

As she spoke, he noticed smaller injuries, scratches and scrapes and bruises over the exposed surfaces of her face, neck, and arms. "And what do they think now?" he asked when she finished.

"Our medical examiner, Patty Ly, spoke with Chicago PD and they've also found loose polyester at recent crime scenes where victims were stabbed. In some cases, they found polyester inside the victims' wounds. Patty thinks someone is making knives."

"Making knives?"

"Out of ice."

It reminded him of those childhood riddles—the hanged man with no chair to stand on, the two politicians and their poisoned ice cubes, the woman murdered by an icicle. Or had she killed herself? Had that been the solution? "That's kind of brilliant," he said. "No prints. No weapon. Even the newest initiate wouldn't leave the murder weapon behind." He folded his suit jacket over his arm and plopped into the visitor's chair.

She held an article up for his inspection. He leaned forward in his chair and read the headline aloud, "Is

Finlox to Blame?" He gave her a quizzical look. "To blame for what?"

"Read on."

The article discussed the role the social network played in facilitating a genocide in the South Pacific. After reading it, Ezra asked, "So Torben brings this to his boss, the boss squashes it, and six months later he gets murdered?"

"Not murder," Lucia said. "No one came in or out of his place. The doors were locked and CCTV footage confirmed it."

"Someone could've put in a feedback loop. Apparently, all these tech people can do it."

"No loop. The cameras show Torben coming and going the whole time. All the way until the music kicked on. Then it shows the neighbor, Saul Posner, coming to the door to check on him."

The sound of morning news poured in through the open door. Someone in the waiting area had apparently turned the volume button on the TV all the way up. Ezra listened for a moment as an upbeat anchor pretended to interview a baby panda, her voice full of the false enthusiasm most often reserved for children. The panda's handler began answering for it. *New life,* Ezra thought. Then the volume suddenly went to a low buzz so Ezra couldn't make out the words.

"So what actually happened?" he asked Lucia.

"We think Torben killed himself, but he wanted to make it look like a homicide. We think he was trying to frame his boss, Benjamin Kirsi."

Ezra brandished the article in her direction. "I don't get it? Why not just leak the story about these islands?"

She shrugged. "You've seen how these situations

pan out. Everyone's to blame, so no one's to blame. If, on the other hand, a jury believed someone murdered Torben Laakso to cover up the role Finlox played in the incident, that would be an easy life sentence."

"Why lock his door?" Ezra asked. "That made your team assume suicide."

"He couldn't risk someone coming in before the knife melted. That's why he left the window open, to cool down the apartment to freezing, and then cranked up the heat right before the act. The building owner had a key to the front door but not the study. That room Torben locked with deadbolts." She considered something. "He also couldn't risk Saul Posner catching the blame."

"The whole thing feels ironic."

Lucia moved in the bed slowly, uncomfortably. "How so?"

"Laakso frames his boss for a minor crime because no one could try Kirsi for the larger one."

"Wait." She moved again, but this time faster. A groan of pain escaped her. "You think murdering Laakso in cold blood is *minor*?"

"One murder compared to a genocide. I'd call that minor."

Lucia rolled her eyes. "But Kirsi didn't slaughter those islanders."

His neck grew hot. "But he helped! The company knew about these discussions and did nothing."

"Did they know?" she asked. "It sounds like the posts weren't being moderated. Nobody spoke this creole language they used."

"Then that's even worse!"

"How could it possibly be worse?"

"It would be like inviting a group into your house and letting them organize a bombing. For months."

"I disagree. It's like letting them discuss the idea of bombings in a public space. It's free speech."

"But Finlox isn't a public space. They're a private company who profited from those conversations."

She laughed, then winced with pain. "This is exactly why you're a Fed and I'm not."

"What's that supposed to mean?"

"Between protecting the Bill of Rights and eliminating a potential threat, the Feds always choose the latter."

"For a well-read person," he said in disbelief, "I thought you'd understand the dangers of unlimited speech. Look at what Hitler did with persuasive speeches."

"Speeches and book burnings." She spat the words. "It's because I'm well-read that I understand the dangers of censorship."

Ezra couldn't believe such an intelligent person could be so cavalier about this tragedy. "What you're defending is anarchy. Anyone can say or do whatever they want."

"They can *say* whatever they want," she clarified. "There's a huge difference between saying and doing. As far as I'm aware, Benjamin Kirsi never supplied sickles or ammunition, and he definitely didn't pull any triggers or light any fires."

He fiercely disliked Lucia at that moment, but he also disliked how much he disliked her. Wasn't this the very freedom he'd sworn to defend? Wasn't she just saying things she had a right to say? "So what're you going to do?"

"Gorecki wants to rule it as a suicide pending further evidence. Chicago PD has a young man in custody who we think sold the knife in question to Torben Laakso. They're going to try to get the rest of the story from him."

"Do you think he'll cop to it?"

"Ha," she said. "I doubt they have enough to build a case, and he's not helping. Even without his confession, though, we can fill in the gaps."

Could they? Ezra still had plenty of questions. For instance, how did any of this relate to the missing heiress, the ransom, or the upcoming merger with MTT? Nélya Kirsi hadn't disappeared until after Laakso's death; Leena had boarded a flight in Helsinki before his death.

"Could Torben have been trying to derail the merger?" Ezra asked.

"Hit Kirsi with the scandal before he cashed in? I'm sure this isn't the only controversy, and MTT will be buying the company warts and all—if that is in fact what they were planning."

"Then Nélya's disappearance is a coincidence?"

Lucia gave him an incredulous look.

"I know, I know, the same day a Finlox VP kills himself, the president's daughter goes missing."

"Maybe she didn't get a warning message after all."

"What do you mean?"

Lucia knitted her brows. "Maybe this heiress of yours knew more than you think. Maybe someone called to tell her about Torben Laakso's death. Maybe she assumed it was murder."

"And what, she worried she was next?" he asked.

"There's so much we still don't know."

He knew someone who could fill in the gaps, if only he could get her to talk. "I suppose we'll find out tonight."

"What happens tonight?"

He poked his head into the hall and, when he returned, lowered his voice. "You can't tell anyone, but there's going to be an exchange tonight."

"Where?"

"West Argyle Street where it crosses the river."

"Are you going?"

He nodded, though he had one stop he needed to make first. He held up the Finlox article. "Can I take this?"

"Sure. Tell me what Leena Åkerholm has to say."

Ezra smiled. "Of course."

Lucia reached out and grabbed Ezra by the forearm. A tiny current of electricity ran through his arm and his heart sped up.

"Before you go, you should read these." She handed him a small packet of articles about Leena.

He cleared his throat. "These were in Torben's lockbox?"

"Gorecki also found cash deposit slips to a Swiss bank account. I wouldn't be surprised if Leena was complicit in some way." She paused. "The Kirsis may have had her on the payroll for years."

She released his arm reluctantly, one finger at a time, the nails tickling his skin pleasantly as they went. When this was all over, he would ask Lucia to dinner, he decided then and there. And it wouldn't be to compare notes.

****

ASAC Cromley put Leena Åkerholm in a hotel only distinguished from the downtown shops, restaurants, and office buildings by its bright red awning. Inside, the brown and gold wallpaper had probably given the hotel an atmosphere of elegance in the 70s, but now it made the space seem dark and outdated. The small wall fixtures, with their tarnished ornate bases and minimal light, didn't offset this impression any. In a way, it reminded Ezra of Leena herself. With her reserve and sudden tempers, she reminded him of a cold-war era official, someone who would've traveled between Finland and Soviet Russia with ease.

Ezra stopped at the front desk before going up. "Leena Åkerholm?" he asked the desk clerk, a black woman with soft eyes and a warm smile.

"Do you know the room number?"

He'd considered texting Leena but feared getting blown off. "I was actually hoping you would know it." He showed her his badge.

She typed in the name, then frowned. "Do you know what day she checked in?"

"Saturday around noon."

"I don't see anything."

"It might be under Cromley?"

She typed. Then asked, "Jeremiah?"

"That's the one."

"Room 307."

He began walking to the elevators, when she asked, "Did you say she checked in on Saturday?"

"That's right."

The clerk shook her head again and called back into the hotel offices, "Ms. Quickly! The system's being glitchy again!"

Ezra took the elevator up to the third floor, but before he could make it to Leena's door, she emerged into the hall.

"On your way out?" he asked.

"I want to stop by the Finlox building before tonight," she said and pointed to a door marked "Parking Garage."

As they walked together, Ezra considered how best to bring up the Durum Islands. Should he feign half-knowledge to see what she knew or come right out with it?

As they pushed into the garage, he blurted out, "They think Torben killed himself."

"Oh?"

"Have you heard of the Durum Islands?"

They continued into the empty parking garage, her high heels clicking like a fire fight from far away. Rat-a-tat, rat-a-tat. "Of course." She stopped at the trunk of her silver sedan. "It was the scene of a genocide last fall."

"And Torben knew what the islanders were planning?"

"Is that what they're saying?"

"Evanston PD believes Benjamin Kirsi coerced him to bury it."

She shrugged and searched for her keys in her purse. "So he killed himself from guilt, is that the idea?"

"Or to set up Kirsi for his murder."

"Ah, this is like something from one of your American movies. You know, not everything is some complex plot, Agent James." She clicked something in her purse and the trunk opened. "Here, I have something to show you."

She pulled the trunk all the way open, but Ezra didn't see what was inside. Something underneath the car caught his attention instead. He leaned down to inspect it. "What is that?"

"Motor oil."

It felt like a sting, like a bee or a wasp, and then something warm flowed into his neck muscles and radiated out through his whole body. It felt, too, like falling into a deep, warm river. It felt like all of this, yes, but it felt nothing like being stuffed into the trunk of a rental car by a rogue Finnish investigator.

Chapter Twenty-Three

Monday afternoon Remy left the busy parish office and took the L south, headed for his after-school chess practice. Either he didn't leave early enough, or Davon came early, because the teenager was already setting up boards and chatting with Reverend Don when Remy arrived.

"Fr. Mbombo!" the preacher proclaimed across the empty theater. "We decided to set up on the stage today."

"I can see that."

Don smiled warmly at Davon. "I thought it would give them a feel for the real thing."

Remy chuckled. "I doubt the rec tournament will have as much pomp. Then again, it never hurts to elevate the game, as it were."

The reverend took him by the shoulder. "Could I speak with you for a moment?"

They walked together down the aisle to the last row of seats, out of earshot of Davon. "He tells me Chuy will be joining us finally," Don whispered.

"I thought Jesus had found himself in some trouble again."

Don laughed heartily. "That's putting it mildly. But no, he's back on the street again." He narrowed his eyes. "I thought today would be a good time to start our real work."

Remy understood the implication. "But we have

already started," he replied innocently.

"You can cut the act, Remy. I'm the warm one, the avuncular one who's good for a laugh. I'm the dream stepdad, sure, but no one's going to tell me anything substantial."

Remy nodded wearily. "And by substantial you mean…"

"Illegal. Actionable. Look," Don said, a bite of impatience in his voice, "I've already laid the groundwork, already spent weeks on this. We had Davon's aunt explain all the priestly confidentiality business, and Chuy's mom did her best, too. All you've got to do is nudge the ball and let gravity do the rest. These young men want to confess. Chicago PD can handle the hard stuff."

Remy gave him an earnest smile. "How will Davon confessing to me help the Chicago police? You know I can't divulge information learned from a confession."

A smile fixed itself on Don's lips as if against his will. Then he forced out a laugh. Under different circumstances, it could've passed for a cough. "Come now, friend."

"I'm not your friend. I once believed we were colleagues, but I stand corrected."

Don squared his shoulders like a retired boxer. "You want a bunch of low lives polluting our neighborhood with God knows what?"

"Are these not souls in need of saving?" Remy asked.

"You said it yourself when we started this little club. They've had chance after chance."

Remy glanced from Don beside him to Davon on the stage, the gesture more instructive than curious. "And when should we stop? How many chances does that young man need? One? Two? Or as many as seven?"

"Don't feed me that shit," Don said.

"What shit?" Remy swore right back, not at all unbalanced by the minister's use of profanity. "Your own shit? Because if that's all it is, if this is a song and dance, then maybe this is not the line of work for you."

The reverend took on a rueful grin. "That Fed warned me about you. He said you papists were unreasonable, that your dog collars cut off the oxygen supply to your brains."

"Unreasonable? The world can have reason," Remy replied. It was plain to see from the way he looked past and around Remy and the way his feet pointed back to the stage that the reverend was no longer listening. Nevertheless, Remy continued. "I've seen enough of reason gone wrong. I've seen how it can mislead human hearts. I will take the divine, however unreasonable it might seem."

"Maybe you'd better bow out if you're not willing to help."

"You let Jeremiah Cromley know this was a failure, and I will get out of your hair," Remy said. "Unless that will put an end to your organization's funding. I assume you have an arrangement with the city too?"

Another forced grin. "Just—" but instead of finishing, Don walked toward the stage. Before he reached it, he turned back. "You knew what this was from the beginning."

"That doesn't mean I agreed with it."

"You've wasted a lot of people's time," the preacher replied.

"No time is wasted. Not on God's green earth."

The words had no effect other than to make Don shake his head in disappointment and trudge up the steps.

****

Twenty minutes later, the entire team sat playing chess together for the first time. While Matt and Joaquin faced off, Don ran through the fundamentals with Chuy, and Remy continued working on more intermediate skills with Davon.

As they advanced into the middle game, Davon pinched the black-square bishop between his fingers. Remy stopped the chess clock. "Are you sure about that?" Remy asked. "Count it out."

The teenager looked puzzled.

"If you take my knight, I'll take your bishop with my bishop," Remy explained

He touched the piece. "But then I'll take your bishop with my queen."

Remy touched his rook, which was lined up on the d-file. His opponent grimaced. "In the eighteenth and nineteenth centuries, Romantic chess predominated. Have you studied Romanticism in school?"

Davon shook his head curtly.

"It was an emotional style of art and literature. Of chess, too. Quick attacks, lots of sacrifices. A bloody version of the game if ever there was one. Then came Paul Morphy and countless others who treated chess not as a game but as a science." He drew imaginary lines with his index finger, all ending on his own knight. "These are all the pieces I have protecting this square. My position is like a coil." He advanced a pawn. "Now it is tighter." He advanced a knight. "Now it is tighter still." He waited to continue until Davon nodded. "Before you strike, you must figure out who will come out ahead—you or me.

"What if I'm outnumbered?"

Remy grasped Davon's bishop and positioned it along a diagonal that threatened Remy's king. "Then you must shift your focus."

The teenager analyzed the new position. It neutralized all of Remy's previous defenses and forced him to move his king. He laughed at the brilliance of the move, then grew contemplative. "This is sort of like my life right now."

"How so?"

"There's all this pressure. Like, I have to do this because of that, and I have to do that because of some other thing, and all the while I know it's not going to end right."

"You don't have to do anything, Davon," Remy said. "That's what free will means."

He ran a hand over his short black hair. "No, I know." Then more to himself, "I know."

Remy thought of the young man's predicament, particularly his dangerous employer. "Have you decided what to do about your well-dressed friend?"

Davon looked winded. "No."

"Did you ask your mother?"

"She says just let it be and go back to school."

Remy nodded. "Can you?"

"Yeah, I think so. I'm not, like, committed." He looked intently down at the board and its crisscross of attack lines. "But is that the best thing to do?" The question didn't sound rhetorical. He wanted an answer.

"You are sixteen," Remy said. "Where I am from, we say, *'Le mieux est l'ennemi de bien.'* The best is the enemy of the good. Don't be paralyzed. Take one step in the right direction today. Tomorrow, you may be able to take a better one."

Davon smiled in relief. "So I don't have to, like, turn state's evidence and go into witness protection?"

Remy laughed. "Just do what you feel is right today. Then, when you wake up tomorrow, you'll be able to do the same."

Reverend Don passed by their table but said nothing. He didn't even make eye contact with them.

"How do you feel about Saturday?"

"The tournament? I'll be there, if that's what you mean."

It was what Remy meant. Their team wouldn't win, but if he could get all four of them to show up, that would be a kind of victory.

****

Mercy Hospital was a short drive from the theater but a long walk. Luckily, Remy had packed his sneakers along with his chess board and clocks. He appreciated the chance to clear his head and also to explore an area of Chicago unfamiliar to him.

Half-way to the hospital, he stopped at a small park sandwiched between office buildings and sat on a bench for a long time. In the distance, the sun dove behind a wall of low-lying cumulonimbus clouds, its light turning the sky a symphony of colors from cobalt blue and burnt sienna to violet and magenta. The colors filtered through the new leaves beginning to bud on a tall oak tree. Along its limbs and branches, a pair of squirrels chased each other back and forth, causing the whole tree to shake like a giant paint brush mixing the colors in the sky.

Spring had indeed come. He wondered briefly how he could work this sight of so much natural beauty into an Easter homily. Not Easter Sunday, of course, but possibly Easter Monday or Tuesday. Those masses were ripe for nature imagery, birth, new life, and continuity. Inspiration abounded, but he had no pen, no notebook, and several miles still to travel. Rather than channel this moment into something productive, he decided to just enjoy it, this instant of time filled to the brim.

When he could put off his mission no longer, Remy stood, wiggled his sore feet, and hailed a taxi.

Chapter Twenty-Four

"Yoo-hoo!"

Lucia looked up from her case files. She'd perused them from her hospital bed all afternoon. Between the pressing and pulling of doctors, nurses, physical therapists and regular doses of morphine, she felt like a rag doll. The Laakso case was the only thing making her feel steady.

"Oh, it's you." she said. "I remember you."

Though the woman in the doorway smiled, her brow knit curiously. "I'm Enni Frost."

"The translator!" Lucia exclaimed. "Sorry, that came out loud. I'm on drugs."

Enni's look changed to warm and understanding as she stepped into the room. "I've been there. I have three kids, and you'd better believe I wasn't having them naturally." She carried a leather-bound journal under one arm. Sandwiched between that and her side, was a coil-bound report with a plastic cover.

"Is that Torben Laakso's journal?"

Enni looked down at it. "Yes, your partner brought it to my office. He told me about what happened. I'm sorry I didn't get it here earlier."

"No worries."

Who was this cavalier person telling the translator not to worry about the timeliness of a key piece of evidence? Lucia wondered. Was this why people did drugs? To be more laid back? What if all drug addicts were secretly type-A perfectionists who had just decided to take prolonged vacations from themselves? Lucia studied the ceiling tiles as if the answer resided up there somewhere.

Enni slid the journal and its translation into Lucia's hands. "Do you want to know what it says?"

"Please. I'll read it myself but give me the high points."

The translator smirked like a woman about to deliver a hot piece of gossip. "Torben was having an affair with someone at work. Actually, it's worse. He was sleeping with a KRP officer investigating Finlox's overseas activities. A woman named Miranda."

Lucia nodded as if she already knew. "It's a reference to *The Tempest.*"

"I'm sorry?"

"Shakespeare. A man, Prospero, lives on a tropical island with his daughter, Miranda. He uses magic to raise a massive storm and cause a shipwreck." She talked lazily, laying out for Enni all the internal workings of her mind. "Miranda is a code name for Leena Åkerholm. Torben was gathering articles about her leading up to the event, and then nothing."

Subconsciously, she'd known this piece of the puzzle for hours now. Its significance to her case, however, eluded her as the effects of the pain medication suppressed her consciousness like a weighted blanket.

"The journal started six months ago," Enni said, "just after—"

"The Civil War on French Halmahera?" Lucia guessed again.

"That's right. When you asked me about a Swedish

island, I thought nothing of it, but now I'm almost certain his email auto-corrected a word. I think he used 'rogue island' as code for French Halmahera. In Finnish, 'rogue island' is *roisto saari*, but 'Swedish island' would be *ruotsin saari*. It's so close. An email provider would almost certainly autocorrect the phrase."

"That's why the Finlox people wouldn't have caught the draft email when they purged his account," Lucia said.

Enni turned to a tabbed page in the journal. "Now read this."

"We are to blame," Lucia read aloud. *"Miranda must know. She must know that's why I had to end things. She will blame Kirsi until her dying breath, but the blame is ours. How could I stay? All I think of when I see her face is what we let happen. Benjamin may have paid us to stay quiet, but we stayed quiet all the same."*

Lucia looked up. "I know what happened," she said. A wave of panic cut through the ether. "I know why Torben died and why Kirsi's daughter disappeared! Oh God, I need to call Ezra!" She began searching frantically for her phone.

"Yoo-hoo!" Another person appeared in the doorway.

Both women turned. "Father Remy!" Lucia shouted. The added stimuli overwhelmed her. Why did everything have to happen at once? She refocused. "Do you know where Ezra is?"

"Let me call him." He dialed and waited. "Voicemail."

"Try again."

He redialed with identical results.

"The field office!" Lucia yelled. "Call his work!"

He tried that next and handed her the phone.

"I need to speak with Agent James," she said to the first person who picked up.

"Agent James is not in his office," a young-sounding man responded. "I can give you his cell."

"I have that," Lucia said. "He's not picking up."

"Maybe he's asleep?"

Lucia didn't point out it was only five p.m. "Can I speak with his supervisor, ASAC Cromley?"

The sound of typing came from the other end. "He's not available either."

She wanted to fling the phone against the wall. She wanted to scream. Instead, she inhaled and exhaled slowly and asked, "Can I have Cromley's cell?"

"No," the voice said after a moment's hesitation.

"Look, I know he's dropping off a ransom at the West Argyle bridge."

The man sighed. "That is not information I have."

"Fine, can I speak with Cromley's supervisor?"

"She is also occupied."

"At the bridge? Are they there already?"

"Sorry, that is not—"

"Information you have. I got it." She hung up and pushed the phone into Remy's hand. "I need you to drive me to the West Argyle bridge."

The priest looked down at his sneakers. "That could pose a problem. I am without a vehicle."

"I have a car," Enni chimed in. "A van. But are you sure you're okay to leave?"

"I don't know what else they need to do to me," Lucia wailed. "They've already fit me for crutches, pumped me full of narcotics, and x-rayed my crotch from every possible angle like I'm auditioning for some kind of skeleton porno—sorry, Father." She swung one leg out of the bed, then the other and nearly toppled over in the process. Remy caught her and helped her sit side-saddle on the bed.

"We'd better get you a wheelchair just the same," he said.

"I'll bring your crutches," Enni added.

Chapter Twenty-Five

Enni Frost, the Finnish translator, drove a mauve colored minivan with TVs in the headrests and soccer balls in the trunk. The TVs switched on automatically, blaring the latest and loudest children's cartoon. The soccer balls made themselves known as they bounced and ricocheted at every sharp turn and stop light.

"I'm sorry about all the junk," Enni said as they drove. "And the noise. Apparently, the TVs are integral to the operation of the vehicle, because I cannot turn them off."

Remy smiled to set her at ease. "Don't be sorry. It just makes it all the more American."

They talked for some minutes about American culture, namely the aspects they were still not used to. Though they hailed from different continents, which had wildly different cultures, languages, even climates, they had much in common.

For one, Remy couldn't believe how often Americans called dessert "breakfast." Enni didn't understand Americans' constant need to fill silences with talking—even with strangers, even on public transit. Neither of them understood how Americans could be both fiercely patriotic and seemingly homesick for "the old country."

Enni became particularly animated on this last topic. "At a New Year's party, a man wearing an American flag as a shirt told me for an hour about the forest in Norway where his ancestors came from," she said. "I couldn't comprehend what was happening. He kept calling himself Scandinavian."

They came to a stoplight. She looked back and forth at the empty cross street as though that might hurry up the light. It didn't.

"Finally, I told him, 'You're not Scandinavian!' I thought that would put an end to it."

"Did it?" Remy asked.

"No. He said, 'Well, I'm not as Scandinavian as you are.' So I told him, 'I'm not Scandinavian either. I'm Nordic.'"

After the light turned green, they drove through the intersection.

"What did he say to that?"

She chuckled at the memory. "He asked me what the difference was."

Curious, Remy asked, "And what is the difference?"

"I told him if he were Scandinavian, he'd know."

In the back seat, Lucia shifted, then groaned. By the look on her face, the exertion of leaving the hospital, even by wheelchair, had taken it out of her. Remy turned to look at her but couldn't tell if she was sleeping or just resting her eyes. The fading light and tinted windows didn't help.

Then Enni Frost glanced over at Remy and said, apropos of nothing, "What a nasty scar."

Remy touched his face. "Oh this? It's an interesting story." He paused. "I was shaving with a straight-razor one morning—and I sneezed."

"No!" she said. Then, "Not really."

He laughed. "No, not really."

She too laughed and hit her steering wheel with both hands. "Now you have to tell me the whole story."

He adjusted the collar of his shirt and pulled at his sleeve, adjusting the wrist button. "Are you familiar with Rwanda?"

"Yes. Oh goodness, were you…?"

"I was. I was there when the violence began. I was visiting a parish that served both Hutu and Tutsi members, those are the two main tribal groups in Rwanda. After the civil war began, I convinced the headmistress of our school, Sister Didi, to transform the parish into a refuge for those being targeted."

Enni clicked her turn signal and waited. "It was good you were there."

He saw it now in his mind, the cathedral on a hill overlooking Kigali. "That's what I thought at the time. For three days, we spread the word from house to house. I felt like Noah collecting two of every species before the storm, but of course the storm was already raging. We gathered as many people as we could.

"On the fourth day, a group of militia men came to the doors of the cathedral with rifles and machetes. They told us to send out the cockroaches. The blood would not be on our hands. Sr. Didi wanted to comply, but I refused. I told them I would not be their Pontius Pilate. If they wanted these Tutsis, they would have to kill me first."

Enni pulled onto West Argyle Street. Remy waited. "Go on," she said.

"Bishop Bahati, who oversaw the cathedral, did not repeat my sentiment but neither did he order me to back down. Sr. Didi went with the men outside where they conferred in hushed tones. The men went away again.

"On the fifth day, they returned, this time with torches and dried palm leaves. They slid the palm leaves under the front and side doors and gave us one final warning. When we didn't comply, they lowered their torches and set fire to the palms. The leaves didn't catch fire easily, but they did fill the space with smoke. We had to constantly push the burning palms back outside lest we suffocate. All day, the militia men did this. Finally, I went to them. I confronted these men, brandishing my Bible at them. You see, these were not random men. They belonged to our parish! I had delivered homilies to them and their families. I had served them communion and taken their confessions. I called them by name that morning. I said I would revoke their confessions—a lie, but it dampened their resolve."

Remy sighed, the reality of what had happened that day returning vividly after so many years. "Then came the sixth day. It was so hot in that crowded space that we had changed into street clothes. The bishop encouraged us to do so. The nuns wore skirts and t-shirts. Fr. Uwawe and I wore shirts and jeans. This was no accident. Bishop Bahati wanted us to look like lay people. He wanted himself and Sr. Didi to be the only sources of church authority that day."

Lucia stirred in the backseat again. She mumbled a few sentences, the end of which sounded to Remy like "Attila the Nun." Remy turned in his seat to ask what she'd said, but her eyes were closed.

"So then the seventh day?" Enni asked.

"If only we'd made it to the seventh day, then perhaps God might've granted us a reprieve. Instead, we were granted different militia men, men who came from another corner of Rwanda and another level of resolve.

The minute they arrived, it became clear to me that someone had called them, perhaps even Didi herself.

"I went instinctively to one of the nuns, a teacher…" he said but stopped. A vision of Sr. Therese, beautiful Therese, flashed in Remy's mind, and he found he could no longer speak.

"It's okay," Enni said. "I shouldn't have asked about your scar."

He shook his head. "It was a harmless question."

The minivan stopped. Through the window, Remy spied a man and woman crossing the bridge. "It's happening," he said over his shoulder to Lucia. Her eyes opened to look.

He pointed to a side road that ran parallel to the river. "Can you take us down there?" he asked Enni.

She made a noise halfway between curiosity and agreement and drove slowly down the side road. She parked and Remy climbed out, followed by Lucia. She positioned her crutches beneath her arms, then staggered awkwardly toward the sidewalk. Together they approached the bridge through a thicket of trees where their presence might not be as conspicuous. The couple walked along the sidewalk, then stopped at the midpoint of the bridge and leaned against the guardrail. The man was in his fifties, the woman substantially younger. Both of them were elegantly dressed, their pale skin like straw in the moonlight.

"Who are they?" Remy asked Lucia. While she and Ezra had been working parallel cases that involved the Finnish company, Remy had been occupied with his own world of Lenten masses, chess club practices, and young men guarding mysterious briefcases. He had found the supercooling briefcase but had no idea its full relevance to Lucia's case.

"The woman in the scarf is Leena Åkerholm," Lucia said. "She's a Finnish police officer. I believe the scarf and sunglasses are to conceal her identity. The man is Benjamin Kirsi, the founder of Finlox."

"This woman police officer is posing as his wife?"

"Maybe," she said.

Remy turned his head and cupped his ear. "Can you hear them?"

They moved slowly to the edge of the tree line. If they came too close to the bridge, they might unwittingly jeopardize the exchange.

"You killed him," Leena was saying. "You know that, right?"

Remy could just hear them now.

"I didn't lay a finger on Torben," Kirsi replied.

"But you're the reason he's dead."

Kirsi forced a weak and mirthless smile. "If you're so sure I forced him to commit suicide, then why are *you* still alive?"

"Take out your phone," she commanded.

"What?"

"Make it look natural, like you're answering a call."

"I'm wearing a wire, Leena."

"I disconnected it before we left the van."

They switched to speaking in Finnish and Remy lost the thread of the conversation.

"You know languages," Lucia said to him. "Is Finnish one of them?"

"Unfortunately not," he replied.

The Finns were moving again, hustling across the bridge. They jogged past Enni's minivan and got into a silver sedan.

An unmarked utility van, which likely contained a half dozen federal agents, turned on its headlights, and the engine began an arduous and unsuccessful attempt at turning over. Its lights flickered and then went out.

Lucia pointed to Leena Åkerholm's retreating sedan. "That's the car that ran me over! We need to follow them!" she yelled.

They made their way back to the minivan, Remy running, Lucia loping behind him on her crutches. Remy had to help her into the back. Finally, they took off in the same direction as the sedan, Enni driving as fast as she could without losing control.

A few blocks west, Leena turned right, running a stop sign, and the minivan fishtailed trying to keep up.

"Stay on them," Remy said calmly.

They were crossing the river again on a narrow bridge. Cars were parked on either side of the bridge and traffic moved slowly both ways. Leena swerved in and out of the lanes, going up on the sidewalk and colliding with the concrete barrier. Sparks flew as the passenger door grinded along the iron handrail. Remy could just make out Benjamin Kirsi, his head whipping left then right like a reflex bag.

"I'm not going up on the curb," Enni said.

The minivan fell back, following from two cars behind, then three.

"We're going to lose them," Lucia said.

Enni stepped on the gas and maneuvered into the empty on-coming lane. When a city bus merged into the lane, she swerved back, right behind Leena now. What was the plan? Just follow? Or follow and ram? What was Enni willing to do? Leena and Kirsi burst through a red-light, and Enni followed.

Remy saw it before anyone, just in his periphery—the colorful roof topper of a pizza delivery truck as it t-boned the right side of the minivan and sent them spinning around twice, their tires squealing and the metal of both cars crunching. Remy's hands flew out in front of him. His left arm collided with the dash and simultaneously his airbag deployed, slamming against his chin, his neck, his nose. Both vehicles came to a stop with a mechanical wheeze. Behind Remy, the door slid open. He heard the tinkle of broken glass, then the splattering sound of Lucia vomiting onto the pavement. He climbed out of his own door and helped Lucia to her feet.

Two unmarked black cars arrived shortly thereafter, their dashboard lights flashing.

"What happened here?" It was ASAC Jeremiah Cromley.

Lucia wiped her mouth. "They got away."

"We think the kidnappers contacted Kirsi directly," Cromley said.

"It's Leena Åkerholm," Lucia said matter-of-factly.

He didn't seem to hear her. "We tried to follow, but our surveillance van wouldn't start."

"It's Leena," she repeated. "She must've sabotaged the engine."

"We can't get ahold of Ezra," he added. "He was supposed to meet us at the bridge.

"It's Åkerholm, dammit!" she said for the third time. "She orchestrated this whole thing. If we find Nélya Kirsi, Ezra won't be far away." She paused, perhaps debating her next words. "Hopefully, they'll both be alive."

Cromley nodded, his face the picture of shock.

"Leena…" he said.

****

An ambulance arrived several minutes later. After clearing all parties of concussions and other major injuries, an EMT discovered that Remy's left ring finger was broken. She bound it to his middle finger with a splint and told him to get to the ER, which he promised to do as soon as they found Ezra.

Remy, Lucia, and Cromley piled into the first cruiser; SAC Banth and Benjamin's wife, Marja Kirsi, took the second. While Banth followed the tracker tucked inside the duffle bag, Cromley, Lucia, and Remy followed the GPS signal from Ezra's cell phone.

Team Duffle Bag struck first, tracking the signal to a silver sedan parked in front of a red brick mansion in an upscale corner of north Chicago. It took the team ten minutes to locate the actual tracker, which had been removed from the duffle and lodged into the undercarriage of the sedan. The car showed no signs of exterior damage nor any markings of a rental company. It wasn't Leena's get-away car, but a lookalike.

Ezra's cell phone GPS led Remy and company right to Leena's hotel. After a careful sweep, it was Lucia who found the phone discarded in a trash receptacle in the parking garage. Beside it lay Ezra's badge and sidearm, a Glock 9 mm.

"How did the Finnish police officer get here?" Remy asked. "Into the country, I mean."

"She flew into O'Hare." This seemed to give Cromley an idea. "But the Kirsis came by private jet. They flew into one of the regional airports. Their plane might still be there."

The ASAC called it in.

Chapter Twenty-Six

By the time they arrived, the two-runway airport was crawling with emergency vehicles. They had the Kirsi's jet surrounded mid-runway.

"There's her car!" Lucia shouted. Despite the adrenaline coursing through her veins, she climbed out gingerly, then pulled her crutches from the backseat.

Remy could just make out the rear bumper of Leena Åkerholm's silver sedan. She had parked twenty meters off the east runway. Lucia hobbled toward it, awkwardly, her legs swinging through the crutches. At one point, she lost her footing and nearly toppled to the ground. Remy stepped toward her, hopelessly out of range to actually help, but she righted herself and continued at an even slower pace.

Cromley approached the jet with his badge held aloft, and Remy followed. Before they reached the plane, a commanding woman in a skirt suit appeared at his side. It was SAC Banth, Cromley's boss.

"Who's going to do it?" he asked her. Remy assumed this meant "who will start the negotiation?"

Wearing a conflicted expression on her face, the woman crossed both her arms. "The official word is either I do it, or we await a negotiator." She uncrossed them and signaled for a SWAT member to bring over a megaphone. "But I have a feeling that if anyone's going to resolve this peacefully, it's you. You've spent the most time with the hostage taker and the hostage." She took the man's megaphone in one hand and passed it to Cromley with the other.

"Technically, Agent James knows Åkerholm the best." He looked back at the parking lot across the runway. "Detective Vargas is checking the property for him."

The wheels of the jet began inching down the runway. The police cruisers tightened around the jet until they bumped nose to bumper. The door opened and Benjamin Kirsi's terrified face appeared in the crack. From behind him boomed the voice of Leena Åkerholm.

"Back these vehicles up! Otherwise, I will start shooting!" she screamed. "The pilot will be the first to go."

Cromley raised the megaphone to his lips. "Let me come aboard."

"Why would I do that?"

"I can help you. Whatever you want, I know how to get it," he said. "Let me show you the collective buying power of the US government."

"There is one thing you could get me."

"What's that?"

"A time machine."

"Maybe you don't need one." He took a few steps closer, lowering the megaphone and placing a hand on the stairway that sat beside the jet. Carefully, he nudged it back into position. "Whatever the situation is, I assure you, we can make it better. Nothing you've done is permanent." The words sounded more hopeful than true.

Leena laughed wildly, a blood chilling cackle. "How do you know what I've done? Only I know. And him." She pressed the muzzle of her pistol into the back of

Kirsi's head.

Remy recognized it as a Glock 17. The firearm manufacturer was a favorite of police the world over. If Remy had the model right, it would be a 9 mm with a seventeen-round magazine. That would provide more than enough ammunition for Leena to put one in the pilot, one in Kirsi, and one in herself. Perhaps she would spare the pilot, but he imagined it playing out something along those lines.

"Someone else knew," she continued, "but he's dead and gone now."

"Torben Laakso?" Cromley asked, edging still closer. For every inch he drew closer, her hand added a few more pounds of pressure to Kirsi's shoulder, digging her fingernails into his shirt until he winced with pain.

"Ben!" she said, choking back a sob. She clutched Kirsi's shoulder and dragged him back inside the jet.

Before she closed the door, Remy called out, "You loved him?"

"Who's that?" she asked, jutting her chin toward Remy.

"He's a priest." Cromley replied. "See the collar?"

"Are you a real priest?"

"Of course," Remy said.

She clutched the edge of the door, her gun's muzzle digging into Kirsi's back. "I don't believe you. This is just what the FBI would do, dress an agent up like a priest."

"Are you Catholic?" Remy asked.

"No."

"Then why would they think a priest would convince you?" Silence. "Never mind. How can I prove it to you?"

She looked to Cromley and then back. "Speak some Latin."

"*Dentes tui sicut greges tonsarum.* Song of Songs 4:2."

"What's it mean?"

"Your teeth are like a flock of newly shorn ewes."

It was the first phrase he ever learned in Latin—his Latin professor giving them especially strange lines to memorize so they would stick—and so it was the first thing that came to his mind in this moment of distress.

Her shoulders waffled as she decided what to do.

"How about this?" he asked then continued before she could stop him, "*Nihil est miserius, quam animus hominis conscius.* Nothing is so wretched as a guilty conscience. That's Plautus."

She pushed the door wide but retained her hold on Kirsi. "Get in."

Remy mounted the steps. From the corner of his eye, he saw the SWAT team inching closer.

****

The sedan was locked of course. Lucia circled around to the trunk and rapped on it three times in quick succession. Two knocks came in response. Then a voice asked, "Lucia, is that you?"

She lowered her lips close to the keyhole. "Is there a release lever in there?"

"How did that slip my mind?" he asked sarcastically. "Let me check."

She wondered how long he'd silently pretend to look.

"Nope," he said finally.

"Then back up as far as you can."

"Wait," Ezra yelled, "you're not going to shoot the

lock, are you?"

She holstered her gun. "Of course not."

Between the parking lot and the runway, she found half a cinder block protecting a sprinkler system shut off valve. Two handed, she lifted it off the valve. Fireworks of pain exploded through her lower abdomen and pelvis as she raised the block and inched back to the sedan. What did Ezra know about her feelings for him? Possibly nothing. Yet still she bore this anguish in silence. Standing beside the trunk of the car, she rested the block on the back bumper for a moment.

"On three, I'm going to get you out of there," she said and raised the cinderblock over her head. If the pain before had felt like fireworks, this new wave felt like a canon blast. "One, two," she counted. Something in her side pinched and the block crashed down of its own accord onto the trunk. The metal dented and the back of the sedan sank several inches before recoiling. She slid the cinderblock off, and the trunk sprung open. "Sorry," she said, "it slipped."

"Where's Leena?"

"I'll show—" Before she could finish, the sound of a gunshot cut her off.

They both ducked instinctively, then looked in the direction of the jet. Ezra climbed out of the trunk then sprinted toward the scene.

"Wait!" Lucia called.

"I have to go," he apologized.

She took his sidearm out of her purse. "You'll need this."

He took it.

****

The scene was beyond tense. Four agents, including

Ezra's bosses, SAC Banth and ASAC Cromley, conferred beside a police cruiser; what looked like a private jet owner's manual lay open on the hood; a SWAT team faced the jet from all directions, crouching and peeking between vehicles like ninjas watching the enemy through long blades of grass; uniformed officers, fire fighters, and EMTs stood around in anticipation, chatting idly; one of the EMTs lit a cigarette and puffed twice before his buddy slapped him upside the head.

"You can't smoke here."

"Why?"

"Jet fuel."

He looked around in a panic before putting it out on the sole of his shoe and stuffing the butt into his pocket.

Ezra passed through this commotion and reported straight to Cromley. "Who fired?"

"SWAT tried to move up and Leena sent a warning shot into the air."

"Why'd they move?"

Cromley hesitated. "They thought she wouldn't notice. She was distracted when…"

"When what?"

"When your priest friend went inside."

"What? Why the fuck did you let Remy go in there?" Ezra felt a pang of remorse over cursing, but anger quickly replaced it. "He's a priest."

"He'll be fine." Cromley shared a look with Banth before adding, "There are things you don't know about your friend. I'm sure he's seen far worse."

"For all you know, Leena Åkerholm is waving a machine gun at him in there."

Cromley shook his head. "She just wants Kirsi."

"But what does she want with him?" Ezra asked.

He saw in their faces then the same expression of bewildered concern. They clearly didn't know what Leena wanted, but they knew this wasn't going to end well.

Ezra turned to Banth. "Leena is going to kill Kirsi, and you let Remy go in there with her?"

"She hasn't killed him yet," she replied.

How could she be so calm? What could she possibly know about Remy that Ezra didn't? And why did Remy make such a point of keeping him in the dark? The priest knew everything about Ezra, the things he couldn't bring himself to tell anyone else, yet their relationship was far from reciprocal.

While Ezra had become more and more of an open book, Remy remained a mystery, a riddle translated and then encoded, the original known only to Remy himself. Well, Remy and Cromley and Banth, apparently. Ezra thought of the CIA's use of priests in South and Central America, pawns against the rise of communism. The same probably held true for Africa. The thought of Remy working as a spy, Ezra was ashamed to admit, made him somehow less of a priest. He understood then why Remy kept back so much of himself. As a fault-filled man, he was compromised, but as a Christ-figure, he had the power to listen and absolve.

Cromley extended an earpiece to him. "SWAT ran a microphone through the landing gear doors," he explained. "It's muffled and there's an echo, but…"

Ezra took the earpiece and put it in.

****

The gun hung precariously in Leena's hand. Would she drop it? If she did, would Kirsi have the wherewithal to kick it toward Remy?

"You can forgive my sins," she said. It was not a question.

"You've been crying," Remy said, deflecting.

"This asshole maced me," she replied, dispassionate.

If Remy were a bee, he would've smelled nothing but self-pity radiating off both the Finnish investigator and the Finnish tycoon. The fight had drained from them both, their faces like straw effigies resigned to the inevitable.

After a long calming breath, Remy asked, "What happened? Where is the girl?"

"As I told Mr. Kirsi," she said, "she was never in danger." She and Kirsi stood face to face now, their backs at opposite sides of the cabin.

Remy strained to put together the little he'd learned about the missing heiress. "You called Nélya?"

"I did. I told her the system had been compromised. I told her to destroy her primary phone. I used a phone from the airplane, knowing they'd put it together eventually. I just needed enough time to find him." She gestured toward Kirsi with her pistol.

Kirsi grunted. "I don't believe you, Leena. They found a shotgun. It had been fired."

"You think I'd harm Nélya?" She laughed. "The gun and the mask, it was all to keep your FBI friends busy and focused on Puck."

"How'd you do it then?"

"It was simple. I told Nélya how to include Puck without including him. I told her to conceal her second phone, to leave the deer mask on that island, to fire off a weapon in the boathouse and then put it in his trunk, all on the off chance that Puck was the threat. I told her she needed insurance."

"You lied to her," Remy said.

"It took convincing. I guess she does love him after all. Good for her." Her face tightened, threatened to crumple. Then she found an inner resolve. "Nélya must've fired the gun just before Puck returned for her Saturday. Ezra and I heard the shot when we searched the property. Luckily, there were hunters nearby for me to blame."

Remy would have to take her word for it. "You still haven't told us where she is. They have her fiancé in custody."

She waved the pistol around again. "She'll turn up. When I called her yesterday, I said to hide out for a few days. She'll see the papers tomorrow and come home. Hell, she'll see it on Finlox tonight." Leena lowered her gun and her expression changed from cavalier to contemplative. Her body language sank an octave. "I had everything—career, respect, love—" she turned to Kirsi again "—and you took it away."

"I took nothing," he said pathetically. "Ben made his choices. I didn't force any of them."

"Just like the islanders?"

"They made their choices, too. You act like my company invented genocide," he said. "One tribe killing another is a practice as old as man."

"Then why did you pay me off?" she asked, punctuating the question by pointing her Glock in Kirsi's face. "If you hadn't convinced Ben to bribe me, you never would've made him an accomplice."

"And you never would've fallen in love," Remy interjected, hoping the reminder of her love for Torben might soften her heart.

"Terävä," she said, nodding. "You are a perceptive priest."

"Don't do this," he said.

"You will forgive my sins." The words took on the cadence of a mantra.

Remy extended a hand toward the gun. "And what if my philosophy is wrong? What if there's no real forgiveness for what you're prepared to do? You really think killing him will ease your conscience?"

Leena clasped her heart and choked back a sob. Now they were real tears.

Remy needed to keep her talking. "Tell me your sins."

"I let Torben come here, his Saint Helena, and accept the blame. I should've seen through his cheery facade. I should've told him it was *my* fault, not his. We should've come up with a plot together."

"You didn't know," Remy said.

"I should've known. If anyone should've known, it was me." She closed her eyes, and when she opened them again, Remy saw a new resolve. "This is the only way."

Remy shook his head slowly. "Killing this man won't undo anything."

"It might prevent more of the same."

"Let the story get out. Tell the truth about what you saw and accept the consequences. That's how you will make true change."

In that moment, he saw their real position—they were two mammals in the wilderness, one urging the other to believe in society, with its rules and restrictions, to believe that it existed and, more importantly, that it should exist. Society might grant her justice, but it certainly wouldn't satisfy her deep need for revenge. Remy wasn't just asking her to choose the more reasonable option, he was asking her to deny herself and her deepest desires. He was asking her to deny the inexorable destiny that love and madness in equal parts had driven her to.

"Start the engine," she called to the pilot.

"We're blocked in!" the pilot shouted back from the cockpit.

"Just start it!"

The engine roared to life, and soon they could hear nothing else. Surely, the SWAT team would intervene now. Every muscle in Remy's body tensed with anticipation.

A sound of metal scraping metal came from the exterior door. SWAT getting into position. Leena sprung across the cabin. In a flash, she was behind Kirsi again.

"Stay out!" she yelled. "Oh God," she added to herself. "Oh God, oh God," she muttered. Her breathing picked up until she was nearly hyperventilating. Remy too spoke to God, praying not for his own safety but for Leena and Kirsi and the men and women who were about to burst into the cabin, and his prayers produced in him an unexpected calm, a surreal, dreamlike peace.

Across from him, Leena too seemed to have calmed. She lowered her gun from Kirsi's back. *Thank God,* Remy thought. Then she raised it to her own temple.

"No!" Remy shouted.

This exclamation caused Kirsi to wheel around. He stood face to face with his captor.

Remy would wonder for the rest of his life if this had been Leena's plan—to elicit a yell from Remy—because the moment Kirsi turned to face her, she grabbed him by the arm and pressed the muzzle of her Glock into his chest, dug it into the very depression where Torben Laakso had sunk a frozen knife into his own heart.

"I'll pay you," Kirsi pleaded.

"Pay Ben," she said and pulled the trigger.

Remy dropped to the ground, closed his eyes, and covered his ears, but still he counted sixteen shots.

Chapter Twenty-Seven

Still unsteady on his legs, which had fallen asleep while in the trunk of Leena's sedan, Ezra leaned against the hood of a police cruiser and watched as the SWAT team mobilized around the jet, the EMTs stood by, and everyone else listened with bated breath to their earpieces as the conversation inside the jet unfolded.

Through his earpiece, Ezra heard Remy yell, "No!" and then the gunshots started. SWAT moved in, and everyone else tore their earpieces out.

SWAT made quick work of the situation, leading the occupants out one by one minutes later. First came the pilot, hands held high, then Leena Åkerholm, hers cuffed behind her back. Two agents led her to one of the unmarked cars and placed her in the backseat. She looked straight down at the floor as if refusing to let anyone see her face.

Next the EMTs climbed the stairs, a stretcher and various handheld equipment in tow. They emerged with Benjamin Kirsi on the stretcher, an oxygen mask on his face and a lake of blood soaking the front of his suit. His skin was as pale as snow.

Remy walked beside him, one hand holding Kirsi's limp hand, the other holding a wooden rosary. The EMTs loaded the stretcher into the back of their ambulance, and a caravan of flashing lights drove off the runway.

Remy stalked back to Cromley's car. "Where are

they taking Leena?"

"That's yet to be determined," Cromley replied.

"What needs to be determined?" Remy asked from behind them. "I just watched her empty a 9 mm into Mr. Kirsi's chest."

"Remy," Cromley said, a note of exhaustion entering his voice. "You know the complexity here."

Remy nodded. But how did he know the complexity? That's what Ezra wanted to know.

"What did you do in Africa?" Ezra asked finally after nearly a year of wondering. "What did you really do? Did you work with the CIA? The KGB?"

It was Lucia who answered. "He was a spy. French Intelligence, am I right?" she asked the man himself.

They all looked at her in surprise.

"You weren't in Rwanda on behalf of the church," she said, "but on behalf of the French government. You're a French priest, not an African one."

He nodded.

"That's why you can't answer the question of what part of Africa you came from. You don't want to lie."

"Detective Lucia has answered correctly," Remy replied. "I never wanted to become a priest. I wanted a career in French intelligence or possibly diplomacy. Although, in the 1980s they were one and the same. I met a recruiter my first year of university in Paris, and she convinced me to go to a seminary in Nigeria." A wistful expression imbued his face with the joy of his youth— and possibly a memory of the nameless "she" who had recruited him. "From there, I would be launched to wherever they needed me."

"I've missed something," Ezra said.

"Your friend here witnessed the Rwandan genocide

firsthand, Special Agent James," Cromley helped. "It effectively ended his DGSE career."

"Your scar," Ezra said, pointing.

The lights and sirens continued to ebb. Uniformed officers roped off the jet and a team in hazmat suits began working the scene.

"Perhaps we should take our conversation elsewhere," Remy said. "They'll need this runway cleared." He pointed to Lucia who balanced uncomfortably on her crutches. "And it looks like you could use a chair." Then he turned to Cromley. "Jeremiah, could you give an old priest and his friends a ride?"

There was something unspoken between them, as though Remy were asking for more than just a ride, as if he were asking for permission—or forgiveness.

"I'd have to be an asshole to say no," the ASAC replied.

****

At Remy's house, the trio were met by Fr. Xavier and Fr. Terry. Remy's housemates were surprised to see Ezra and Lucia, and they were concerned at Remy's long absence that day. Where had he gone after chess practice? Why hadn't he called one of them? Even though they'd already eaten dinner, Fr. Xavier reheated the leftovers, a vegetarian Moroccan stew, and they all sat down to eat.

Remy recounted his tale from the beginning, covering the same ground he had related to Davon and those parts he'd only told to Lucia and Enni Frost. Then with a heavy heart, he continued.

"Sister Therese. I finally went to her and told her how dire our situation was. 'They are going to kill us,' I said. She only nodded. There were tears in her eyes, and I realized she had known this fact even longer than I had. We hatched a plan. I would get the keys to the bus, and she would get our passports. I also told her about a listening device." This was new information, something he hadn't told anyone in nearly thirty years. "I had affixed a small recorder to the bottom of the bishop's chair in the confessional. It helped me gather intel on the Interahamwe's strategies, but also it proved the bishop's complicity."

His eyes darted sheepishly to his fellow priests, gauging their response to his ex-communicable offense. They frowned sympathetically.

"We decided to gather as many people as we could and sneak away that night. I knew where they kept the bus, and because it was too dangerous for her, I went alone.

"She grasped my hands then—I can still feel the pull of her fingers. The sight of her face against the pale spring sky recalled a line from Baudelaire. Without thinking, I asked, 'Will I see you no more before eternity?' She smiled and replied, 'Elsewhere, far, far from here!' She had read the book of poetry I'd left for her. Not just read it, but learned by heart, the same poems I had. I was a priest, and she was nun. We couldn't be together, but we knew that in another life we would've, and that was enough.

"I ran from that place as a man on wings—how could I know what would happen? I made it to the garage in what felt like an instant. I can still remember dropping the keys a dozen times as I fumbled with the padlock. I can remember grabbing them from the ground one final time, my hands muddy with sweat and dust. I can remember driving up that hill, too fast, and nearly plunging off the side of the road and into a ravine. And too, I can remember what I saw once I arrived there.

"Sr. Didi and Bishop Bahati were carrying gasoline cans out the side doors of the cathedral. A large red canister swung from each of their hands. I followed them with my eyes, down a set of stairs that led to the school. I turned off the engine and climbed down to get a better view. I watched from behind a row of *umubunda* trees on the downward slope of the hill. Through the cover of pine needles, I witnessed a sight I will never forget—not even if I live to be as old as Methuselah himself, not even if eternity exists."

As Remy narrated his tale, people ate and drank, passed dishes and tidied their spaces, but slowly one by one they became still, entirely absorbed in his words, until all stared transfixed at the man, their ears straining to hear what Remy would say next.

"The militia had lined the refugees up and forced them to kneel. These new soldiers ran coarse rope around the kneeling Tutsis, around their waists and around their arms and legs, lashing men, women, and children together. My eyes searched back and forth for Therese, but I couldn't find her. Didi distributed the canisters to the militia men and watched as they doused the refugees with gasoline. Then other men came with torches. One by one, they lowered the lit torches to the heads and backs of the Tutsis.

"They struggled, they fought to break free. The few that did break away ran burning alive or were shot directly. The rest died screaming and writhing, held tight by the ropes. There was no remorse on the face of the murderers. No joy either. They were the faces of soulless creatures, not even creatures but automatons, set into motion without feeling or wills of their own."

"Hollow men," Lucia echoed.

Remy nodded. "I too felt a sudden loss of will. Without thinking or meaning to, I began to run. I ran as fast as I could into the cathedral, searching high and low.

"When I found Therese," he said and choked back a sob. "When I found her…" but he stopped again. "Her arms…splayed like an angel's wings."

He did not speak for several minutes. No one did.

"Fear alone saved me. Fear alone drove me downstairs where I found my passport. Fear drove from the cathedral, that animal fear that screams to survive even when the mind says there is no longer any reason to live. I ran and ran, only knowing that I needed to head in the direction of the setting sun, in the direction of Zaire.

"Barricades blocked the streets in many places. In others, the bodies of soldiers and civilians choked the shoulders and ditches from where they'd been pushed off the roads. Still more roads were made inaccessible by machine gun fire. I was almost out of the city limits when I saw a group of young men swinging machetes. They wore nothing official, no flags, no fatigues. They were scarcely more than children, and they didn't seem to care who they harassed. I knew my Zaire passport would not matter to them, so I ran the other way. I ran, and they followed. They were younger and faster. I could hear their feet hitting the pavement like a dozen fingers on a *djembe* drum.

"At a turn in the road, I dove sideways into the river of corpses, praying the light had faded enough for me to blend in. These over-grown children arrived, four of them. Two moved on, but two remained, examining the pile of bodies. Apparently, I was not the first person to hide among the dead. 'Where are you little *inyenzi?*' they asked. That's the word they used for the Tutsis. Cockroach. For days, the radio had called for nothing but the extermination of these cockroaches who plagued the country, and now there I lay among their lifeless shells, their feelers and thin stiff legs, hoping to be mistaken for one of them—not a live *inyenzi* but a dead one."

Remy ran a finger down his scar. "One of the soldiers began slashing hard into the mass of bodies. I wondered if I should try to wiggle away or position myself beneath another body as a shield. Before I could decide, I felt the blade sink down into my cheek. The warm blood spread over my skin, but it sent a cold chill down my spine. I must have winced, but the light was all shadows now. I bit my tongue, clenched every muscle in my body, and by some miracle I did not cry out. I prayed the fresh blood would not glisten in the thin moonlight. I prayed it would blend in with the dried blood all around me. He began poking the bodies with the end of his machete. 'Come out, *inyenzi,* and we might let you live.' I didn't move. I didn't breathe. I tried to pray the rosary in my mind, but I kept getting lost, kept coming back to the first line of the creed. *I believe in God, the Father Almighty...I believe in God, the Father...I believe in God...I believe...* Then his poking stopped. He studied the pile for a moment, the longest moment of my life.

"Finally, he joined the others, and they moved on."

The company around the table exhaled collectively. They knew Remy had survived, but the release of tension still brought them relief.

"How did you make it out of Kigali?" Lucia asked now.

"I walked all night. The moon was new, barely a crescent. It cast a negligible amount of light, but I knew how to travel by the stars. I was thankful for the cover of darkness. Outside of Kigali, I found an abandoned jeep, the keys still in the ignition, and I drove west. I encountered soldiers from both sides of the conflict and passed through several checkpoints. Each time, I showed them my Zaire passport, my letter from the bishop, and then I convinced them that I was on their side. A medic from the UN refused to let me pass. She first insisted on stitching up my face and locating a bottle of antibiotics.

"Sunrise found me just across the border into Zaire, sitting on the banks of Lake Kivu. As the sun rose, it turned the horizon a burning red. The light caught the feathers of the bright pink flamingoes that covered the water. The redness in the air and on the surface of the water, all of it reflected double in the lake. It produced a vision like the apocalypse—the world being consumed by fire. I felt like a soldier from the First World War, wounded, shell-shocked, convinced I was witnessing the end times first-hand—and too exhausted to care."

He pushed back his chair and sighed with the weight of the remembrance. "I didn't know what to do," he said. "I returned to Zaire, to Fr. Khonde, and I said nothing for several weeks. We resumed our business, our routine, and we tried to forget that I'd ever left for Rwanda or what I had witnessed there. He even took to looking me in the right eye, to avoid my scar. Then one day in the confessional booth, I told him everything—what I had seen, what I had failed to do, and who I really was—not an African priest but a French spy. 'What should I do?' I asked through tears. 'Say it, and I will do it.' Fr. Khonde did not respond at first. I thought he was going to excommunicate me then and there or have me arrested. I was so tired and afraid.

"Instead he told me that only I could decide. Either I was a priest, or I wasn't one. 'Under these conditions, no one can hold you to your vows, but no one can deny you have said the words,' Fr. Khonde said. He spoke like that, his meaning moving in two directions at once. Either the words I'd spoken were true and the responsibilities that came with them were mine, or they were a lie, and I could lay them aside. But I had to choose."

Again they waited breathlessly.

"I decided then and there and every day since that I could do more as a priest, an ordinary pastor, than I'd ever done as a spy. I told Fr. Khonde as much. He nodded solemnly and told me the sanctuary needed dusting. We never spoke of Rwanda or the DGSE again."

Fr. Terry, who had been silent throughout the story, spoke now. "The priesthood must be renewed each day."

Fr. Xavier agreed. "We have all broken our vows at some point—in thought, if not in deed."

"Have you ever regretted your choice?" Lucia asked.

"Lucia!" Ezra said reproachfully.

Remy laughed. "It's okay. Of course I have."

The other priests snickered as well.

"There is no life free of regrets nor any life full of certainty," Remy continued. "I have seen utter certainty with my own eyes, and it looks a lot like what Leena Åkerholm and Torben Laakso witnessed—a mob wielding machetes and torches. No, I will take my quiet life with its quiet regrets." He gestured around the table. "Now our plates are empty, and my story is finished."

"It was an honor to hear it," Lucia said.

Fr. Terry rose from his chair. "I understand that you two need a ride."

"Please," she replied.

Chapter Twenty-Eight

As Remy had still not paid a visit to the ER, he rode in front with Fr. Terry, while Lucia and Ezra sat in the backseat, their hands resting on the armrest between them, their fingers perilously close to touching.

Terry parked in front of Lucia's apartment building. It was not exactly raining, but a light mist made the streetlamps glow and the new green leaves glisten. At the sight of all this natural softening and blending of form and color, a few stray notes of classical music played in Lucia's mind, something minimalist and somber and French, the intro to a piece by Erik Satie maybe, or Claude Debussy. Something lovely but sad.

Soon the evening would be over. Ezra would leave, and Lucia would be alone again. Was it the aloneness that bothered her? Or the absence of Ezra? She'd never felt this sad when Adrian left the room.

"Are you sure you want to get out here?" Terry asked Ezra.

"A walk will do me good."

"Even in the rain?"

"What rain?"

After the priests drove off, Ezra walked Lucia to the front door of her building. She leaned her crutches against the wall, and they lingered beside the door like two teenagers on a first date. Above them, the moon had grown full to bursting with an impossibly bright light, its edges also softened in the faint mist.

"You saved me again," he said.

"I found you. That's all."

His gaze traveled from her eyes to her lips and back again. She watched it. "And here I thought I found you."

"That's so corny."

Then he slid his arm behind her back, and it didn't seem corny at all. He leaned in, but she stopped him, a palm laid lightly on his chest.

"What about Julia?"

"We're divorced."

She raised an incredulous eyebrow. "I saw her. The last time she visited you."

Ezra hung his head. "I don't know what that was. A relapse, I guess."

"Maybe you should explore it."

He looked away. "There's no future there."

"Does she know that?"

"She told me as much herself."

Lucia didn't mention her own interaction with Ezra's ex-wife, who had reacted like a lioness whose den had just been invaded. "How about you?" she asked, the incredulity returning in full. "Do you know there's no future?"

"Let me take you out this Saturday, not for lunch and not to compare notes."

Lucia felt herself on the precipice, the highest point of the rollercoaster before the drop. "Okay," she said.

He leaned in again; this time she let him. His warm lips met hers, then his hands found her lower back again and pulled her body into his. His tongue found hers, and she could feel his heart beating through his chest and into her own. As his mouth traveled to her earlobe and then her neck, she whispered into his ear, "I have a cracked pelvis."

"Oh, right."

He pulled away carefully, but she pulled him back in for one final kiss.

"Saturday night." She patted his face playfully, then took her crutches and disappeared inside, her heart beating like a hummingbird's and her face smiling so broadly she knew she must be dreaming. Hearts didn't beat this fast in real life, and no one could feel this much pure joy.

She peered out the crystal window that ran alongside the building's entryway and watched Ezra walk into the night. And, though she pinched herself, she did not wake up.

Epilogue
Saturday

Reverend Don made two passes through the recreation center parking lot before finding a spot. Sitting anxiously in the passenger seat, Remy worried that the vehicles all belonged to chess tournament participants. His fears were allayed when they came upon a large gymnasium bustling with a basketball tournament, the stands filled with spectators.

This must be tournament day, Remy thought. His fears vanished entirely, replaced with a hint of disappointment, when they entered a nearly empty room. Two scraggly teenagers with pale, acne-covered skin stood awkwardly beside eight unoccupied chess boards.

"Is this the tournament?" Remy asked.

A spectacled gentleman introduced himself as "Mr. Wentworth" and invited them to sign in. He seemed on edge. Remy couldn't tell if his anxiety stemmed from the racial and socio-economic make-up of the arriving competitors, or if he simply suffered from social anxiety.

"This is everyone who signed up, so we can begin whenever you're ready," he said, pinching the skin of his upper arm through his white button-up shirt. "I thought we might have some walk-ins, but this is probably better for a first tournament."

Remy directed his team to take their seats at the boards. "This is more people than came to my first

289

tournament," Remy said.

The host perked up. "You played tournaments growing up?"

"I learned how to play from the pastor at my first posting in Zaire. He was a talented chess player and insisted I take up the game as well. One summer, we hosted a chess tournament as part of a youth outreach program." Remy laughed at the memory. "Only one boy came. He didn't really know how to play, just how the pieces moved, but still he beat me."

Mr. Wentworth seemed impressed. "You were a priest in Zaire? That's the Congo?"

"That's right."

He smiled genuinely, more at ease now, and invited Remy to one of the unoccupied boards. While the two of them played, the six competitors set up their own boards and began warming up. The young men went through their practice games quickly, then they came over to watch the adults.

Remy fell down a pawn on an early exchange. Then he lost a pinned knight. They continued, grinding into the end game, until Remy stopped.

"What's the matter?" Wentworth asked. Then he blinked twice at the board and nodded. "Yes, it is unavoidable. I didn't realize."

They shook hands, leaving their spectators perplexed. Remy rose and began setting up chess clocks.

"Why did you stop?" Davon asked.

Remy turned the hands of the clock until it displayed a half hour. "Their coach had me in an unavoidable checkmate in two moves."

"You could've forced him to do it."

"Stopping was a kindness to me, not to him," Remy

explained.

The games began shortly thereafter, the two Evanston players beating Matt and Jesus easily and Davon beating Joaquin not long afterward. The round robin tournament proceeded until there remained only one game. Davon had earned two wins, and one draw by repetition. Trevor in turn had won all of his games easily. On a wrestling mat, Trevor would've been shaking like a leaf, but here in his element, the teenager only sweated slightly, the droplets gathering on his peach-fuzz mustache.

Trevor opened the game with the king pawn and Davon responded with the Sicilian defense. They progressed into a closed game. Trevor seemed surprised at his opponent's ease with the cramped position. Hope began to swell in Remy's chest, impossible hope. Davon could actually win and what would that victory do for the teenager's self-esteem?

Then Davon moved an integral pawn two spaces instead of one. Trevor pounced on the unprotected pawn. On the next move, he forked Davon's king and queen. How would he react? In past games, Remy had seen Davon fling pieces, curse at himself over errors, and glower menacingly at his opponents. The hope that had arisen so suddenly deflated just as fast, replaced with a father's dread.

Davon just laughed. "I was with you there for a while."

Trevor nodded. "You play a mean Sicilian. I've never liked closed games."

"Do you want to play it out or can I quit?"

Trevor smiled and gestured toward Davon's king. "By all means."

He tipped his own king over. The two young men shook hands and began setting the board up again. Even though the game was finished, and the tournament decided, Trevor still agreed to show Davon his mistakes, which started long before the ill-advancement of his pawn. The Evanston teen seemed to have a photographic memory, replaying the game exactly as it had occurred.

Meanwhile, the other competitors played new games and the host discussed with Remy and Don how the tournament had gone.

"We've been meeting every day for practices," Remy said.

Don rocked back on his heels and buried his hands in his pockets. "We have a space in north Chicago, an abandoned movie theater."

Wentworth raised his eyebrows. "You could move your practices here to the rec. Then we could combine the teams."

The young men commented and corrected one another, serious faced one moment, then joking over blunders the next.

Remy frowned. "We appreciate the offer, but I don't know if our fellows could commute every day. There isn't a car between them and the van we brought today belongs to Don's church."

Wentworth thought it over. "Then we'll come to you."

"It's not the best neighborhood," Don said apologetically.

"I know the area," he replied. "It's not dangerous." He beamed now at the two of them. "I think this could do Trevor a lot of good."

Remy wondered if he meant the act of charity.

"Trevor's a little…he could use some more friends."

"We're all a little…" Remy added helpfully.

Outside, the afternoon sun melted the last ice in Evanston, a trickle of water running off the sidewalk and into the grass, which was just beginning to green.

****

It only seemed appropriate that Lucia would collect her things from Adrian's place on a Saturday. It was a Saturday that he first invited her over to his ritzy apartment in the Loop. The monthly rent for Adrian's apartment with its views of both Grant Park and Lake Michigan, must've exceeded what Lucia paid in a year. She'd already picked up her clothes, which fit into an overnight suitcase. Now she held the various and sundry items she'd left over the last few months, all of it fitting loosely into a cardboard box. It felt like the last day on a job, and in that context, she realized just how short their relationship had been. If it had been a job, she'd leave it off her resume.

"I am sorry," she said.

He shrugged. "Don't be. In the long run, who's going to even remember?"

Adrian was probably right. Ten years from now, would either of them remember this conversation or why they broke up or even why they got together in the first place? Still, she couldn't help feeling sad. She wanted to say something that would bring them both closure, but that wasn't really her role. Instead, she nodded and turned to leave.

"What was my word?" he asked.

"Your word?"

"You told me once that you always summarize people you meet with a word. You said Ezra's word was *nonchalant* because he's always trying to act more casual than he feels. What was mine?"

"Principesco."

He smiled. Then he shook his head. "I don't get you, Lucia. Then again, I guess that's why things didn't work out." He gave her one last hug and then shut the door behind her.

****

Ezra rubbed his palms on his knees. "And that's everything."

"What do you mean that's everything?"

They were sitting in Dr. Palacios' spare office, the psychiatrist at the edge of his ratty office chair and Ezra leaned back in the loveseat. After everything that had happened, Ezra thought it only prudent to meet with his psychiatrist to talk things through.

"That's how it ended. Leena Åkerholm put sixteen bullets into Benjamin Kirsi's chest, and we shipped her back to Finland to await trial. They're allowing her to attend Torben Laakso's funeral today in Helsinki."

He could picture her there, a light mist in the air, a guard on either side of her as she watched them return the only man she'd ever loved to the earth. Ezra had spent the majority of his hour-long session recounting the case. He gestured now to the newspaper on the doctor's desk. "You've read the write up by that pop psychologist, Müller?"

Palacios swiveled his chair in the direction of the paper. "Ah yes, Complicated Grief Disorder. The suicide of her lover inducing psychosis in Leena Åkerholm, leading her to kill Mr. Kirsi."

"Do you believe it?" Ezra asked.

"Dr. Müller makes a compelling case. What do you

think?"

"She seemed sane to me," Ezra answered. "During the two days I spent with her, she never exhibited psychosis. She carefully worked the case while simultaneously redirecting Nélya Kirsi. She ran over Lucia just to keep her off the trail, a premeditated action, and then she drugged me when I came too close. No, Leena was level-headed, rational, and calculating."

"External signs are not always predictive."

Ezra considered this a moment. "Can grief cause a psychotic break?"

"If Leena Åkerholm had an underlying mental condition it could."

"But she didn't."

"That you know of." The doctor frowned. "How long did you keep your own disorder a secret?"

This was a fair point.

"At your last session," Dr. Palacios said and shifted in his seat, "we discussed your mother."

He shuffled through a row of books on his bookshelf until he found what he was looking for and handed it to Ezra. The title read, *Unraveling Your Epigenetics.*

"Some light reading material," Ezra quipped.

"Someone told me you had a master's degree in psychology."

Ezra was that someone. He mentioned it frequently during their sessions, usually when he was feeling contradictory. "Forensic psychology is different."

Palacios reached to take the book back.

"Sorry," Ezra said. "I don't know why I'm so resistant."

The doctor narrowed his eyes. "Maybe because you know what this theory suggests."

"And what is that?"

"The absence of free will—for you and the people you spend so much of your time and energy bringing to justice."

Ezra didn't respond. They waited through a minute of silence before the doctor continued.

"But that's not what it means. An action, a behavior, a way of thinking—these have a myriad of influences. The less we understand them, the more they shape our decisions. The more we understand them, the more free will we actually have. Picture a smoker who doesn't know nicotine is addictive, doesn't realize she's being chemically compelled to smoke. Understanding may not set her free, but at least she will see the situation correctly." Palacios acquired a thoughtful expression. "Epigenetics suggests that how we act and react can guide our genes, that is all. You have seen firsthand the effect of a genetic predisposition and a chaotic childhood. It is like pouring gasoline on a fire."

Ezra was having trouble following the doctor. "But my childhood is long past."

"Yours is, yes, but what about your children's?"

Momentarily, he thought the doctor was confusing him with another patient. "What children?"

"The ones you may want to have? Do you want to continue this cycle in the lives of your own children?"

Ezra laughed. "I don't think I need to worry about that anytime soon. I'm not exactly in a child-rearing position at the moment."

The doctor smiled. "Maybe not, but if you work through these things now, then when you are, you'll be ready." He rose from his chair, circled around the desk, and placed a hand on Ezra's shoulder, a rare show of physical comfort. "You are not a bad man, Ezra, and not a bad looking one either. It has been a year of treatment. It's time you stop looking backward and start looking at what comes next."

Ezra looked down at the book in his hands. "I will. And I'll read this." He checked his watch. "Shoot, we're over."

"It's my fault," Palacios said, squeezing Ezra's shoulder and then releasing it. "Here I kept you talking about your work this whole time. We can go long today if need be. I don't have any appointments after this."

Ezra smiled. "I actually have something."

"Oh?" A grin spread over the doctor's face. "Something you'd like to discuss?"

"Let's see how today goes first."

"Fair enough."

****

For the first time in a long time, Ezra was genuinely excited for the evening that lay ahead. As he pulled into his driveway, however, everything changed.

There in his parking space sat a yellow jeep. His ex-wife's. The driver's side door opened, and Julia stepped out. She waved half-heartedly at him.

"Julia," he said, stepping out to meet her. "Didn't have anywhere better to be on a Saturday night?" He had aimed for playful sarcasm but it came out serious. He didn't correct himself.

She flashed two tear-filled eyes at him.

"What's wrong?"

"You act like this thing has only happened to you."

"What thing?"

"The CTC case, the manic episode, the probation," she said. "I went through all of it, too."

297

Ezra scoffed. "I didn't see you in the mental hospital, getting shot in the ass with Thorazine."

"No, but you saw me at the cafe with Louis. You pulled a gun on me, need I remind you?"

"I pulled it on Louis."

"You pointed it at both of us."

"I never would've shot *you.*"

She turned away. "How was I supposed to know that?" She opened the door of the jeep and slid a leg into the footwell.

"Don't go," he said. "Come inside." He scanned the street for any sign of Lucia. "I'll make some coffee."

"It's after five," she said, still looking away.

"Then tea," he said. "I have some peppermint. I didn't realize…"

She turned back to him, eyes glossy still, and bit the first knuckle of her finger. "I shouldn't have come. I feel foolish."

"No," he said, half-hearted.

Julia removed her leg and closed the door of the jeep. Together but not touching, they mounted the stairs of the porch. Before they reached the door, she plopped down onto the wooden bench swing.

"I always loved this swing," she said, a wistful note in her voice.

"You can have it. I'll have it shipped to KC."

His ex-wife buried her face in her hands and, when he sat beside her and placed an arm on her back, she buried her face in his chest. He felt the dampness of her tears through his shirt. "I had no idea you were so upset," he said. "I thought you left because we lost the baby. That or because the world turned on me."

She wiped her eyes. "I left because you turned on

me." It was an accusation. "I left because I'd been through trauma after trauma and I didn't know if I could survive another one."

Ezra thought of his own childhood. "I can't blame you."

She looked surprised.

"What can I do?" he asked. "How can I make amends?"

"Oh, Ezra." She studied the wooden boards of the porch.

"What? Whatever it is, just tell me."

She said it in a muffled whisper.

"What?" he asked softly.

She looked into his eyes, her face an expressionless mask. "I'm pregnant."

When she'd announced their first pregnancy, Ezra popped a bottle of champagne and they went to a French restaurant. Now she looked utterly terrified and all he could think to do was rub her back and puzzle over a question that ran through his mind like a broken record, the question Dr. Palacios had just asked him.

Do you want to continue this cycle in the lives of your own children?

He looked down at her flat abdomen, trying to peer inside at the child just beginning to form, a child with all his potential, good and bad. Looking down, he didn't notice the car that slowed in front of his house nor the driver who peered at him through her driver's side window before speeding away.

A word about the author...

Steven earned his undergraduate and graduate degrees in English from Kansas State University. He started his writing career as a lowly student worker for the prestigious literary journal The Southern Review. (If you received a formal rejection letter from the mid-2000s, he probably sealed the envelope.) He has published fiction, poetry, and nonfiction in various newspapers, magazines, and journals since that time.

He lives in Southwest Kansas with his wife and three children.

http://www.stevenjkolbe.com